"And what would you be thinking of, woman, when there's work to be done?"

Amelia sighed and fanned herself with her hand. "It's awfully hot, don't you think?" Deliberately, she looked at the water.

Garrick sighed but, truth be told, didn't resist. Still, he felt compelled to say, "Houses don't build themselves, you know."

Her eyes danced with merriment. "You're sounding more like a Puritan Elder every day, going on about work to be done and no time for pleasures."

His eyebrows rose. "Puritan? Me? That's an insult, woman. Take it back."

She put her hands behind her and assumed an expression of complete unconcern. "What will you do if I don't?"

He stopped halfway through stripping off his shirt and said, "What I've been wanting to do for quite a while now...."

Dear Reader,

This month we bring you the first book in a delightful trilogy by author Maura Seger. Set in Belle Haven, a fictional New England town, *The Taming of Amelia* is an adventurous tale of two people destined to forge new lives for themselves in the Colonies. It sets the stage for stories of the town's future generations—right up to the present day, with a tie-in book from Silhouette's Intimate Moments line.

Prolific newcomer Kit Gardner is sure to please with *The Stolen Heart,* a high-spirited romance between an aristocratic English girl and the Pinkerton detective whom she thinks is an outlaw.

New to Harlequin Historicals but certainly not to romance, Virginia Nielsen has written a moving story about a privateer and the Creole woman who rescues him in *To Love a Pirate.*

Knight's Lady, Suzanne Barclay's new book, features another of the irresistible Sommerville brothers. Introduced in *Knight Dreams* (HH #141), Gareth is the eldest sibling and heir to a fortune, yet the granddaughter of a lowly goldsmith holds the key to his heart.

Look for all four titles at your favorite bookstore.

Sincerely,

Tracy Farrell
Senior Editor

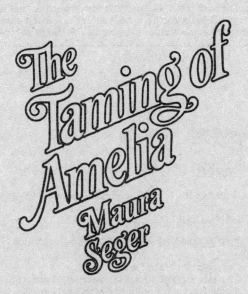

The Taming of Amelia

Maura Seger

Harlequin Books

TORONTO • NEW YORK • LONDON
AMSTERDAM • PARIS • SYDNEY • HAMBURG
STOCKHOLM • ATHENS • TOKYO • MILAN
MADRID • WARSAW • BUDAPEST • AUCKLAND

Harlequin Historicals first edition February 1993

ISBN 0-373-28759-3

THE TAMING OF AMELIA

MAURA SEGER

began writing stories as a child and hasn't stopped since. Her love for history is evident in the many historical romances she has produced throughout her career. But her interest is not confined to the early periods of history. She has also written romances set in the more recent eras of World War II, the sixties and contemporary times.

A full-time writer, Maura experienced her very own romance in her courtship and marriage to her husband, Michael, with whom she lives in Connecticut along with their two children.

Chapter One

The wind blowing off the bay gusted suddenly. It struck Amelia Daniels square in the back and almost wrenched the latch out of her hand. She struggled through the doorway into the small building.

Quickly, she slammed the door shut and held her shoulder against it for a moment to be sure it would stay. Only then did she straighten up and look around.

The room that took up most of the first floor was dark on this cloudy, dank day of March, 1650. Winter battled to keep its grip on the land even as spring remained tantalizingly out of reach.

Beyond the settlement in the marshes around Boston town, the first soft green shoots could be found. But for the people gathered in the rough wooden buildings chinked with mud to stave off the frigid cold, the months-long struggle to endure went on.

Scant light filtered through the cloth covering the few windows, barely illuminating the dozen or so men gathered inside. They sat on benches set around rough-hewn tables, playing at pegs or dice.

Without exception, they were big men, hard-faced but well dressed in fine woolen breeches and gaily hued doublets of velvet and silk, more color and grandeur than was to be found anywhere else in the settlement. But then they, almost alone among the several hundred souls clinging to the edge of this new world, were not Puritans.

Their religion was commerce and the sea, bound inexorably together. The small building was an inn used solely by the captains and officers of the great vessels that were putting into Boston harbor in greater numbers every year.

The Puritans tolerated them because they had no choice. No one else could deliver the goods and people the colony desperately needed in order to survive. But they also struggled to keep the rough and irreverent seamen apart, making it clear they were not welcome in their homes or other gathering places.

That seemed to suit the men fine. They were solitary by nature, content with their own company or the company of others like themselves. Certainly, they did not welcome the young woman in plain Puritan homespun blown into their midst by a winter wind.

Amelia clenched her teeth to keep them from chattering. The warmth of the fire had not yet penetrated her damp cloak. She still felt cold to the bone but beyond that she was also sensibly nervous. Proper young women did not come to such a place.

The men's faces reflected their surprise, but only for a moment. They deliberately turned away, ignoring her in the expectation that she would realize her error and vanish as quickly as she had appeared.

She did not. Instead, she cleared her throat and said softly but distinctly, "I am looking for Captain Marlowe. Is he here?"

Silence. She took a breath and tried again. "I said I am looking for Captain Marlowe. Do any of you know his whereabouts?"

There was a guffaw from a table at the far side of the room but it was quickly muffled. Nearer to where she stood, a bewhiskered man wearing a broad-brimmed hat decked out with a flamboyant feather looked up and down slowly.

"Marlowe, you say?"

She nodded. Beneath her cloak, her hands were clenched tightly together to stop their trembling. But her head was high and she faced him unflinchingly. "He came into port four days ago."

"I know when he came," the captain rumbled. "Question is, why do you want him?"

From the far end of the room, a voice called out, "Maybe Puritan women ain't so different after all?"

In the general laughter that followed, Amelia struggled to remain calm. She could feel her face flaming but she told herself not to be daft. She'd known what she was getting into when she decided to seek Marlowe at the inn. The decision hadn't been lightly taken. She had struggled over it for several sleepless nights, and she wasn't about to give up now.

"I wish to see him on business," she said firmly. Her small, rounded chin lifted. "My name is Amelia Daniels. My father was Jonathan Daniels." She had the satisfaction of seeing them glance quickly at one another before she went on. "I perceive that means something to you, as it should. I have business to discuss with Captain Marlowe—*Daniels's* business—and I'm sure he won't thank you if I'm not able to do that."

"Don't get on your high horse, lass," said Captain Feather—as she had privately dubbed him. "He's upstairs... sleeping. When he comes down, we'll tell him you were looking for him.''

Amelia frowned. It was the middle of the day, and besides that, if Marlowe wanted to sleep, why wouldn't he go back to his ship to do it? She eyed the captain skeptically. He seemed sincere enough but she had no reason to trust him, and if she had learned anything in the last few months it was that she had to look out for herself.

She took several more steps into the room, shook the dampness from her cloak and said, ''Thank you but I will wait.''

This brought deep scowls and grumbling. Shaking their heads, the men went back to their amusements but they kept a careful eye on her. Clearly, a woman who would intrude on their privacy was a woman to be watched.

Amelia sat on the edge of an empty bench. She kept her back and shoulders straight, and her gaze fixed on the small, winding staircase that led to the second floor. Time passed slowly. She began to wish that she had brought some diversion—her needlework, perhaps, or one of her precious store of books.

Marlowe might be planning to sleep all day. She could wait hours and achieve nothing. And the longer she remained inside the inn, the greater the danger that word of her presence there would spread beyond. It was quite possible that the Puritan elders would send someone to drag her away. She might even end up in the stocks for being so unseemly.

Despite such fears, she kept her expression calm and her attention on the staircase. At last, her patience was rewarded, although not as she had expected. A young woman emerged from the upper floor. She had a good-natured, rosy face, pretty blond hair and a buxom figure that her plain servant's garb could not disguise.

Amelia did not know her by name, but she recognized her as a bondwoman in service to a Puritan family. So, too, did the young woman recognize Amelia. She took one look at her and flushed to the roots of her hair. *"You,"* she exclaimed before she could stop herself. "What would you be doing here?"

Amelia tried to come up with some explanation for her presence that could excuse it. But she had no success and fell back on the truth. With as much dignity as she could muster, she said, "I am waiting to see Captain Marlowe."

The girl gave her a curious look as though she still couldn't believe what she was seeing. Before she could ask anything more, Amelia interjected, "Are you working here now?"

The girl's flush deepened. She cast a quick glance around at the men who studiously looked away, hiding their amusement.

Speaking very fast, she said, "I came to fetch ale for my master, that's all. I'll be going now."

Hastily, she gathered her cloak around her and departed into the wind. Amelia stared after her for a moment, contemplating the strangeness of sending a girl for ale without providing her with anything to carry it in. She might have thought more about it had not a footfall sounded on the stairs.

Quickly, Amelia straightened up. Her throat was tight and her hands, still beneath her cloak, once again clenched. So much depended on what happened in the next few minutes that she could hardly bear to think of it. Taking a deep breath, she stood to face the man coming down the stairs.

He was very big, she noticed instantly. Bigger even than the other men in the room. He had to bend his dark head far over to clear the low ceiling above the stairs. His hair was black, combed straight back from his broad forehead and secured at the nape of his neck. His features were chiseled and long burnished by the sun and wind. His eyes were deeply set beneath slashing brows, and they held a pewter sheen. His jaw was square, his mouth firmly etched and his nose appeared to have been broken at least once.

He had several days' growth of beard but was otherwise neatly turned out in a loose white shirt untied at the collar and tucked into black breeches. If his expression was anything to go by, he was in good humor until he saw Amelia. Then he stopped short and stared at her.

"Who the hell are you?" he demanded.

Amelia was growing tired of explaining herself. Besides, she'd had enough of arbitrary men in the past few months. Now, here she was, face-to-face with what was surely the most arbitrary of all.

Before she could think better of it, she said, "Who I am is my business—unless you're Captain Garrick Marlowe. Are you?"

His brows drew together in a scowl that under ordinary circumstances might have set her looking for the way out. Unfortunately, there was none. The door let out into the town, and that was not where she wanted to go. She half hoped the portentous man would tell her that the captain was still snoring upstairs. Instead, he nodded slowly, his eyes raking her, and said, "I'm Marlowe. Now I'll ask once more, who the hell are you?"

Before she could reply, one of the other men answered. "She says she's Jonathan Daniels's daughter. Any chance she's telling the truth?"

"Of course, I am," Amelia began indignantly—only to be cut off as Marlowe took a quick step toward her, seized her chin roughly and turned her face to the light.

Her instinct was to struggle, but there was no point. The mere touch of his fingers was enough to remind her that he was vastly stronger than she. With no other choice, she forced herself to stand still as he studied her insolently.

He saw a woman in her nineteenth year, slender and above average in height, with flushed cheeks, flashing hazel eyes, a full mouth, and, tucked beneath a white starched cap, russet hair that matched her slanted brows. Her bone structure was delicate, but there was an innate sense of strength about her. Moreover, when she defiantly met his eyes, he saw the unmistakable glint of intelligence.

His hand dropped. Slowly, he said, "It's her alright."

"I told you that," she snapped. Rubbing her chin rather more than was necessary, for he hadn't actually hurt her, she said, "You came to our house in Amsterdam several times when I was a child. My father invested in the first voyage on which you were captain."

She didn't add, although she could have, that Jonathan Daniels had taken a considerable risk when he agreed to underwrite the youngest captain ever to put wind to sail, for Garrick Marlowe had been scarcely twenty when he took the first ship under his own name to Boston in record time.

His reputation made, he had never again lacked for investors, and he and her father had continued to do business in the decade since. Jonathan had always spoken well of Captain Marlowe despite what he admitted was a streak of wildness in his nature. Her father had speculated this came from being a combination of Irish and Scots, which he characterized as a volatile mixture. Amelia couldn't help but think he had been right.

"Aye," he said quietly, his gaze still on her. "Your father was a good man. I'm sorry for your loss."

To her dismay, Amelia felt her eyes sting. She blinked hastily and looked away for a moment. "Thank you," she murmured. Taking a deep breath, she added, "Is there someplace we can talk?"

"What's wrong with right here?"

She glanced around at the men who were making no attempt to conceal their curiosity. All eyes—and ears—were turned their way.

"I'd prefer somewhere more private," she said.

Marlowe shook his head in amazement. Gruffly, he said, "If you had any sense, you'd prefer nowhere at all. Don't you know you're not supposed to be here? And you're certainly not supposed to be going off alone with the likes of me. Have you no sense at all girl?"

Amelia's mouth tightened. "I'm not a child, Captain Marlowe, and I'm not a fool, either. My father taught me well. As fond as you undoubtedly are of these fine gentlemen—" she cast a withering glance in their direction "—I would think you'd prefer to keep your business dealings private. Or have you not the sense for that?"

For just a moment, she thought she had gone too far. The captain's dark gaze turned thunderous, not unlike the sea as a great storm strikes it. But as quickly as it appeared, the anger disappeared, suppressed beneath his iron control.

Steadily, he said, "As you will. There's a room in the back." Without looking at her further, he turned and led the way.

She followed gingerly. Behind her, she could feel the stares and hear the scornful murmurings of the other men, but she refused to heed them. Having come this far, she could not possibly give up now.

The room was little more than a closet used for storing plate. A tiny window framed a view of the water. Garrick positioned himself near it, leaning comfortably against the wall with his arms folded over his broad chest and looked at her.

Amelia drew her cloak more closely around her. It was cold in the room, but he didn't seem to feel it. She, on the other hand, was close to trembling.

Telling herself it was the cold, and not the man, which affected her so, she said, "I wish to leave Boston."

He shrugged. To him, anyone with any sense would want to do that. "Ships leave every week. You can have your pick."

"They sail for England. I do not wish to go there."

His eyebrows rose. She had managed to surprise him. Cautiously, he asked, "Where do you want to go?"

She took a deep breath. This was it, she thought. The moment the words were past her lips, there was no going back. The long, sleepless nights after her father's death, the anguished debate within herself, the worrying and wondering all came down to this.

Quietly, she said, "I wish to sail southwest along the coast."

He frowned, for her meaning was not clear. "To Nieuw Amsterdam?" he guessed. "You want to go to the Dutch? Is it that you're seeking a ship to take you back to the Lowlands? I know the Netherlanders gave you Puritans sanctuary when you were driven out of England, but I didn't realize any of you were anxious to return there."

"I'm not," Amelia said. "It isn't Nieuw Amsterdam I seek, it's the colony of Connecticut."

"Connecticut?" he repeated. "That's Pequot land. Why would you want to go there?"

"The Pequot sachems sent emissaries to Boston to discuss the founding of new settlements on their lands. They seek allies against their traditional enemies, the Mohawks. The Massachusetts Bay Colony—and the Puritan council—are preparing to send parties out soon to explore the possibilities. The best lands will be taken quickly."

"Probably," Marlowe agreed, "although if you ask me, the Pequots will rue the day they invited any of us to come among them. All the same, what's it got to do with you?"

"I was my father's only child, and indeed, his only close family. He left me well provided for. It is my intention to use that wealth to found a settlement myself."

Garrick looked at her for a long moment as though he had suddenly found himself in the presence of an extraordinary creature unlike any he had ever seen or imagined. Abruptly, he threw his head back and laughed. The robust sound bounced off the walls of the small room and was undoubtedly heard well beyond it.

"You're mad," he said when he was at last able to speak again. Grinning broadly, he added, "Beautiful, and definitely a diversion, but stark raving all the same."

"I am not—" she began, only to stop when he held up a hand peremptorily.

"Lass," he said soberly, "I know Jonathan was an indulgent father. He had all sorts of notions about education for women that most men reject. But despite that, surely even you realize that no one is going to let a female found a settlement? The good gentlemen of the Puritan council would have apoplexy at the mere idea."

"Which is why," Amelia cut in swiftly, "I don't intend to inform them. It may interest you to know that the Pequots—those so-called savages—hold a more enlightened view. They are willing to negotiate with me provided I can get myself and a suitable group of settlers to Connecticut."

This, at least, brought him up short. "Do you mean to tell me," he demanded, "that you've actually talked with the Indians?"

She nodded. "I met with one of the emissaries privately while he was in Boston. We came to an understanding."

"By God, girl, you've the brass. I'll give you that much. But the whole idea's lunacy. It's not worth talking about."

"Why not?" Amelia demanded.

"Because of what you said yourself. You have to get you *and* a suitable group of settlers to Connecticut. No one's going to follow a woman."

"Don't be so sure of that, Captain Marlowe. There are a good many people here in Boston town who are unhappy with the Puritan council. They left England seeking greater freedom, and found repression as severe as any king ever managed. They can't afford to strike out on their own, but given the chance, they'll come with me."

"You might be right, lass," he said thoughtfully. "I certainly wouldn't want to live under the good council's rule. But it doesn't matter."

"Why not?"

"Because the idea is still mad." Before she could protest, he went on. "You're talking about going into a harsh and wild land. You've no idea what it would take to survive there. Do you know how many died when Plymouth was settled? Barely half the colonists were left alive the very next year. You've only seen this place, Boston town, fully twenty years after its founding, and it's still hard enough to live here. The wilderness will kill you, lass. Make no mistake about that.''

Amelia would be lying if she'd said she wasn't afraid. He spoke with the unmistakable ring of experience, reminding her of the voyages he was said to have made deep along the inland waterways. Garrick had seen the land in all its savage beauty, and he was telling her she could not survive there.

He might be right, she conceded.

He saw the look in her eyes and realized she was thinking seriously about what he had said. To drive home the point, he added, ''If you don't want to go back to England, stay here. Surely there's no lack of good Puritan lads happy to marry Jonathan Daniels's daughter?''

That was a mistake, for it struck the sorest of her nerves. She blanched and shook her head. ''My father came here seeking freedom of conscience. He took sick at sea and died within days of our arriving.''

Her voice fell as agonizing memories swept over her. She had loved her father dearly. The struggle to go on almost overwhelmed her but she forced herself to continue. ''He never got a chance to see the way it really is here—how harshly the council has imposed its rule. I know that if he had, he would never have stayed.''

''Maybe not,'' Garrick admitted, not unsympathetically. He respected all things with spirit, even when they were misguided young women. ''But he was a man, lass, and that's all the difference in the world.'' Decisively, he added, ''I'm sorry, but I truly cannot help you.''

Amelia's throat tightened. She had hoped so much.... But it did no good to regret. If the past few months had taught her anything, it was that.

"Then I will ask someone else," she said.

"You'll get the same answer." He cocked his head toward the outer room. "Those are good men out there, rough around the edges, but honorable. They won't do what you want for any amount of money. But there's another kind of man who will do it—for the coin and more."

Garrick's eyes raked over her, making her painfully conscious of her femininity. Harshly, he added, "If you continue on this, you'll find yourself hooked up with that kind, and then you'll pray the wilderness will indeed take you."

He took her by the arm and led her from the room to the door of the inn. Opening it, he said above the wind, "I called your father friend, so I won't say anything about this to anyone. Take my advice and bury this mad notion deep. You're a woman, lass, and there's nothing at all you can do to change that."

She tilted her head back to look him straight in the eye. Softly, she said, "I don't want to change it, Captain. But I will be free."

A frown marred his brow as he watched the straight, slim figure walk away, her proud carriage carrying her unfalteringly into the wind.

Chapter Two

"You did the right thing, Garrick," said the man Amelia had called Captain Feather. He took another mouthful of ale, swallowed and wiped his mouth with the back of his hand before continuing.

"You've problems enough with this stiff-necked lot. We all do. The last thing you need is for the council to think you're up to something with one of their women."

He paused, as though inviting Garrick to either deny the possibility or provide the details. The captain did neither. Instead, he frowned into his ale and said, "She's Jonathan Daniels's daughter."

"Aye, we knew that. You said it yourself."

"He helped me when no other man would give me a by-your-leave," Garrick said.

"He was a good fellow, for all he was a Puritan and a merchant. Everyone said that. How did he die, anyway?"

"She says he took sick at sea and perished a few days after they arrived."

"Hard on her," the older man mused, "being here alone and all, but I don't suppose that will last. Once she's done mourning, one of them will have her wedded and bedded quick enough."

Garrick's frown deepened. He did not know why he so intensely disliked the notion of Amelia Daniels married to a whey-faced Puritan, but dislike it he did. So much, in fact that he felt a moment's regret for having sent her off.

It was a grand idea she had, to go founding a settlement down Pequot way. The land there was rich, well watered and plentiful with game. A man could do far worse for himself.

He shook his head in disbelief at his wayward thoughts. Since when had he, Garrick Marlowe, hankered over a farmer's patch? He was for the sea and the wind, for the freedom of sail and the wealth to be wrested by braving storm and current. Not for him the servitude of plow and hoe. He had grander dreams to follow.

As for Amelia Daniels, she was only one woman among many, and a proudful one at that. The Puritan who took her on would have his hands full taming her. Good luck to him, whoever he was, and let that be an end to it.

And so it should have been. Yet much later that night, as Marlowe made his way to where his ship, *Venturer,* rode at anchor, he was still thinking of Mistress Daniels. The pain in her eyes at the moment he told her no, rankled him still.

So did the conviction that while any sensible woman would give up such a mad notion and accept her proper place in life, Amelia Daniels was cut from less predictable cloth. He wanted to believe she would heed his warning and not place herself in even greater danger, but he couldn't be sure.

Grumbling over the ill-conceived stubbornness of women—and of Jonathan Daniels's daughter in particular—Garrick retired to his cabin. Stripping off his clothes, he bathed in cold seawater and dried himself briskly.

On the deck above, he heard the watch changing and was satisfied that his crew had matters well in hand. They thought him a stern taskmaster, as he was, but no one resented him for it.

The conditions on *Venturer* were the best to be found anywhere, and the crew shared in each voyage's profit. Men competed to sail with Garrick Marlowe. He chose only the best of them.

Stretching out on the bunk that had been constructed for his larger than usual length, he folded his arms behind his head and stared at the timbered ceiling within hand's reach. Despite the battering wind and the chill air, the cabin was snug.

A carefully shielded lantern burned nearby, illuminating the solid wood furnishings, the soft Araby rug covering the floor, the leather-bound books on the work table and the silver plate in the cabinet nearby. Without doubt, he had come far from the boy raised in a wattle and daub hut where hardship was a way of life and suffering was taken for granted.

He'd had a letter from his factor in London not long before sailing. A few more successful voyages and he would realize his hope of buying a second ship.

Once that was done, he'd finally be out from under the constant threat that his single vessel could suddenly be destroyed and all his hopes with it. With a second ship, he could put into operation his carefully nurtured plans for ventures to the Caribbean and beyond.

Thinking of that, he turned onto his side and closed his eyes. *Venturer* rocked gently at her moorings. Her master was well satisfied in mind and body; sleep should come readily. Instead, it remained elusive, held at bay by images of the flashing hazel eyes and delectably full mouth of a woman who defiantly refused to be put in her proper place.

"I won't," Amelia said. She spoke quietly, but with unmistakable firmness. In her experience—and she had several months' worth by now—it did no good to be overly delicate with Mistress Barton. The stocky farmer's wife would not have recognized a hint had it risen up and bit her on the nose. Moreover, she would have bit it back.

"You're wrong," the older woman said. She sat on a small stool by the fire, industriously scraping carrots. The peelings went into a copper pot that bubbled night and day over the fire. Every scrap of meat, fish or vegetable, every bone and bit of gristle, found its way to the pot. Amanda Barton wasted nothing, and for that Amelia admired her. But admiration was not liking, and nothing could make it so.

"Peter Harkness is a fine man," Mistress Barton went on. "You should be honored that he wishes to come calling."

"It is unseemly," Amelia insisted, taking refuge in the only argument she had yet to find that carried weight with the Puritan elite. Inwardly, she sighed. It had been so much easier back in Amsterdam, where she and her father had gone to escape the persecution of the English Crown.

Although she had grown up in the Puritan community there, she had also spent a great deal of time with non-Puritan children. Her father taught her the best of his beliefs and for that she would always thank him, but he had not truly prepared her to deal with the way those beliefs were being twisted by others.

"I am still in mourning," she added when she saw that Mistress Barton was disposed to argue. "My father had been dead scarcely five months. A year would hardly be too long to grieve for him."

"A year? In Amsterdam, perhaps, or in England such nicety is expected, but not here. Here, a woman cleaves to a good man as soon as she is able. She becomes his helpmate, bears his children and prays God will not make her burdens too great. To do otherwise is to invite the Deity's displeasure, Mistress Daniels. Beware, lest others think you too much indulged to be as we all must be— servants of the greater vision."

"I shall strive to avoid that," Amelia said calmly. Never mind that the slur on her character made her bristle. She had done her share and more in the months since her arrival in Boston town.

The ordinary chores of a Puritan housewife were also her own—the spinning and carding, the weaving and dyeing, the soap and candle making, the preparation of foods and medicines—all the endless rounds of labor necessary to support life on the edge of the wilderness. She had done it all, and without objection.

Moreover, since coming to stay with the Bartons her father's death, she had also paid board. Truly, no one had reason to complain of her, even if she refused to receive Peter Harkness and hear his suit.

Yet, for all that, she understood Amanda Barton's motives well enough. William Barton was a member of the Puritan council, the elect presumed chosen by God to rule over their less fortunate brethren. So, too, was Peter Harkness of the elect.

Undoubtedly, they had decided among themselves that Jonathan Daniels's fortune had lain fallow long enough. It was time to put it to use for the great cause of furthering Puritan growth in the New World, and not incidentally, enriching the elect.

Once Amelia was safely married off, her husband would control her wealth. He could do with it—and with her—as he would.

Was it any wonder she was anxious to leave? Yet, despite her disappointing encounter with Garrick Marlowe, she was still convinced that returning to England or the Lowlands was no solution.

Nothing remained there for her. For better or worse, her future was in the beautiful but harsh continent before her.

"Master Harkness will be very disappointed," Amanda Barton warned. "He won't take this well at all."

"I'm sorry," Amelia said without repentance, "but I must follow my conscience."

She turned away, but not before she saw the stern frown of rebuke that strained Mistress Barton's features. To Amanda, conscience was not a private matter.

It was for one's betters to say what should be, and in the case of Mistress Amelia Daniels, that meant the Puritan council. Let the elders decide what was best for her, and the sooner the better!

As soon as she was able, Amelia escaped from the confines of the Barton house. Although the weather remained cold, she thought there was a hint of spring in the air.

Chill or not, Boston town bustled. Indians of several tribes, a few Frenchmen down from the wilds of Canada and Englishmen of every stripe hastened through the narrow streets.

The ground was muddy, but the streets were laid with reeds and the cast-off bark of trees normally used for the houses, making them at least passable. All the same, she had to lift her skirt clear of her ankles to keep it even somewhat clean.

When she was at last beyond the town, she breathed a sigh of relief. Here on the hills above the bay she could be alone with her thoughts—and her dreams.

Not that the solitude cheered her much that day. She found a place out of the wind that gave a good view of the harbor and sat down with her knees drawn up and her arms twined around them. The hood of her cape was pulled up over her head and she had warmly knit mittens on her hands, but still she felt the wind.

Ignoring it, she stared at the half-dozen vessels at anchor in the harbor. They belonged to the most daring sea captains—Garrick Marlowe included—who had braved the winter ice floes of the north Atlantic to bring the colony scarce goods, and in return, to wring the best prices for them from the settlers.

As a merchant's daughter, she thought the arrangement fair. The other Puritans did not see it in the same light. They grumbled over every length of timber, every barrel of fish and every skin of fur they had to pay.

Indeed, complaining about the unfairness of their lot seemed to be a favorite pastime. She guessed they had fallen into the habit early on, when the complaints were justified, and had kept it up even when conditions improved. It had become part and parcel of who they were.

Sighing, Amelia leaned her head on her knees and looked out over the ships. Any one of them could carry her to Connecticut. Tomorrow, she would have to take her courage in hand and go back to the inn. Despite what Marlowe said, about the other captains, she would not give up until she appealed to each of them.

She closed her eyes for a moment gathering her strength. The weight of her father's death still lay so heavily on her that there were times she thought she could not bear it. When her doubts and fears grew strongest, she forced herself to remember all he had taught her about the faith that could, need be, move mountains.

A slight smile curved her mouth. She had only to move one man. Garrick Marlowe had washed his hands of her. But sitting on the hillside looking out to sea, she realized she was not yet ready to do the same with him. There might yet be a way to reach him. All she had to do was find it.

"I have no better nature," Garrick said. He looked astounded that anyone would have thought otherwise. Glaring at Amelia, he went on, "I thought I made myself clear to you yesterday. I will have no part in this mad scheme."

She sighed and did her best to appear calm. She was dareful to come back to him like this, but she didn't know what else to do.

"My plan shocked you, I realize that," Amelia said, "but you have had a night to think it over. Surely, your friendship with my father and the very real dangers you pointed out should I approach the wrong person combine to stir your conscience."

His eyes narrowed. It was all she could do not to flee from the fierceness of his gaze. "I cannot decide whether you are truly as daft as you sound, or if your father so indulged you that you cannot understand when you are told no. Which is it?"

Amelia flushed. His derision hurt her deeply for reasons she did not wish to contemplate. With dignity, she asked, "Have you never wanted something so badly that you were willing to risk all to attain it? Has nothing in your life ever been that important?''

He frowned, remembering suddenly the thoughts he'd had the previous night. Deep inside, the proud, defiant child he had been stirred restlessly.

"This is different," he insisted, although he wasn't sure exactly how.

"Because I am a woman. Yet women came to Massachusetts. No one suggested they stay safely at home while the men went out to found a colony. It was recognized from the beginning that they had an important role to play."

"They were married women," he said. He thought, he had found it, the irrefutable reality out of which she would not be able to squirm. "They were under the guidance—and might I add, the control—of their husbands. You have none, and your father is dead. Lacking the prudent care of a man, you will flounder and only succeed in harming yourself."

Amelia took a deep breath, reminded herself of how much was at stake and smiled. "Exactly my point, Captain. Should you agree to my venture, I would accept your authority in all matters. After all, the captain is master of his ship, isn't he?"

Marlowe looked at her dubiously. He thought her strong-willed and overly independent. This sudden attempt to play the deferential female rang hollow. And yet, he had to admit, it had a certain attraction.

"No," he said hastily, before he could be tempted by the hazel-eyed beauty before him. "It matters not what you say; the answer is no. Now get you from here. I have work to do." Deliberately, he added, "*Men's* work."

Amelia bit back the angry retort that rose to her lips, clenched her hands in frustration and turned on her heel.

Damn the man! Never in her life had she met anyone as arrogant, as stubborn, as infuriating, as . . . as *male*.

Her cheeks flamed as she walked away from the wharf and into Boston town. She was dimly aware that the people she passed shot her curious looks, but she paid scant attention. All her thoughts were of Garrick Marlowe, and they were not remotely flattering.

Fine, if that was how he felt about it, she would not trouble him again. She would get to Connecticut another way—even if she had to walk!

She was actually considering whether or not that might be possible several hours later as she finished milking the Bartons' Jersey cow and carried the wooden pail inside.

"Careful," Amanda Barton admonished as Amelia entered the kitchen. A few drops of milk sloshed onto the floor that was scrubbed and sanded every week.

Amelia put the pail down and was about to clean up the spill when Mistress Barton surprised her. The older woman took the rag from her hand, smiled and said, "Here, now, I'll be doing that. You go tidy up for supper."

It would have been uncharitable of Amelia to show her surprise. She was not accustomed to such consideration from her hostess. But Mistress Barton was insistent. Before Amelia could think of any reason to object, she was sent on her way.

The small room she used was tucked under the eaves on the second floor. It was barely large enough for a single rope bed, a trunk and a rough-hewn table that held a candle and porcelain bowl for washing.

Amelia hung her cape on the peg beside the door and smoothed her plain black dress that she wore with a starched white apron. Sitting on the edge of the bed, she untied her cap, set it aside and took the pins from her hair. With the russet mass tumbling around her shoulders, she began slowly and steadily to brush it.

As she did so, her thoughts turned back to the barely remembered time when she had sat on her mother's lap to have her hair brushed. She could still hear—if only faintly—the soft, sweet melodies her mother had sung to her and recall the subtle scent of violet that had lingered on her skin even in the depths of winter. That was still how she thought of her mother, as something rare and wonderful whose delicacy could not long withstand the harsh, cold world.

Amelia was made of sterner stuff, fortunately, for when she went down the narrow steps to the kitchen, she found Peter Harkness waiting for her.

Chapter Three

The Bartons exchanged looks of sheepish triumph. They had engineered this meeting against Amelia's objections and they meant for it to follow exactly as they planned.

William Barton rose and gravely inclined his head. "Good eve, Mistress Daniels."

"Elder Barton," Amelia said, nodding in his direction. He was a short, compactly built man with thinning gray hair and pale features.

In England and later in the Lowlands, Master Barton had worked as a lawyer and had been content to remain as such while his more adventurous friends went off into the wilderness. But with the improvement of life in the colony and the lure of a large land grant, he at last felt the call to go.

To his pleasant surprise, he discovered that young as the colony was, it had its share and more of disputes requiring a lawyer's assistance. He put his land out to lease and unpacked his legal books.

Within a year, William Barton had a flourishing practice and had sufficiently impressed the Colony's leaders to be elected to the Council of the Elect. He took his responsibilities seriously and never hesitated to step in where he thought his wisdom and guidance were needed—exactly as he was doing now. Amelia's gaze shifted to the big, blunt-featured man beside him. Peter Harkness was in his mid-twenties, young for the position he held in the community. He had a full shock of light brown hair and a flourishing beard that she suspected he had grown to make himself look older. He was large-boned with long limbs, broad shoulders and a leonine head.

His face, where it wasn't covered by hair, was reddened by the long hours he spent outdoors farming his considerable holding or supervising the work of his bond servants. His eyes were blue and not unattractive, although they rested on Amelia with an intensity she did not like.

Brought to the Plymouth colony as a child, Harkness believed fiercely in the superiority of the Puritans over all other men and in their God-given right to make the New World their own. He was known to have complained that anyone who thought otherwise was a backslider not worthy of the great task on which they were embarked.

Amelia suspected he considered her father to have been one such weak link in the Puritan chain, although he had been careful never to say so to her face.

Now he inclined his head in acknowledgment of her and said gravely, "It be time for prayers, mistress. Join us."

Amelia knew perfectly well that there was always prayer before supper. The custom was followed in the Barton household as it had been in her father's. Master Harkness's reminder was intended solely to demonstrate his right to give her direction.

She deliberately ignored his gesture for her to stand beside him, instead taking her place on the opposite side of the table. Master Barton shot her a reprimanding glance, but he shied away from correcting her.

He had learned in the months she had lived under his roof that while Mistress Daniels could be the soul of courtesy and consideration, she possessed an iron will he did not wish to challenge. Better to leave that to Elder Harkness, whom he both admired and vaguely feared.

Although William Barton was the eldest male present—and it was his home—he showed his respect for his guest by deferring to him. "Would you lead us, Elder Harkness?" he asked, handing him the Bible.

The burly farmer contrived to look surprised at the request, but only for a moment. Clearly, he accepted it as his due.

"By all means, Master Barton." Taking the Bible in his large hands, he opened it gently, found the passages he sought and began to read in a voice that, though deep and gravelly, had a melodic quality that was not unpleasant. Nonetheless, the words chilled Amelia for they were from the Book of Judges and dealt with the abuse of women unfortunate enough to be given into the hands of strangers.

Telling herself she should not read too much into Elder Harkness's choice, Amelia kept her features blank. She stood with her hands folded and her head bowed.

Firelight flickered in the hearth and in the pure beeswax candles set in pewter sticks on the mantel and table. The kitchen was pleasantly warm and filled with good smells.

Outside, darkness had fallen and the wind rattled against the window frames. Yet Amelia found herself thinking longingly of the hills above the water and the free, wild places where she would much rather have been.

At length—longer than was usual—Elder Harkness finished. He closed the Bible, returned it to Master Barton and took his seat opposite Amelia. The Bartons sat at either end. Two young bondwomen appeared to serve the food.

Amelia's appetite had deserted her, but she forced herself to eat at least a small portion of everything. Her strength was her best—indeed, only—protection. She could not afford to let herself weaken.

Silence reigned for an uncomfortable time until at last it was broken by Master Barton who was responding to his wife's telling glance. "Well, now, Elder Harkness," he said with strained joviality, "how goes the tilling?"

"Well enough," the younger man responded. "Three new fields will be laid to the plow this season. The stony land plagues us as always but we press on. The bondmen complain about their burdens and give scant work for the keeping, and constant vigilance is needed lest the Indian rise against us." He shrugged as though saying no more than was obvious to everyone. "It matters not. The great work continues."

Mistress Barton murmured approvingly and called for more turnips. Amelia took a sip of her cider and remained silent. She sensed more was coming and thought it best to get it over with as soon as possible.

"Only three fields?" Master Barton repeated, urged on once again by his wife's silent glare. "I thought you had meant to add more?"

Elder Harkness chewed a portion of salted beef, swallowed it and said gruffly, "I did, but the cost is too great. Steel plows must be bought as well as oxen, labor is dear, and then there is the matter of seed." He shook his large head in frustration. "Until we can provide more fully for ourselves, the heathen captains will continue to rob us."

"Heathen?" Amelia repeated. She had not meant to speak, but such provocation could not go by unquestioned. "I was not aware that any captain of a vessel putting into Boston proclaimed himself a heathen."

"Then you be ignorant of the truth," Elder Harkness said bluntly. "They are loose, immoral men driven by their greed to the exclusion of all else. They care nothing for the Almighty or those who do his work. Indeed, they mock our sober, God-fearing lives. But," he added with satisfaction, "they will not mock when the fires of hell torment them. They will repent throughout eternity while we bask in the glory of salvation."

Amelia pressed her lips together tightly. She despised such self-righteousness and thought it deserved only contempt. Moreover, Elder Harkness's obvious pleasure at the thought of how others would suffer dismayed her.

And this was the man the Bartons thought she should marry? She really *would* walk all the way to Connecticut before she let that happen.

She managed to sit quietly through the rest of supper but as soon as it was over and the table cleared, she seized the chance to escape.

"If you will excuse me," she said as she rose, "I have had a long day and would like to retire."

The Bartons looked surprised, for they knew her to be a light sleeper who preferred to read much of the night away. Indeed, they had chided her about her extravagance with wood and candle, ignoring that she paid for both. "Surely you will stay awhile," Mistress Barton said.

It was not a question, but Amelia chose to treat it as such. "How kind you are to want my company," she said with exaggerated courtesy. "Another time I would be delighted."

Pausing for dramatic effect—and smiling inwardly at her daring—she touched the back of her hand to her forehead. "I fear this long winter has sapped my strength."

Mistress Barton's eyes narrowed, for she held the opinion that her young boarder had the strength of ten when she chose to use it—or at least the stubbornness of ten. Before she could insist further, Amelia dropped a slight curtsey and withdrew.

Behind her, she heard their muttering voices—among them Peter Harkness's, demanding to know if she was "commonly subject to such weakness."

Let him think so, Amelia urged silently. Perhaps he would judge her unworthy of the honor of being his wife and leave her in peace.

But much as she longed to believe that was possible, she knew better. Her wealth made her attractive to him, and nothing she could do would change that. Except leaving.

Reluctantly, she climbed the stairs to her room. It was cold in the small chamber. Not having expected her to retire so soon, the servants hadn't warmed her bed. She climbed into it shivering, having left on most of her clothes, and drew the candle as close as she could.

She settled down to read by the flickering light. The book was one of her favorites: a translation of the journal of Marco Polo recounting his adventures in the East. Although she had read it many times before, it never failed to hold her attention.

Until tonight. Try though she did, she could not concentrate on the familiar passages. Instead, she found herself thinking of Garrick Marlowe.

She should despise the man by now—and a part of her did. But she also found herself remembering the flash of his eyes, the broad set of his shoulders, the rough, almost caressing timbre of his voice.

A groan escaped her. She was behaving like an addle-pated idiot, and she had to stop right now. "The Polos—father, uncle and son—had reached the court of the Great Khan where all manner of splendors awaited them," she read.

Amelia tried to concentrate on the tale's telling but the image of Garrick Marlowe kept distracting her. At last, she gave up and extinguished the candle beside the bed.

She lay under the covers, listening to the wind and did not really expect to sleep. But the stress of recent days overcame her. She slipped almost unaware over the boundary of consciousness and knew nothing more until the sunlight peeping through the window woke her.

"They're driving a hard bargain, Captain," Jacob Dykler said, "or at least they're trying to. I've never seen prices like this for stores in all my born days. You could feed a fleet for what they want."

Garrick leaned against the ship's railing and stared out over the water, in the opposite direction from the port. Just then, he was fed up with Boston town. Were he to never see it again, it would suit him, well.

"They think it's turnabout and fair," Garrick said with a shrug. "We sold nothing cheaply, so they don't want to either."

"Aye, but we brought luxuries that they could have said nay to," Jacob pointed out. He was a Hollander and the first mate on *Venturer* for the past five sailing seasons. Ten years older than Garrick and a grizzled veteran of the seas, he commanded both respect and trust.

"No man has to have fancy French furniture or silver from England or fine Irish wool spun in Flanders," Jacob continued. "They're supposed to be plain folk here, aren't they? But since they've gotten a little prosperity, they want to buy only the best. They have to expect to pay for it."

"And they want us to do the same, even though all we're buying is flour and corn, dried fish and cider."

"Aye," Jacob rumbled. "You'd think we were planning to eat and drink gold all the way back."

"We're not," Garrick said emphatically. He came away from the deck railing, a lean, powerful figure austerely dressed in black breeches and a loose white shirt. The day had turned warm with the dying of the wind. It was possible to believe spring had truly arrived.

"They forget," he added, "they are not alone in this place."

Jacob nodded. Softly, he said, "Passicham says the tribes have good stores left from the winter and will trade for them if we wish."

Garrick did not reply at once. He walked over to the other side of the deck and stood for a few moments, watching the bustle along the pier. Jacob came to stand beside him.

An ox cart passed bearing lumber and several kegs of nails. It was only one of several to be seen around Boston. Everywhere they looked, the town was expanding. New streets were being laid out, and new houses built. The pace of growth was almost dizzying.

Nor was it limited to the town. They had only to journey a few hours inland to find new villages going up at a startling pace. Each month brought new immigrants to the colony's shores. Some of them stayed in Boston but many others ventured westward in search of the cheap land that had drawn them to the New World.

And all the while, the Indians watched. Some of them said the white man would stop coming, for there could not be many more of them willing to make such a long journey to an unknown future. Others said it was useful to have new allies.

And some said the tribes should make peace among themselves at last, and together stop the strangers who had come into their land—before it was too late.

Quietly, Garrick said, "Tell Passicham to come on board tonight. We will talk."

Jacob nodded. "What shall I tell the merchants?"

"That I don't like their prices and they should reconsider them, what else?"

"They won't be pleased—and if they get the idea we're willing to trade with the Indians, they'll be angrier still."

Garrick shrugged. "I didn't come three thousand miles across the ocean to be cheated of a fair profit and neither did you. Before I pay blood money for salted cod, I'll chew Pequot jerky all the way back to Bristol."

"It may come to that," Jacob said with a touch of grimness. "I'll get the word to Passicham. Where will you be?"

"Stretching my land legs," Garrick said with a grin. "If you need me, try the inn."

"Upstairs or down?" Jacob asked with feigned innocence.

The captain shook his proud head ruefully. "Boston's a cold town even on a warm spring day."

"It is that, yet you've a way of heating it up." More seriously, Jacob added, "Be careful, Garrick. I can't put my finger on it, but there's a certain tension in this place that I don't like. These people are getting stronger, that's for sure. The hardest days are behind them. But they're not showing any signs of appreciating their good fortune. They're a stiff-necked lot, sure they've got the answers to everything. Men who think that way will do the damnedest things and still call themselves holy."

"They can do anything they please," Garrick said bluntly, "so long as they don't cross swords with me." He cuffed his old friend on the shoulder. "You worry too much. Maybe you're the one who ought to be visiting the inn."

Jacob laughed but shook his head. "I'll wait for home and my own sweet Vilma. Thanks all the same."

"As you will," Garrick said. He swung down the gangway and was soon lost in the passing crowd.

Amelia took a basket from a hook by the kitchen door, looped it over her arm and slipped out into the yard beyond the house. Mistress Barton was in the drawing room, the most recent addition to the house and by far that lady's private joy.

She had several friends in for conversation and precious cups of chocolate. Amelia had pointedly not been invited.

This pleased her no end. The last thing she wanted to be doing on such a bright, warm day was sitting with Mistress Barton and a half-dozen ladies like her, enduring their censorious looks and pointed conversation. She was in disgrace for shunning Peter Harkness, and she was enjoying every moment of it.

In addition, she had work to do. While the matter of how to leave Boston remained unsettled, she still had to reassure those who were counting on her to succeed. Market day offered the perfect opportunity to do so.

Neatly garbed in a plain black dress, her hair concealed by the usual white starched cap, she set off for the center of the town, where farmers from the outlying villages gathered to sell their products. Most of the goods were roughly made compared to those being brought in from Europe, but they appealed greatly to the large number of colonists who could not afford such luxuries.

The stalls were already set up and the traffic brisk by the time Amelia arrived. She made her way past the tanners and wheelwrights, the barrel makers and coopers, the weavers and sail makers to find the small booth where the Whitler family offered its wares.

Samuel Whitler was haggling with a townsman over a length of cloth that Lissy Whitler had woven during the winter. The townsman offered tuppence, but Samuel was holding out for more.

As he said to Amelia when the townsman had gone away empty-handed, "What will tuppence buy me? A handful of seed, a piece of cod? A man needs more if he is to live."

"Be patient," Lissy advised softly. She laid a hand on her young husband's arm and smiled at Amelia. " 'Tis early yet. We'll sell the cloth before the day is out."

"I'm sure you will," Amelia replied. She touched it lightly, admiring the snugness of the weave. Lissy had made it from the wool of their own sheep. They also had several tanned hides to offer along with smoked hams and sides of bacon.

On the surface, they were doing well, but Samuel complained that the council had denied him the right to acquire the land next to his even though he was confident he could farm it well. Moreover, they would not let him build a small dam to help irrigate his fields unless he paid a hefty tax for the privilege. Every time he turned around, he met new restrictions and limitations. And he knew why.

"They save the best for themselves," he said bluntly. "If you're one of the elect, you're set for life. If you're not, well then, good luck to you, for it's the short end of the stick, for sure."

"It wasn't supposed to be like this," Lissy said sadly. "When the man came from the Massachusetts Bay Colony to speak in our town, he promised the chance to build something we could never have had at home. But now..." She broke off, sadness shadowing her eyes.

Amelia knew of her pain because Samuel had told her that their first child had been born dead in the steerage hold of the ship that brought them to Boston. Before they ever set foot in their home, the cost of it was already higher than they could have imagined. And now they had to face the fact that it had not been worth it. At least, not yet.

"Any news?" Samuel asked, lowering his voice.

Amelia shook her head. She did not want to add to their burdens by telling them about her problems with Captain Marlowe. Instead, she chose to be hopeful.

"Nothing yet, but now that the good weather has come, more ships will be in harbor. You understand, I must be careful about who I approach. We don't want word of what we plan to reach the council."

The Whitlers nodded quickly. No one had to tell them what the consequences of that would be. "We will be ready when the time comes," Samuel assured her, "and so will the others. It can't be too soon to suit us."

Amelia felt the burden of the trust they placed in her, but she did not resent it. Life had prepared her for such responsibility, for all that men like Garrick Marlowe thought it unsuitable for a woman. The Whitlers and the others were counting on her. She would not let them down.

She was still thinking about that as she made her way among the stalls and did not see the large, bearded man who approached her until he stood directly blocking her path.

Abruptly, she stopped and looked at him. "Elder Harkness ... good morn. I did not expect—"

"Obviously not, Mistress Daniels," he said gruffly, although to give him credit, he did attempt a smile. "You looked deep in thought or perhaps in prayer."

"Thought," she said, and moved to go around him. He shifted slightly—enough to stop her. "Excuse me," Amelia murmured, and tried again.

"Why so hurried?" he asked, and took her arm.

She flinched at the touch and tried to pull away, but he would not have it. His smile turned grim as he stared down at her. "You are defiant, Mistress Daniels," he said.

"You are presumptuous, Master Harkness," she shot back. With an effort, she wrenched herself free and turned on her heel.

If she could not go around or through him, she would simply find another route. But she would not spend another moment in the company of this man who was beginning to frighten her.

Elder Harkness had other ideas. Before she could get more than a few paces, he was beside her. His hand gripped her shoulder as he turned her to him. "Your father did you no favor when he raised you in so unwomanly a fashion," he said. "But fear not, the fault can be corrected. Be guided by me and you will be spared the pain of eternal torment."

Amelia paled. She stared into his overly bright eyes and tasted bile. "You are mad."

"Mad?" he repeated as though the word was foreign to him. Bemusedly, he shook his head. "Truly, you are possessed by devils. That must be why the Almighty sent you here—that your soul be saved from damnation. When we are man and wife, you will bend before the rod of correction. Pain will purge you and in it you will find salvation."

"I will roast in Hell first and think myself fortunate. Now let go!"

Startled by her vehemence, he almost did just that. But after an instant, his grip tightened even more fiercely. Amelia had reached the end of her patience. She was angry, frightened and disgusted.

It was that disgust, more than anything else, that prompted her to lash out at Elder Harkness. She kicked sharply, catching him in the shin. Taken by surprise, he gasped and let go of her.

Amelia ran. She was not so foolish as to stay to examine the extent of the damage she had inflicted—either on his person or his arrogance. Later, she would deal with the repercussions that were bound to come, but not just then. Or so she hoped as she darted down the narrow street. However, her thwarted suitor recovered quickly and was after her in a flash. Red-eyed and panting in his rage, he caught up with her near the fishmonger's. She had only a moment's glimpse of his features contorted with anger before his hand caught her full across the face.

She screamed and stumbled against the stall. The fishmonger yelled at Harkness to stop and several other people cried out in shock, but he paid no heed. Starting after Amelia, he paused long enough to unbuckle the broad leather belt he wore around his waist.

"Let your correction begin now," he snarled, "for truly it comes not a moment to soon."

The belt raised, he advanced on her, only to stop suddenly in midstride, his hand still stretched above his head and his face frozen in shock.

The side of his black woolen jerkin was pinned to the stall, held there by the protruding hilt of the dagger embedded in it.

Chapter Four

Her eyes fastened on the weapon, Amelia got to her feet. She was shaking all over and only just managed to stay upright. Dazedly, she looked around.

Garrick Marlowe stood a short distance away, observing the scene. His smile was chilling. He stepped forward, removed the knife and slipped it back into the leather sheath on his boot. His smile deepened.

"Elder Harkness, isn't it?" he asked, almost pleasantly. His calmness—even his good humor—made him all the more threatening, Amelia realized. He appeared to fear nothing.

The two men were almost the same height, both broad-shouldered and heavily muscled. Each was in peak condition.

Harkness was fueled by rage and, just possibly, madness. Marlowe was coldly lethal. He easily sidestepped the blow Harkness aimed at him, grabbed the elder by the scruff of the neck and sent him hurtling into the wall of a nearby shop.

Reeling, Harkness climbed slowly to his feet and stood shaking his head like a dazed bull. Marlowe spoke quietly.

"Come on, try it again. Let's see how you do against someone your own size. Women are easy. They're smaller, weaker, and they aren't trained to fight. Any coward can go after one of them."

Harkness made a low, guttural sound, bent his head and charged again. This time, Marlowe met him squarely.

The hard thud of the men's bodies colliding made Amelia wince. She looked away hastily, only to find that she was irresistibly drawn to watch.

The struggle went on for several minutes. Harkness was so used to enforcing his will through his fists that he had trouble believing how outmatched he was. Although he did manage to land several blows, they had scant effect.

Marlowe, on the other hand, was relentless. Step by step, he drove Harkness back until the elder was bent over, gasping for breath, blood streaming from his nose and his eyes swelling shut.

The crowd watched with rapt attention. Although many among them were Puritans, none stepped forward to help Harkness. By the looks on their faces, Amelia guessed that more than a few were not sorry to see him brought so low.

For her, the sight was sickening. She was on the verge of crying out to stop it when Harkness fell heavily to his knees and made no attempt to get up.

Marlowe rubbed his knuckles absently as he came over to where Amelia was standing. He frowned as he saw the bruise rapidly forming across her cheek.

"You need a keeper," he grumbled, and taking her hand marched off toward the harbor.

So numbed was she by what had happened that Amelia let him lead her away without protest. Not until they were standing in front of the inn did she realize what was happening.

"That's far enough," she said quickly, and grabbed her hand away. Hastily, she added, "I thank you for your help, but I must be going now."

He made a low sound of derision and ignored her. Instead, he threw the door open and with a firm but gentle shove, pushed her inside. For once, the main room was empty. The captains and officers were taking advantage of the fair weather to see to tasks about their vessels.

Marlowe guided Amelia to a bench, told her to stay put and disappeared into the back room. He returned to find her halfway out the door.

With a low curse, he dropped the basin he was carrying on the table, sloshing water in the process, and crossed the room in rapid strides. Her protests availed nothing as he placed her firmly on the bench.

"Sit still," he ordered. Glaring, she set her mouth mutinously and shook her head. That was a mistake. Pain washed through her, making her cry out.

Marlowe cursed again. He dropped to his knees in front of her, took both her hands in his and said, "For the love of God, it won't kill you to do what you're told just this once!"

The fervency of his tone stunned her into obedience. She sat quietly as he gently bathed the bruise and, while he was at it, the cuts she had gotten on her hands as she raised them in a futile effort to defend herself. As he worked, he had several comments to make about Harkness, all to the effect that he had let him off too lightly.

When he finished at last, he sat back and observed his handiwork. "You look better," he said gruffly. "Now drink this and tell me what happened to set him off."

Amelia took a sip from the mug he held out to her, sputtered and eyed him accusingly over the rim. The liquid burned all the way down her throat, but it also eased the queer, melting sensation she had been experiencing ever since he began ministering to her.

"What is this?" she asked, wheezing.

"Rum. Haven't you ever had it before?"

"Of course not. Proper Puritan woman don't drink spirits."

He grinned broadly. With an odd note of tenderness, he said, "You don't look very proper." He stared at her for a long moment before abruptly getting to his feet.

He took the basin away and emptied it out a window. When he was finished and had set it aside, he did not return to where she was sitting, but stood some distance away from her.

"Did Harkness find out about your harebrained scheme?" he demanded.

"Of course not. I have been very careful."

"Then what set him off?"

Amelia hesitated. She took another sip of the rum and discovered that it did not burn so badly this time. The terrible fear of the past hour was fading swiftly. In its absence, she felt strangely calm.

Softly, she said, "I rejected his suit."

Garrick's eyes narrowed. Incredulously, he asked, "He wanted to marry you?"

"Why so surprised?" Amelia demanded, the softness fading. "Isn't that what you recommended? Marry some Puritan, you said, as though that was the answer to everything."

"I said some good Puritan lad," Garrick shot back. "Not a heavy-handed bully who was left out under the moon a time too often."

"He sits on the council of elders," Amelia said. "He has the respect of the leaders of the community. *And* he is determined to have my father's money." Almost to remind herself, she added, "I could be forced to marry him."

"Then leave," Garrick said bluntly. "The *Bristol* sails tomorrow. Captain Bradley's a good man. He'll give you passage."

For a moment, Amelia was tempted. If she did as he said, her struggles would be over. She could go back to England, take up the threads of her life among cousins who had made it clear she would be welcome, and perhaps in time, find a man to her liking.

She could have a full and good life. Any sensible woman would have leaped at the chance. Which only showed, she thought ruefully, how singularly lacking in sense she really was.

She stood and with quiet dignity said, "I can't. I know you think that means I'm mad, and perhaps you're right, but there's such tremendous opportunity here to create something of true worth. I can't give that up."

"Even though it could cost your life?" he asked harshly.

She answered thoughtfully. "I'm not a very brave person, captain. If anything, this experience with Harkness showed me that. I'm deeply grateful to you for your help. But we all die eventually. It's as natural as birth itself. What matters is what we do in between."

She turned to go. Garrick stepped forward and opened the door for her. He looked at her intently as he said, "I still believe you're wrong, mistress, but Jonathan Daniels would be proud of his daughter."

Amelia flushed. "Thank you," she said. "If you change your mind, Captain, there is still time to join us."

He inclined his head to show that while he wasn't about to take her up on it, he respected her persistence. They exchanged smiles before she departed.

Garrick went into the inn slowly, his thoughts on Amelia. Long ago he had decided that emotion was a weakness he could not afford. Lesser men fell prey to anger, fear, love, lust and all the rest distracted from what they might otherwise have achieved.

But not him. He fought when he had to, enjoyed a woman when it was convenient and otherwise kept his mind on business. At least until now.

He could have killed Peter Harkness. The urge to do so had been so strong within him it was almost irresistible. If he hadn't stopped when he did, it would have been too late.

And afterward...sweet heaven, what he had felt as he touched her poor, bruised face, shocked him. Never had he felt so driven to possess a woman and yet equally compelled to protect her. He shook his head disbelievingly. He called *her* mad, but what of himself?

Water lapped against the pilings behind the inn. Not far away, *Venturer* rode high, her cargo emptied. Soon she would be reloaded, and when that was done he would catch the first tide out of Boston town. It could not be soon enough.

By the time Amelia returned to the Barton house, word of what had occurred in the market had spread. She was met at the door by a scowling and red-faced Amanda.

"How dare you?" Mistress Barton demanded. "Elder Harkness beaten in the streets over the likes of you! You belong in the stocks, you ungrateful wench. To think that we took you in, sheltered you, gave you—"

"Gave nothing," Amelia interrupted flatly. "You are incapable of charity, Mistress Barton, and we both know it. You have been well paid for anything I have received here. As for Elder Harkness, *he* attacked *me*. Captain Marlowe came to my defense. If he hadn't, I might be dead by now. I will say that in public and at the top of my lungs should the council or anyone else try to deny it."

"Why, you—" Mistress Barton sputtered. Her eyes bulged. Though she continued to move her mouth, no sound emerged. Amelia's defiance so astounded her that she was struck dumb by it.

That was at least some small satisfaction—yet it comforted Amelia little. She brushed past Amanda and went upstairs to her room where she fell exhausted onto the bed.

Her face had begun to throb again, but she could not think about that. Clearly, it was impossible for her to remain under the Bartons' roof. Her departure from Boston was more urgent than ever. Yet the problem of how to achieve it remained unsolved.

Despair weighed down on her, but she refused to give in to it. There had to be a way... She was so close. The Indians were willing to deal with her, so all she had to do was... She sat up suddenly, struck by the realization of what she had overlooked.

She remembered her meeting with the Pequot emissary on the Whitler homestead just outside of town. With him had come a party of several dozen braves. Together, they had traveled to Boston by land and water. The birchbark canoes they used had been brought ashore near the farm. She had seen them herself.

The Pequot had said she could deal with them for land if she came to Connecticut. At the time, she had not expected to face such a formidable problem in getting there.

It hadn't occurred to her to ask them for help. But now it did.

She had heard rumors that the emissary was still in the town. All she had to do was find him. But in daylight, the risk of detection would be too great.

Downstairs, she heard Mistress Barton moving around. She was slamming pots and berating one of the bond servants. Sighing, Amelia resigned herself to a long afternoon. She lay on her bed, her head pillowed in her hand, and watched the sun slowly sink toward the hills.

Passicham came on board *Venturer* shortly after dark. He came alone and so silently that he was on the deck striding toward the forecastle before the watch realized he was there. Garrick waved the watch into silence and stepped forward to greet the Pequot.

"Welcome," he said. "I was about to sup. Will you join me?"

Passicham nodded. He was in his late twenties, of moderate height and well built with sharp eyes and a steady manner. Garrick liked him.

"Gladly," the Pequot said. His English was slightly accented but fluent. He had learned it as a child when he had shown a gift for such things.

Among his other accomplishments were Algonquin, Mohegan, Penobscot and French. Garrick was unsure of his precise standing among the tribes but he sensed it was high.

They adjourned to the cabin where they would be assured the greatest privacy. The cook's boy brought platters of stew and freshly baked bread. They ate in silence.

When the stew was gone and the last of the sauce dipped up, Garrick sat back in his chair and studied the Indian across from him. He was uncertain how to begin, but decided that the direct approach was best. Besides, he'd be willing to bet *Venturer* herself that Passicham already knew what prices the Puritans had demanded.

"Greed does strange things to men," Garrick said by way of opening.

The Pequot nodded thoughtfully. "So I have observed."

"Fairness and honor can be forgotten."

"If they ever existed.

"Indeed."

Silence reigned as the two men regarded one another. Each waited for the other to speak, sensing advantage in a seeming lack of eagerness. Finally, Garrick bowed to the fact that it was his men who needed their stomachs filled, not Passicham's.

Quietly, he said, "I still have goods to trade. Bolts of cloth, nails, rope and several fine saddles. Does that interest you?"

"The cloth and rope, possibly. The nails, no. As for the saddles..." Passicham smiled slightly. "We shall see."

From this, Garrick concluded two things—that a deal would be done, and that the saddles would bring the highest price. Although the Pequot did not depend on horses, being mostly a forest and shore people who traveled by water or by foot, they were beginning to develop a fondness for the animal introduced to them of late. The usefulness of the saddle, especially in combat, had not escaped them.

The bargaining proceeded smoothly. Both men enjoyed haggling to some degree, but neither was interested in wasting time.

Before the candle had drawn down an inch, the deal was set. Garrick would have the provisions he needed for the homeward voyage and he would have them at a fair price. The Puritans be damned.

He smiled with grim satisfaction and held out his hand to Passicham, who took it readily. "I am anxious to depart. Can you begin bringing the goods on tomorrow?"

"I can," the Pequot agreed, "if that is what you wish." Passicham paused delicately, his silence making the point that if the good citizens of Boston town saw a party of Indians loading goods onto *Venturer,* they would be none too pleased.

Garrick took that into account, but his growing frustration with the Puritans outweighed it. He thought it time and past time that they learned a useful lesson, namely that there were always alternatives for those bold enough to seize them.

"Do it," he said.

Chapter Five

In the shadows beyond the wharf, Peter Harkness stirred gingerly. He was hurt badly but determined to ignore the pain. Some would say mere instinct had inspired him to watch Marlowe in his lair. He preferred to believe it was the favor of the Almighty shining as it always did on the elect. A brittle smile twisted his mouth. The Indian was on board, the one Harkness had already warned the council about.

He could not say exactly what made him so dislike the one called Passicham, but it had something to do with the way the man so steadily and calmly looked at him, as though he saw clear through to his soul and did not care for what he found there. Harkness did not want a person like that to exist in the same world as him. It was really that simple.

And now he had found him with Marlowe. It was almost too much to be hoped for, he thought. He trembled with eagerness as he stood and slowly made his way into the town. He would inform the elders. He would insist on his rights. He would have revenge.

An unwelcome thought suddenly crossed his mind. What if they refused him? Already, he had seen in their eyes a certain displeasure over what had happened in the market. Several had made comments about embarrassing the elect. Some even seemed to suggest that he could have been at fault.

Harkness's next thought caused him to gasp for air.

They were against him. He saw it now that he thought about it carefully. Oh, yes, they had elected him to their precious council when his growing wealth and the fervency of his belief could no longer be ignored.

But he couldn't really trust any of them. They were all weak when it came down to it—lawyers and scholars whose idea of struggling for the Lord meant talking, talking, talking until a man grew sick to death of words.

He preferred action.

If he went to them, they would debate what should be done. There would be proposals, counterproposals, arguments. Even, perhaps, a vote before it was over. God save them all.

Had they voted at Sinai when the commandments were handed down? Had there been debate over when and where the Savior should be born? Faith—true faith—did not allow for such things.

He knew what must be done. He always knew, even when the little, sniveling men couldn't decide.

Grinning, he walked quickly away from the pier and was soon lost in the swirling night mists.

Amelia left the Barton house shortly before midnight. She moved on tiptoe down the steps and almost held her breath when the door creaked as she opened it. The moment it shut behind her, she began to run.

Quickly, quickly, like a deer in a field racing for cover before someone saw it. The Whitler farm was an hour beyond town. Moonlight ribboned the road, turning it

silver. Solitude and silence closed around her, punctu-
ated by the muted sounds of an early spring night.

A few early waking frogs croaked hopefully. A doe
raised its head from nibbling, but sensed no danger. A
dark shape close to the ground ambled across the road
before her—a woodchuck, perhaps, or a raccoon recently woken from its winter sleep.

She wrapped her cloak more closely around her and
kept going, glad that her father had long ago taught her
to appreciate the night. While others fled from it in fear,
barricading themselves inside their houses and their
dreams, Jonathan Daniels had taken his small daughter
outside so that she might see the moon with all its faces
and the stars, gleaming, as he said, like the promises of
the Almighty in the inky infinity above.

She had loved it all as she loved him. The memory of
that love wrapped her in comfort snugger than any cloak.
Her thought was to find the Whitlers and get word
through them that she needed to meet with the Pequot
again. As soon as that could be done, she would broach
her plan. With luck, it would prove acceptable.

But first, she had to cross the marshes beyond the
town. She was concentrating fully on the road when some
unknown sound perceived at the edges of her mind
caused her to turn.

She stopped, staring in the direction of Boston as her
heart rose in her throat. There, above the town, twisting
gray in the moonlight, was the unmistakable sign of fire.

She was a merchant's daughter, bred to the narrow
streets of London and Amsterdam, where a single tinder
bursting free could wreak havoc. Bred, too, to the tales
of ships destroyed and dreams dashed when vessels perished in flame. Terror curled at the edges of her soul and
set up a keen howling deep within her.

She ran, faster than before, feet pelting, back toward the town. Never mind that she had grown to despise the elect and everything they stood for. They were human, too, as were all the others threatened so suddenly with destruction. Fire banished all differences.

Her breath came in short, painful gasps when at last she reached the town and saw that the fire was near the piers. That was a mercy, perhaps. If it was a ship ablaze, it could be confined; the vessel would be cut from its moorings and set to drift on the tide where the fire would do the least damage.

If the tide was outgoing. Amelia struggled to remember, realized that it was and gave a sigh of relief. The fire roared, and she could hear its deep-throated voice. But this night, at least Boston town would be spared.

Spared not was the proud vessel engulfed in darting tongues of flame. When Amelia saw which ship it was, she gave a cry of dismay. *Venturer* was in her death throes, alight from the tip of her mast to the last few feet of hull showing above the waterline.

She had been cut loose and was drifting out on the tide like the Viking burial ships her father had told her about, Amelia thought. There was a terrible, majestic sorrow to the dying vessel. She cried out again and moved closer to the pier.

The crowd there was thick. Many had come out at the call of fire, bringing buckets and burlap sacks—anything they had to fight it with. And they had tried, at risk to themselves.

Men of the town had helped get the sailors off and even saved the captain's precious instruments. But it was the captain, they were saying, who had gone back into the inferno to carry the first mate, slung over his shoulders and moaning with the pain of his burns, to safety. The captain, himself, was so darkened by smoke and flame as to seem like something from the netherworld.

They had done what they could; there was no more except to stand in the roaring darkness almost as bright as day and watch the great ship die.

She was awhile at it. First, the mast fell with a mighty crash into the consuming flames, then the roof of the forecastle gave way. Little by little, the flame ate, growing hungrier with every bite.

The smoke thickened and the heat grew almost unbearable. Now the ship was ten feet beyond the pier, now twenty, thirty... The air cooled, the tide pulled and she drifted farther, a skeleton now engulfed in fire, her shrieks growing quieter.

Amelia choked back a sob. It was only a ship, she told herself. Not a living thing—only wood and resin, rope and sail, hopes and dreams. Nothing, really. She stumbled away from the pier and turned without thinking toward the inn. There was a crowd there, too, but they parted to let her through the door.

The first person she saw was Captain Feather. She did not know him, nor he her, but she went up to him without hesitation.

"Captain Marlowe," she said, her voice low and rasping from the smoke, "where is he?"

He gave her a long, level look. Swiftly, he pointed, "There, but don't go over."

"Why not?"

"They're caring for the mate. He's badly burned. You don't want to see." Ignoring him, she took a step forward. His hand closed on her arm. "Easy, lass," he said gently. "I be Charles Bradley, captain of the *Bristol*. I'm a friend of Marlowe's and of his mate. They're both good men and neither would want you to see this."

"He said the same of you," Amelia murmured.

"What's that?"

"Garrick said I should take passage with you because you were a good man."

Bradley looked surprised for a moment before he laughed grimly. "I'll remind him of that next time the winds run more in my favor than his. But for the moment, come away."

He meant well, she knew that. He was a kind man and he wanted only to spare her. But there were things he didn't understand.

"Let me go," she said quietly, for indeed she felt that way. A great calmness had settled over her, so different from the frantic fear that had struck her on the road. "I can help," she added.

Her voice, or the steadiness of her regard, was enough to make him loosen his hold. She went quickly—before she could think about it.

Dykler was badly burned, she saw at a glance. Mercifully, he was unconscious. She hoped he would remain that way for some time yet.

"Don't," she said as she saw one of the men nearby gingerly touch the skin on the mate's face. "Step back."

Remarkably, they obeyed. She had no way of knowing that it was the swift glance Garrick shot her, his quickly concealed surprise, that drove his men away from her.

Garrick was beyond anger and in some far distant world where there was only guilt. It was his fault. No one had to explain that to him. He had smelled the fire first, been the first on deck and seen it when it was no more than an infant cluster of flames.

He had tried to stop it, but without success. It had taken him precious moments to understand that it was the tar spilled over the decks that was fueling the fire making it unbeatable.

By that time, it was too late. It was all he could do to shout to the crew to abandon ship, and even then Jacob hadn't obeyed. He'd gone back, trying to get the instruments that in the end some townsmen had managed to save by swimming off the pier and climbing through the porthole.

Garrick would remember forever the smoke and fire he had walked through to reach Jacob. He had felt death licking at him as though deciding whether he was worth the devouring. Incredibly, it turned away, letting him go by so that he might live to another day.

Looking at Jacob, Garrick prayed silently: Please, God, don't let him die, not like this, so far from his beloved Vilma.

Amelia's hands were very slender. He noticed that as they passed over Jacob, inches above him, not touching but doing something Garrick couldn't understand. After a few moments, she stopped. Her hands fell into her lap. "We need ice," she said.

He looked up at her, startled. "And fat," she added. "Pork is best, but beef will do. He must be coated with it, then wrapped in cloth with the ice set around him."

When Garrick still hesitated, she raised her voice. "Now. It must be done or he will die. There is no time to waste."

He obeyed, shouting the order so that others leaped to do her bidding. And he stayed with her, marveling at her gentleness and courage, as she did what had to be done.

Not for an instant did she flinch. Her hands were sure, her compassion unyielding. She stood, a slim, pale shadow, between Dykler and the looming darkness of certain death.

He was carried to a pallet on the floor and the ice in great blocks placed around him—the straw the blocks had been stored in still clinging to them. His clothes were cut away, the fat applied and the bandages wrapped. She did it all aided by Garrick. When she was done at last, she sat back on her haunches, paler still, and said, "Get some sleep. It will be a long night."

"What about you?" he asked.

She looked surprised by the question. This was what she did, this waiting, this silent struggle. Ever since childhood when she had found the skill within her. And her father, understanding somehow, had arranged for her to be taught. So much there was still that she did not know, but could only sense, hovering off in the shadows beyond her awareness.

It didn't matter. She knew it was there, and knowing meant much. She could summon it if she tried hard enough, and she would on this night, for this unknown man. She might fail, it had happened before, but she would try all the same.

Her father had died. She reminded herself of that as she bent closer to Jacob Dykler and listened to the shallow rhythm of his breathing. For Jonathan Daniels, there had been no way to turn back the devouring presence that descended so suddenly into him. She had struggled with all her strength through dark, endless nights, and he had died anyway.

This time was different, although she couldn't say why. Some spark remained in Jacob that had been missing from her father. Some hope.

She thought Garrick would leave, but he did not. Exhausted as he was, he stretched out on the floor beside where she knelt. His hand reached out, the fingers curling around hers.

She stiffened. This was an intrusion she was not accustomed to. Yet it was comfort as well. His touch was warm, reassuring, strong. After a time, the tension left her. She smiled faintly and returned the pressure of his touch.

He slept.

The long and terrible night passed as even the worst of them do. Morning came, and with it the need to confront new realities.

Venturer was gone. And Amelia's night-long presence at the inn—added to all else—had not gone unnoticed. The council had been alerted, a hue and cry raised and dire repercussions threatened.

"They're saying the stocks are too good for her," Captain Bradley told Garrick. "They're saying she led Harkness on and deserved the beating he meant to give her when you intervened. They're crying shame to the rooftops and demanding justice."

"Justice?" Garrick croaked. He had managed to bathe in the water from the well behind the inn, but his clothes were still encrusted with grime. He could barely speak, as sorrow remained a crushing weight on him.

"If they want to talk about justice," he said, "they should concern themselves with finding who burned *Venturer*. I smelled the tar."

Bradley frowned. "What's that?"

"Someone spread tar over the decks. It couldn't have happened by accident. She was burned deliberately." Although he'd had hours to think of it, sleeping and waking, the realization stunned him. Only a madman would deliberately destroy a vessel.

"Who?" Bradley demanded.

Garrick shrugged. The effort hurt him, so stiff and sore did he feel. "My guess is Harkness. He looked like a crazed animal when he went after Amelia, and he wouldn't forgive me for besting him."

"You've an enemy, then, lad, for he's a powerful man."

"He's insane. They all are who use God as an excuse for evil."

"You won't have any argument from me over that. All the same, you ought to think of leaving here."

Garrick smiled bitterly. "How? Every shilling I own is in England now. It will take months to contact my factor and have funds sent. In the meantime, I'm trapped."

"I'd like to help you, but—"

"No need. I understand well enough. Most of us have every pence we've ever earned tied up in ships and cargo."

"Aye," Bradley mused. "But there's some that wouldn't mind changing that. Did you know Gleick wants out?"

Garrick's brows rose. Jan Gleick was one of a company of sea captains who regularly voyaged to the New World. He was in Boston now, having arrived only a day or two after *Venturer*. Although Gleick was beyond his prime, his reputation was spotless.

"He's tired," Bradley said. "Got himself a little spread outside Amsterdam and wants to enjoy it."

"You jest?"

"Nay, I don't, lad. There's some of us who don't think land's the worst place to be. Comes a time when a man feels an urge to settle down."

"Not me," Garrick said quickly. "As soon as I can, I'll get another ship and—"

Another ship. But he didn't have enough for that. To get it, he would have to sign on another man's vessel and go back to being crew instead of captain. After the years of being his own master, that was bitter indeed.

Unless . . .

He looked toward Amelia where she lay asleep beside Dykler. She looked very small and slender, inconsequential really, he thought. It was utterly ridiculous that such a woman would even think about going into the wilderness, much less for the purpose that drove her.

Her own settlement.

His own ship.

He took a deep breath, closed his eyes and said to Bradley, "Tell Gleick I'll be by to see him."

Chapter Six

"Do I understand this rightly?" Jan Gleick demanded. "The two of you be wanting to buy *Lady Star* together?"

"No," Amelia replied. "I wish to buy your ship. Captain Marlowe will take charge of her for me."

Gleick raised his eyebrows, impressive growths of salt and pepper that covered a large part of the top of his face, and said, "It that so? And to what purpose?"

"Does that matter?" Amelia inquired.

"Aye, it does." The grizzled captain smiled slightly as though suggesting that he found the situation amusing. Garrick did not share his view. He shifted from one foot to the other and devotedly hoped the discussion would end soon.

"If you're planning to sail her to hell and back, I'd just as soon know," the Dutch captain continued. He took a puff of his long-stemmed pipe. "She's a good ship and deserving of the best."

Garrick felt a twinge of sympathy. He, too, had known a good ship—but she'd found only a watery grave. He intended to do better by *Lady Star*. "She'll have it," he said. He pointed to the chairs beside the table. "Do you mind if we sit?"

"I guess not," Gleick said after a pause. "Might as well. This looks to take some time."

"Not really," Garrick told him after they had taken their places. He shot a warning glance at Amelia. She'd said enough. Now it was men's business.

They were alone in *Lady Star's* cabin. It was as well appointed as his own had been. He felt the now familiar ache and pushed it away. Later.

Time to be straight with Gleick. The man demanded it.

"We plan a little voyage down the coast. Nothing too adventurous."

Gleick frowned, struggling to follow the train of his thought. "To Virginy?"

"Not that far," Garrick said.

The frown deepened. "There's not much in between save Nieuw Amsterdam and the settlements of my own people."

"Not there," Amelia said hastily, only to fall silent again when Garrick glared at her. Let him take care of it then, arrogant man that he was, she thought.

"I'm too old for guessing games," Gleick said. "Spit it out."

"The Pequots are welcoming settlers in Connecticut," Garrick said. "We'll be heading there."

"Then the council has approved you?"

Slowly, Garrick shook his head. "It's Pequot land," he said. "The council has nothing to do with it."

Gleick whistled softly. He looked bemused, but he was also smiling. "I'll give you credit. You've the brass."

Despite her nervousness—or perhaps because of it—Amelia laughed. "Captain Marlowe said the same about me," she explained, "when I brought the scheme to him."

"It was your idea then?" Gleick asked.

By answer, she said, "I don't like Boston."

It was his turn to laugh. "Neither do I. Too hidebound by far. But mark my words, it will change. Take time though."

"More than we've got," Garrick said. "What say you to the offer?"

Gleick did not answer at once. He rose and walked over to the porthole. Quietly, he said, "She's been my life for well on twenty years. I hate to part with her."

From another man, that might have been a bargaining ploy. But Garrick knew the older man was telling the simple truth. "You don't have to," he said. "You could go on as you are."

Gleick sighed. He broke off his contemplation of the view beyond the porthole and turned back to them.

"My joints creak like the timbers of an old yawl caught in a mighty blow. I forget things I used to remember without even trying. I sleep less but need it more often, and the other night I went to take a sighting and realized I couldn't make out the numbers. No, lad, it's time for me to hang it up."

He sat down again at the table and looked at them steadily. "I don't know you, mistress, but I knew your father and respected him. If you're anything like him, you just might manage to pull this off. As for you, Marlowe..." He shook his head ruefully. "I'm tough but you're tougher, that's the fact of it. A man can go far on that. Still, I'd say you're also lucky, and that doesn't hurt either."

"We'll need luck where we're going," Garrick said.

Gleick nodded. He restocked his pipe, took a draw and settled back in his chair. "Let's get to it then."

The haggling began. Amelia had agreed ahead of time that Marlowe would handle it. She had no real way of judging the worth of the ship, but she knew it would be high. Such vessels came on the market rarely and were snapped up when they did. Silently, she set herself to wait.

An hour later, it was done. Garrick rose and offered Gleick his hand. Both men were smiling.

"You drive a hard bargain, lad," the Dutchman said, "but a fair one." He inclined his head to Amelia. "Mistress, your ship will be in good hands. But I advise you to carry out your plans without delay. We don't need any more proud vessels burning in Boston harbor."

She shivered at the thought and glanced at Garrick. He met her eyes and silently nodded.

They sailed at the turn of the tide. Men were still scrambling to secure the cargo when Garrick called the order to cast off. Boston lay wreathed in darkness. Only a few red-eyed rats observed their departure. *Lady Star* slipped smoothly from her moorings and turned her prow into the wind.

Garrick stood at the wheel, his feet planted slightly apart as he surveyed his new ship. She felt different from *Venturer,* lighter in certain ways, heavier in others.

He wished he'd had the chance to take her out on a shakedown but that was a luxury they could not afford. As it was, they were lucky to get away without trouble.

Passicham's supplies were in the hold, paid for by trade goods that had fortunately been warehoused when the fire hit. Jacob was resting in the captain's cabin, Garrick having insisted that he take it. Amelia was keeping a close watch on him, although she had said he was doing better than she'd really expected.

Garrick turned the wheel slightly, nudging *Lady Star* on to a southwesterly course close to the shore. The wind on his face was fresh and damp. A few clouds scudded across the sky, but the night was clear. A mile beyond the town, he ordered the mainsail struck and let the vessel tack gently toward shore.

They were waiting on the beach beside the pitch torches set up to guide the ship in. There were three dozen in all—eight couples and the rest small children.

Young families, he thought, the kind who would be most likely to rebel against the harsh rule of the council. Their belongings were heaped around them—barrels, sacks and crates, farm tools, blankets and furniture that had been taken apart and strapped together for easier carrying.

Off to the side, tethered to the scrub trees, were the animals—a sturdy pair of oxen, several cows, a ram, several ewes with their lambs, and three fat pigs one of which looked soon to bear. Crates held geese and ducks that flapped their wings as best they could and squawked at the indignity.

"We'll be all night loading," Garrick said. He had come onto the beach with Amelia and a few of his men to see what had to be done. The renegade colonists eyed them warily. But Amelia was there, murmuring reassurances, and the solid bulk of the *Lady Star* riding at anchor helped convince them that all was on course. Still, they were afraid.

As well they should be, the captain thought grimly. They were about to embark on a struggle they might very well not survive. Yet they didn't lack for courage, he had to grant them that.

Here and there, he noticed couples holding hands, exchanging smiles of comfort. The children were quiet, and they showed no sign of fear. Most of the babies and toddlers slept as the work swirled around them.

By dawn, they were finished. The decks of *Lady Star* were crowded. Garrick had to step over bundles and passengers to reach the wheel deck. Several of the children had awakened and were peering curiously around from the safety of their mothers' arms. One or two of the more daring had begun to explore.

From the prow, the tethered oxen lowed plaintively. The sheep baaed, the geese honked, and before long, the whole lot of them—children and animals together—was setting up an excited clamor that seemed to increase as the sun rose higher and day burned away the uncertainty of the night.

"Just as well Gleick isn't here to see this," Garrick said when Amelia came to join him for a moment.

"Why is that?" she asked. Although she'd had almost no sleep in two nights, she was smiling. Her white starched cap had long since been discarded, and the neat braid she had made of her hair had come undone. Russet tresses fell over her shoulders. The sun warmed her cheeks, her eyes were bright and—though she didn't know it—her lips were invitingly soft.

Garrick looked away. He reminded himself that women were bad luck on a ship. Some old rules still had good reasons behind them.

"He'd not be too happy seeing his proud boat turned into a cattle hauler."

"Oh, I don't know about that," Amelia said. She glanced at him teasingly. The more distance they put between themselves and Boston, the happier she felt. She was almost light-headed, standing there on the rolling deck in the bright sunlight looking at Garrick Marlowe. He was very rumpled, she thought, needing a shave, and weary, too.

As she was herself. Ever since the fire, time seemed to have slowed down, each moment etched clearly on her mind. Yet, there was still barely enough of it. She had felt pushed along, as though by an irresistible wind.

Now, the wind seemed to have lessened, if only briefly. She drew a breath and took a moment to look around.

"It's like an ark," she said, gazing at the people and animals spread out over the deck. "Captain Gleick wouldn't object to that, would he?"

"The passengers on the ark survived," Garrick pointed out. "It remains to be seen whether we do the same."

"Not we," Amelia pointed out reasonably. "Remember our arrangement, Captain, for I surely do. We make landfall in Connecticut and come to terms with the Pequot. You and your men stay to help us begin our settlement but once the first harvest is in, you are free to go along with the *Lady Star*. She will be your ship then."

"None too soon," Garrick muttered under his breath. He didn't know which rankled more—the fact that he had agreed to stay with her for several months, or the fact that eventually he would have to go.

It made no sense to feel that way, he thought. He should be counting the days until he would see the last of her. She was an unwelcome weight around his neck, a detour in a carefully planned life, a high-handed, independent-minded woman with no notion of her proper place in the world.

In short, she was Amelia.

"You don't look well," he said just a bit nastily. He was very tired and should have wanted nothing but to sleep. Yet looking at her as he was, his body tightened and he had to resist the urge to take his hands from the mighty ship wheel and put them on her instead.

He was not used to this. Women came at his bidding, not the other way around.

"Go and lie down," he added, and then turned away from her the way a man ought to do lest women mistakenly come to think themselves of importance.

"Alright," she said as though it sounded reasonable to her. No offense taken there, so far as he could tell. He might have been an older brother giving a useful piece of advice.

Damn the very notion. He did not feel in the least brotherly toward her. If she'd had any idea in that prim little Puritan soul of what was going through his mind just then, she would have—

A swell hit *Lady Star*. She sheered slightly. The deck angled portside, and Amelia lost her balance. She would have fallen had not Garrick's arms been there to catch her. Strong arms, not at all inclined to let her go not even after the ship righted itself. Strong, protective, possessive arms, holding her so very close.

"Garrick..." she murmured, her eyes meeting his. Below on the deck, the weary but exalted colonists were going about their business, heedless of whatever happened on the wheel deck.

She should not have said his name, not the way she did, slightly breathy and with a note of longing that was unmistakable. Had she been more experienced—or experienced at all—she would have known that.

And he—he should not have held her as though it mattered not what she did or didn't say. It was for him to let her go, to turn his back and to pretend he didn't notice when she walked away. And after that, for him to look at her as if he neither saw nor felt the bright, leaping warmth behind the cool Puritan facade, the woman, Amelia, in her drab clothes and plainspoken ways, just waiting to get out. Should not...should have... All was lost in that moment as the sea surged, the ship rocked and, as though that weren't enough, the sun broke from behind a violet cloud to spill gold across the surging decks.

He bent his head. Hers was tilted back so that she seemed to meet him halfway. Certainly, she did not resist or make any effort to retreat. Rather, she waited, as though some secret, wiser part of her had half expected this, half hoped.

"Garrick." She did not say his name again but he heard it anyway echoing deep within him like the sea and the wind and the ribbons of sun beckoning him onward.

His mouth brushed hers. Her lips were warm, slightly moist and soft. She smelled of sun, salt and woman. His arm curled around her waist, drawing her to him. Supple as the willow, she bent to his strength.

He could feel her surprise, but she did not try to draw back, nor did she show any fear. A jolt of pleasure, so intense that it was almost painful, roared through him when her mouth opened tentatively beneath his own.

Abruptly, reason reasserted itself. This was madness. She was a proper Puritan woman, gently reared and with no notion of what she was about to unleash. Moreover, she was under his protection. He scoffed at men who prattled on and on about honor and ignored it at the earliest possible opportunity. For him, it was the bedrock of life. Without honor, there was nothing else but need. And yet, the temptation was so great that for a moment he teetered on the edge. But circumstances conspired to save them. A child shouted exuberantly, a man called to a friend and a cloud returned to hide the sun and cast a dampening chill over them.

Garrick drew back. He stood staring down at her as he fought for breath. She was flushed and trembling and could not meet his eyes. With a soft murmur, she turned and fled the deck.

He watched her go, grim satisfaction mingling with regret. Better, by far, for her to understand that she needed to be warier around him. She had bought his services as captain, not as lapdog. Let her bind up that glorious russet hair again, hide behind the dull Puritan garments and keep her distance from him.

His eyes were narrowed and his face taut as he turned his attention back to the foam-flecked sea. Here was the only mistress he truly wanted, and the only one he could trust.

Lady Star surged beneath him. Starboard, the low, dark edge of the land stretched away into the distance. Broad beaches gave way to dense pine forests. Sparkling rivers surged down to the sea. Out over the water, birds circling for their prey called mockingly.

His hands tightened on the wheel. He called the order for full sail and urged the proud ship on.

Chapter Seven

The inlet was framed by golden sand beaches dotted with scrub grass and small, thorny bushes. A broad, sun-splashed river ran into it. Stately pines rose on either side. Beyond, on the gently rolling hills that stretched inland as far as the eye could see, oak and maple were coming into leaf.

Even Garrick, who had spent as little time as possible ashore in the last ten years, had to admit that the aspect was pleasing. Certainly, it thrilled the would-be settlers who clustered along the ship's railing, eagerly pointing out to one another the various attractions of their new home.

Or what they hoped would be theirs. That had yet to be confirmed. Passicham, who had sailed with them out of Boston, was noncommittal. It was for others to decide.

The Pequot emissary went ashore first. Garrick, Amelia and a handful of sailors accompanied him in the ship's longboat. While the men pulled the boat up onto the beach, Passicham stepped out. He stood tall and dignified in the morning sun. Looking toward the fringe of pine trees as though he could see what lay beyond them, he said, "I will return at midday."

Amelia nodded. She hadn't told Garrick, but sea voyages did not agree with her. Fairly or not, she had come to associate them with dread events, first her father's sickness on the journey from the Lowlands and now the patient but heart wrenching suffering of Jacob Dykler. That he had survived this long gave great hope for his recovery.

"I'll wait here," she said.

Passicham inclined his head, shot Garrick a quick glance that held veiled amusement and disappeared up the beach.

"*We'll* wait," Garrick corrected her. "You can't stay here by yourself."

The color deepened in Amelia's cheeks. Since the encounter on the wheel deck, she had scrupulously kept out of his way. Honesty forced her to admit that she had found pleasure in his touch, but that only made it worse.

She didn't understand the strange, disturbing feelings he unleashed in her. She wanted herself back, the calm, strong Amelia she knew she could count on, not this bewildered creature of unseemly longings and unsuspected needs.

Her eyes averted, she said, "I'll be fine. I'd like to look around a little."

She didn't hear whatever he muttered under his breath, and perhaps it was just as well. A quick glance in his direction was enough to confirm that he was less than pleased.

"You cannot go wandering around here by yourself. Any ninny would know that."

His words stung. She lifted her chin and glared at him. "I will stay on the beach within sight of the ship, Captain. As for my safety, I have been taking care of myself for some time now and I haven't done too bad a job of it."

"Not unless you count Harkness," he reminded her relentlessly.

She paled and some of the anger left her. He hated to see it go. Without it, she looked weaker somehow, and far too weary.

"Sit down," he said gruffly. When she hesitated, he almost pushed her onto the cool, damp sand. "You look like a stiff breeze would knock you over. When did you sleep last?"

"This past night," she insisted. Granted, what little rest she had gotten had been on the floor beside Jacob Dykler's bunk, but she saw no reason to mention that.

"It couldn't have been much. There's plenty of time to look around later. If you don't want to go back to the ship, then stay here for a while and get some rest."

The thought was tempting. Too bad that it was also impossible. How could she possibly rest with him nearby? The moment she closed her eyes she would see him there—his lean, dark face smiling, or scowling more probably, his eyes alight as they moved over her, his voice caressing even when he was angry.

She squeezed her eyes shut, not because she was taking his advice—heaven forbid!—but in frustration with herself. She had to stop thinking about him, absolutely had to, or she would not be accountable for whatever happened next.

"I prefer a brisk walk," she said stoutly. For good measure, she added, "Alone."

He laughed. Very clearly and without apology, he put his head back and laughed. The sailors turned in their direction, smiling cautiously. They had no idea what had put their captain in such a good mood, but they were glad of it.

Amelia was not. She felt ridiculed and turned away in a huff, only to find that she could not get very far with Garrick holding her arm.

He was still smiling broadly, but he spoke with unexpected gentleness. "Settle down. I know it's hard to wait until Passicham gets back. But you don't know this land. It may hold dangers you haven't even thought of. You can't go alone."

"Then what do you suggest?" she asked, struggling to ignore the warm tingling in her arm where his hand touched her.

He shrugged as though it should be obvious. "I'll go with you."

Her eyes widened. He had to be joking. "It isn't proper," she blurted.

The struggle in him was obvious. He was trying very hard not to laugh again. Quietly, he said, "Mistress Daniels, in case it has escaped your notice, nothing you have done is proper. One more transgression will hardly count. And besides, who do you fear offending? Your fellow renegades from Boston town who are too busy celebrating their liberation to notice what anyone else is doing? My crew, perhaps? Honorable men all but not precisely models of strict behavior. Or the Pequot, any of them as may be concealed about to get a look at you?"

At her startled response, he said, "It would be perfectly reasonable of them to want to know more about you before allowing you to stay. But whether they're here or not, there's no one who will care what you do. Except yourself."

Amelia stared at him as she tried to digest all this. He was right, of course. She realized that in a flash.

Even though she hadn't consciously planned it, when she cut her ties to Boston, she also cut them to the stifling Puritan propriety that had so distressed her. By coming to Connecticut without the approval—or even the knowledge—of the council, she had declared her intention to set her own standards and go her own way.

Standing there on the golden beach staring into Garrick's eyes, she realized that for the first time in her life, she was truly free.

The knowledge was as terrifying as it was exhilarating. She felt like a bird suddenly tossed from the nest, unsure that it can really fly.

"I hadn't really thought of that," she murmured.

"It's a bit late to start now. You can't go back."

"I wouldn't dream of it. I just hadn't quite understood all the implications, that's all."

She gazed down the beach to where the shining river ran into the sea. Softly, she said, "Alright, we'll go together. I would like to see what lies inland of the river. Is that agreeable?"

Her grave courtesy touched him. He understood full well that she was choosing to trust him and found himself moved by that more than he would have thought possible.

"Perfectly," he said with equal gravity, and went to tell his men to return to the ship. Although one or two of them might have been tempted to make some comment, the look in Garrick's eyes was enough to stop them. They departed in the longboat in good order and a few minutes later tied up again beside *Lady Star*.

Garrick and Amelia were left alone on the beach.

Without a word, he strode off in the direction of the river. She followed. Her feet sank into the damp sand and her heavy skirt slowed her down, but she managed to catch up with him. They walked in silence until they came to the river's edge.

Here, the bank was lined with lichen-stained rocks that glistened in the sun. A few turtles sunned themselves in the slow current. An egret, pausing to feed, lifted its graceful neck to study the intruders. As they watched, a sudden flash of silver below the water's surface announced the presence of fish.

Amelia bent down and looked more closely at the rocks. They were thickly coated with black-shelled mussels. As she stood again, there was a sudden clamor as a flock of ducks swooped in and landed amid much squawking. Near the shallows, she caught the white flash of a deer darting back into the woods.

"This is a beautiful place," she said softly.

Garrick looked down at the delicate curve of her cheek visible to him in profile, the slender line of her throat and the swell of her breasts beneath the proper Puritan clothes. A hard, hot knot of longing clenched within him.

He shook his head at his own susceptibility and pointed. "There's a trail." Amelia had not noticed it until he drew her attention in the right direction. Only then did she see the narrow defile of bare ground leading off into the forest.

"Do you think there's a Pequot village near here?" she asked worriedly. It was fine and good to have neighbors but not too close.

"Maybe a summer camp for fishing. The main settlements will be farther inland."

"You sound very knowledgeable for a man who's spent his life at sea."

He hesitated a moment before answering her truthfully. "I've spent some time with the Pequot. They're an interesting people."

Amelia stepped ahead of him into the trail. "The Puritans call them savages."

Garrick snorted. "No more than you or I. Surely, if God had meant all people to be the same, He would have taken care of the matter Himself."

"I think so," she acknowledged. "Passicham seems an honest man."

"He is that—although a tough one. As for the others, they have a particular idea of what they want. It may not also be what you intend."

"You think there will be problems?" she asked.

He held a low-hanging branch aside for her and said, "Aren't there always? What matters is whether or not some common ground can be found."

"I will do my best," she pledged. "As you have pointed out, we can hardly go back to Boston."

"I wouldn't recommend it. Have you thought what the council will do when they discover your whereabouts?"

"Wring their hands and call curses on our heads, I suppose. What else can they do?"

Garrick shrugged noncommittally. They had come to a fork in the trail. One side led off toward a ridge that stretched inland. The other ran parallel to the coast and vanished into a copse of trees.

"Let's see what's over there," Amelia said, pointing toward the copse.

She lifted her skirt and stepped lightly over the mossy ground. The trail led deeper and deeper into the trees.

The air grew cooler and the light took on a verdant hue as it was filtered through the overarching branches. All was silence and the faint but unmistakable sense that they were treading on ground that was in some way special.

"The Pequot believe the earth has great power," Garrick said softly. "In places like this, they say the surface is worn thin and the power can be felt very clearly through it."

Amelia shivered slightly. The idea was different from anything she had been raised to believe, yet it carried the stamp of truth. She began to wonder if they might not be trespassing in some way.

"Perhaps we should go back," she said reluctantly. She didn't want to return to the beach yet, but the silent coolness of the copse made her feel as though they had slipped away from the rest of the world.

The sun-bright beach and the ship anchored immediately off of it suddenly seemed very far away. She almost felt as though she needed to go back to make sure they were still there.

"If you like," Garrick said. He turned to go.

Amelia held out a hand to stop him. She was being foolish. Of course the world was still there. They had merely stepped out of it for a short time.

"No, wait," she said. Her eyes were soft with yearning, but she had no idea of that. She only knew that, after all the turmoil and sadness of recent months, this sylvan sanctuary drew her irresistibly. "I would like to stay. That is, if you don't mind?"

Garrick took a firm grip on every ounce of decency and chivalry he possessed, and shook his head. "Not at all."

She wanted to stay. Fine, that's what they would do. Stay here in this secluded enclave hidden away from everyone except a few inquisitive blue jays that were perched in a nearby tree.

They'd stay and...do what? Talk, perhaps. Unfortunately, there was damn little he could say to her. His life up to that point had not exactly prepared him for polite conversation with a proper—or even improper—Puritan woman. She was exactly the sort he'd always kept clear of—a stiff-backed female of independent mind and willful nature.

She was also startlingly beautiful there in the glen, in her white starched cap and her drab black dress with wisps of russet hair trailing around her forehead and her cheeks pinkening under his scrutiny.

Garrick cleared his throat. "There's a dry patch here," he said. "Why don't you sit down?"

She did as he suggested, but kept her eyes averted. He sat nearby, close but too far away to just possibly give in to the temptation to touch her.

She was so very touchable—soft yet strong, pliant yet responsive, he thought. A sudden, vivid memory of the taste of her mouth shot through him, hardening every muscle in his body. He jerked slightly, drawing a startled glance.

"What's wrong?" she asked.

"Nothing," he said through gritted teeth. How in God's name did they do it, those proper Puritan gentlemen? Whatever else he thought of them, he had to give them full marks for their restraint. And when it came to walking the straight and narrow, they couldn't be beat.

Not Harkness, of course, but Harkness was an animal, as much a renegade from the Puritan ideal as the would-be settlers themselves, although in a very different way. The fault of the council lay in not recognizing what he was and dealing with him properly.

Garrick, on the other hand, was made of far frailer stuff, if only in that regard.

"Something *is* troubling you," Amelia said and, kind young woman that she was, reached out a hand to him.

Her reservations forgotten in the light of his obvious distress, she asked, "Is it Jacob you are worrying about?

Be assured, he is doing very well. When I left him, he was sleeping comfortably. The burns were not as extensive as I feared at first, and he is very strong. I believe he will surprise you with the speed of his recovery.''

Garrick offered a silent prayer of thanks for that, hardly realizing that he was doing it. His attention was focused on keeping the hand she touched completely still.

If he flexed his fingers even the smallest bit, he was convinced he would take firm hold of her. And once having done that, he doubted very much that he would be able to let go.

"I'm grateful for that," he said thickly.

She nodded, sensing nothing amiss. So far as she was concerned, he was simply a man concerned about his friend. Such was the protection of her innocence.

For a fleeting moment, he wished he could have been the same. When had he been innocent? As a child growing up in Ireland where he had seen firsthand the anguish of poverty and despair? As a young man when he first went to sea and quickly learned that only his size, his strength and his relentless will protected him from debauchery?

And later, when he had grown to power, had he ever once felt that pure unquestioning faith in the ultimate goodness of the world that glowed within Amelia like a fine, rare gem?

He could stand apart, recognize it for what it was and even admire it, but he could not claim the smallest piece for himself. For a moment, resentment filled him, but it vanished as quickly as it appeared. He was a man— strong, solitary and self-reliant. He had no room for regrets.

"Let's go," he said, and stood up quickly.

She looked surprised. "Passicham will not be back for a while yet."

"I know, but there is more to see. You should at least make an effort to judge the fertility of the land and to examine any other sources of fresh water as may exist."

"You're right," Amelia said as she, too, stood. Her laxity embarrassed her. Once again, she reminded herself that others were depending on her judgment. Indeed, they had staked their lives on it. It was not the time to be indulging private urges.

They stepped back onto the trail, but as they did so, she turned for just a moment and looked toward the copse. Daring greatly, for such was the strictness of her conscience, she let herself hope that she would return there before too long.

And that she would not come alone.

Chapter Eight

"It is done," Passicham said. He rose, smiled at Amelia and added, "All the lands from this Asmatuck River westward to the Patomuck Creek are yours to settle. You are welcome here."

She nodded a little shakily. There were six other Pequots in the group, one a very old man called Amogerone, who was described as the sachem, and another a younger man named Owenoke, who was the chieftain.

The sachem had said nothing, during the meeting only observed her carefully. The chieftain had spoken through Passicham, asking various questions about what they intended to grow, how many others they thought might join them, and so on.

In the end, the Pequot leaders were satisfied. The trade goods they had brought were accepted along with their assurances of enduring friendship. Amelia understood full well what that meant. If the Pequot were attacked, she and her fellow settlers would be expected to fight with them. From now on, they were not merely neighbors, but allies.

It was a heady responsibility but only one more to add to an already long list. Her knees trembled as she considered the enormity of what she had just done. She, who until recently had never bought anything more significant than a bolt of cloth or some new china, had just purchased several square miles of rich, fertile land.

Not a single man in Europe could have said the same, much less any woman. Not even her father had ever been party to an arrangement of such size. But she knew exactly what he would have done had he been.

"We must have a document," she said. "Something that states all this clearly."

Passicham's smile deepened. "We have noticed how much your people like things written down on paper. You put more faith in them than in any person's word."

"Words can be forgotten," Amelia said gently. She did not wish to offend them but she wanted a deed, if only so that future generations would be able to look at it and understand how it had been in the beginning.

"Not by us," Passicham assured her. "However, if it matters to you, it will be done. Draw up what you think to be appropriate and we will consider it."

Garrick stepped forward with the small, portable writing desk he had brought from the ship. Amelia sat down with the desk on her knees. She thought long and hard before she wrote.

We, Amogerone and Owenoke, sachem and chieftain of these lands, do sell unto Amelia Daniels and the settlers of the vessel called *Lady Star*—henceforth to be called the Lady Star Company—all their rights and interests in the lands between Asmatuck River and the Patomuck Creek to be held in common by all, or else divided in such manner as may be mutually agreeable. The little neck of land called Monakewego, henceforth Daniels Neck, will be the property of aforesaid Amelia Daniels, her heirs and her assigns forever.

Passicham had told her that Monakewego, now Daniels Neck, was what his people called the land where the
copse stood. It had not been in her mind to claim land for
herself, in particular, but the charter of the Lady Star
Company, drawn up so speedily even as they departed
Boston, gave her the right to do so. She could think of no
place she might want more.

When she was done, she blotted the paper carefully
and handed it to Passicham. He read it slowly, then spoke
to the others. The chieftain, Owenoke, laughed.

"What does he find funny?" Amelia asked Garrick.
She had noticed that although he did not announce it, he
seemed to have some understanding of what the Pequot
were saying when they spoke among themselves.

He leaned closer to her so that his breath touched her
cheek and said, "He thinks it's amusing that you were
able to pick out such a good piece of land for yourself so
quickly. He says there is great energy there and that you
must be sensitive to it."

"Do you believe that?" Amelia asked softly.

He shrugged, his broad shoulders moving lightly under the linen shirt he wore tucked into black breeches.
The shirt was untied at the neck, revealing the bronzed
column of his throat. The wind ruffled his dark hair as
he looked down at her.

Standing so close to him, she was aware of the considerable difference in their size. Although she was tall for
a woman, he towered over her by a good head. And while
she had never thought of herself as delicate, the sweep of
his shoulders and chest made her feel exactly that.

It was a strange sensation and not particularly welcome in these circumstances when she needed to call on
all her confidence and strength. The teasing smile he shot
her didn't help, either.

She really had to stop thinking about this man. He was only a means to an end, and although she would deal with him decently as she did with all people, there could never be anything else between them.

Absolutely never.

She would do well to remember that, but at the moment she was having trouble doing anything except look at him. With an effort, she wrenched her eyes away. Her cheeks were hot. For a frightening instant she almost forgot why she was there and what she was supposed to be doing.

Passicham reminded her. He handed the document back with a nod of approval. "It is acceptable. Amogerone and Owenoke will make their marks."

When this was done, Amelia also signed on behalf of herself and the Lady Star Company. Garrick added his name as both a participant and a witness. It was over.

It had begun.

Sam and Lissy Whitler were the first off *Lady Star*. They came ashore with broad smiles and whoops of laughter, and were quickly followed by the rest.

"You did it," Lissy exclaimed as she threw her arms around Amelia and hugged her fiercely. "You actually did it. I can hardly believe it."

Amelia stepped back slightly, a bemused look on her face. To come so far and not be sure? she asked herself. "Did you not think I would?"

"Oh, I prayed hard enough for it, but that didn't mean it would happen. Imagine, land of our own, free of the council. It's almost too good to be true."

"That it is," Sam agreed, "but it doesn't change the fact that there's work to be done. I'll give you my thanks later, if you don't mind, mistress." He squinted at the sun. "We've maybe six more hours of daylight and we'd better make the best of them."

Celebrations would have to wait, as a new sense of urgency gripped the small group. Although they had been lucky in the weather so far, there was nothing to say it would hold. A shelter had to be raised and the cattle and cargo brought ashore as quickly as possible.

Amelia saw little of Garrick in the hours that followed. She was too busy to pay much attention to anything except the work that had to be done. But she was aware of him always in the back of her mind, sensing when he was near. He moved back and forth between the ship and the beach, urging his men on, but doing his share, as well. She took note that he wasn't one to merely give orders but lent his own strength in carrying them out.

By mid-afternoon, a canvas shelter had been rigged and a rude enclosure built to hold the animals. The oxen could be heard all the way onshore. They smelled land and wanted to be on it.

"We'd better get them off now," Sam said.

Amelia agreed. She went on the longboat the next trip and spoke with Garrick.

"The oxen are getting impatient. We shouldn't leave them here much longer," she said.

He looked at the brooding-eyed animals and frowned. "I thought they were supposed to be the long-suffering type—just plod along and do what they're told. Why are they bellowing that way? And while we're at it, have you *seen* what they've done to my deck?"

Amelia laughed. She was too tired and still too giddy to do anything else. "Do I take it you've never transported livestock before? They're animals, and they're behaving just as they ought. The sooner we get them onshore, the better for everyone."

"We barely managed to get them on board. How do you plan to get them off?"

"I'll push them," she said, straight-faced.

He glowered at her. "Be serious. You couldn't move one of those beasts if there were ten of you."

She walked over to where the oxen stood, undid their fetters and moved behind them. They turned their heads to keep her in sight. The rest of them followed, neatly positioned in front of an opening in the deck rail. Amelia leaned her weight against the ox who stood on the left, put her shoulder to his rump and shoved.

The ox started violently and lurched for the opening. The others instinctively followed. They landed with a great splash that sprayed water all over the deck.

She shot Garrick a triumphant look, only to have it abruptly vanish as she realized too late that she had shoved hard enough to knock herself off balance. Teetering on the edge of the deck, she struggled to regain her balance but to no avail. With a cry of dismay, she followed the oxen into the water.

Garrick lunged for her. He almost made it. His hand was outstretched, within inches of her, when she fell. The skirt of her black dress billowed out around her as she slammed into the water. Almost instantly, it filled with water and began to pull her down.

He told himself she would be alright. There were only a few yards between her and the oxen. All she had to do was swim that distance and grab hold of one of them. She would be out of danger.

But instead, Amelia cried out something he couldn't hear and promptly sank from view. Garrick cursed as the truth dawned on him. The twit couldn't swim.

She'd crossed the ocean, bargained her way onto his ship, turned his life upside down, actually convinced the Pequot to give her land, and after all that, she couldn't *swim*.

He was still cursing moments later as he hit the water in a clean dive and shot straight down, searching for her. Without taking the time to remove his heavy leather boots and belt, he was at a distinct disadvantage.

But that didn't matter. Not for a second did he let himself consider that he might not find her.

The water this close to shore was less than forty feet deep but only the first ten feet or so were clear. The rest was obscured by the tides and currents stirring up the bottom silt.

He strained through the murk to catch sight of her. If he had miscalculated and was in the wrong place, time would run out and she would be lost.

His lungs burned and his heart hammered against his ribs, but he refused to give up. He did not think—that was beyond him. He merely reacted to the quick, flash-fire images of Amelia, proudly defiant at the inn, achingly compassionate as she cared for Jacob and terrified but still valiant in the face of Harkness's brutality. Amelia in his arms, in his dreams—like it or not, in his life.

And now, slipping from him down that eternal passage from this world to the next.

Darkness swirled. He saw sparkling lights in front of his eyes as his lungs emptied and unconsciousness threatened. There was a great roaring in his ears. Every instinct for self-preservation that he possessed screamed for relief.

High above, seemingly an infinite distance away, sunlight glistened and blessed air beckoned. He could still save himself.

The light grew dimmer. He continued plunging down-ward until—*there*—in the murk-strewn bottom, he caught sight of the black skirt billowing cloudlike.

This time when he reached for it his fingers closed around the sodden fabric. With the last of his strength, he hauled Amelia to him and gave a mighty shove, driv-ing upward against the darkness and the pain, against the pull of death, up and up to the light, to life, to the water opening above their heads and the great rush of air surg-ing into their lungs.

Or his, at least. She was not breathing. A single, fran-tic glance was enough to tell him, that. He struck out for the shore, swimming as he had never done in his life, and swiftly felt the rocks beneath his feet.

Dragging her onto the sand, he turned her onto her stomach and knelt over her, his legs on either side of her bottom. Hands pressed flat on either side of her back, he pumped the water from her.

She retched—music to his ears—and moaned faintly. With grim reassurance, he turned her onto her back, tipped her head and locked his mouth to hers.

His breath filled her, life to life, pushing away death, dragging her into the sun-washed world until at last her eyes flashed open and she sat up, coughing.

He held her until the worst of the spasms passed, then abruptly he stood and glared down at her. They were both soaking wet.

The drab black dress clung to her, outlining the slen-der contours of her hips and thighs. The starched white cap had come undone and trailed down her back. Thick, gleaming russet hair spilled over her shoulders. Her teeth were chattering and fierce color stained her cheeks, but otherwise she looked undaunted.

Belatedly, he became aware of the crowd gathered around them. Lissy Whitler was the first to act, rushing forward to fling a blanket around Amelia. The others pressed closer, looking all set to make a great fuss.

Of the two dozen wayfarers looking on, most were still unknown to Garrick, but the few he had gotten to know on the brief voyage he couldn't help but like. Fools they might be, but brave ones for all that, and inspired enough to find something better in this world.

Still, he felt a driving surge of resentment at the thought that they might bear Amelia away from him. He was, after all, the one who had saved her. Irrational or not, that made him feel as though she somehow belonged to him.

"She's alright," he said gruffly as he pushed several of the men aside. They were being too attentive for his taste. "She's just had a scare."

"She could have been killed," Lissy insisted. She shot him a look of admiration. "You saved her life, Captain. We're all very grateful."

The murmuring assent of the crowd confirmed that they were indeed. Embarrassed, Garrick shrugged off their thanks. It was as well that they did not know what had gone through his mind during those dark and turbulent moments on the edge of the abyss.

It was not charity or chivalry that had sent him into the deep after Amelia Daniels. It was the driving urge to possess, mingled with a strange protectiveness, that he could not fathom.

He wanted to tell them that their gratitude was misplaced, but he knew where that would lead. Where it always did with such upstanding and well-meaning people. He would demur, they would insist, and the whole conversation would go on far longer than it ought.

Instead, he cut it short. "Daylight is fading. I suggest the rest of you get back to work. I'll see to Mistress Daniels."

He all but held his breath, thinking for sure at least one of them would object that it wasn't proper. But they seemed to have shucked off such concerns the same way they'd shucked off Boston town, without so much as a backward glance.

Only Lissy hesitated. "She'll need dry clothes. Her trunks are here somewhere. I'll find something, if you like."

Garrick gave her a smile that warmed her cheeks and sent her scurrying off to see what she could do. The rest dispersed to their tasks.

The oxen had reached shore and had to be secured. There were goats and cows to see to, several pigs, ducks and chickens, not to mention the half-dozen or so small children who were underfoot.

More shelters had to be raised and food prepared for the evening meal. Under such circumstances, there was little time to think of anything except what had to be done before nightfall.

Garrick bent to pick up Amelia. She lay very still in his arms. For a moment he feared she might be unconscious, but her eyes moved. The light seemed to have gone out of them. They were left great pools of darkness in which only fear flickered. She was shaking violently.

His mouth set grimly, he carried her into the canvas shelter.

Chapter Nine

"I can do it," Amelia said. She tried to slap Garrick's hands away without great success. Her weakness stunned her. She could barely stand. Without the strength of his long, hard body to lean against, she would have fallen. It was humiliating, but more than that, it was terrifying. She had never felt so dependent on anyone.

Garrick ignored her feeble efforts and went on unbuttoning the back of her dress. He considered telling her that she was being foolish, that he felt no more for her than for a limp rag, which by the way she distinctly resembled, and that she might be advised not to flatter herself by presuming otherwise.

But he would have been lying.

The skin of her back shone like alabaster. Beneath the damp, fusty smell of the dress, he breathed in lavender. Bemusedly, he shook his head. After all she had been through, how could she smell like lavender? Her hair was soaking wet and smelled of the sea, but even that was enticing.

She crossed her arms over her breasts and, holding the dress in place she squeezed her eyes shut. He cursed when he saw that she was fighting tears. It was all he could do to let go of her and take a few steps back. A rough brown blanket lay nearby. He grabbed it and threw it over the supports, creating a simple privacy screen.

From the other side of it, he said, "Get out of those clothes. Lissy found something dry for you. It's there on the floor."

She didn't answer, but he could hear her moving inches away. He heard the slither of fabric as she pulled it away from her body and dropped it on the floor, the soft sound of her sighing, and the intermittent pitter-patter of water as she wrung it from her hair.

He touched the tips of his fingers to the rough blanket and struggled mightily for control. The canvas shelter was open at the far end. People were passing by. Privacy was no more than an illusion, and for that he was deeply grateful. Otherwise, he had little doubt that he would do something he would regret.

"Get dressed," he repeated. He was relieved when the sounds from the other side told him she was doing that.

A hand reached tentatively around the blanket. It was a small hand, slender and absurdly delicate for the tasks it undertook. He found himself staring at that hand and actually feeling angry that she did not take better care of it.

Amelia herself emerged from around the blanket. She looked at him doubtfully.

"I'm not sure I should wear this."

"Why not?" What did she mean, she shouldn't wear it? he pondered. How could that possibly matter? It covered her, didn't it? Not as well as the awful black thing, but it did the job. Was it out of style, perhaps? Not quite the height of Puritan fashion? Was that the problem?

"It isn't black," she said in a faint voice. Her head was bent, her eyes focused on the skirt she held spread between her hands.

She had dried her hair fairly well. It gleamed in the fading light as it fell over her shoulders and the exposed swell of her breasts. "Also, it isn't very modest."

He had been at Whitehall, he had visited Hampton Court and he was not completely unknown at some of the finest and most exclusive brothels in more cities than he cared to remember. He had seen women dressed immodestly. They did not look anything at all like pink-cheeked Mistress Daniels. The very idea was ludicrous.

Until he remembered her father. She was in mourning for Jonathan Daniels, a man he respected and missed. By her standards, his death should be remembered for more than just a few months, and the most visible symbol of that remembrance was his daughter.

To put off black, to don the simple but undeniably pretty white dress Lissy Whitler had found for her, was to turn away from the past and set her eyes firmly to the future.

"Your father loved you," Garrick murmured, hardly knowing what he had said.

Amelia raised her head and looked at him. "That's a strange thing to say."

"Is it? Do you really think it would matter to him whether you wore black or not? He'd want you to do what was best for yourself." He gestured toward the beach. "I'm not sure he'd agree this is it, but he wouldn't want you mourning him, either. He loved life too much for that."

"You knew him better than I thought," Amelia said softly.

Garrick shrugged. He didn't want to give her the wrong impression. Whatever Master Daniels would have thought of his daughter founding a new settlement, he most certainly wouldn't have approved of Garrick Marlowe helping her do it.

Particularly when that involved standing very close to her, admiring the curve of her breasts. He reminded himself that his own standards of honor were not as forgiving as he might have wished.

"Wear the dress," Garrick said softly. "You're starting a new life here, Amelia. It shouldn't be garbed in mourning."

It was the first time he had used her Christian name, and they both knew it. She could have objected, but felt no impulse to do so. It all seemed so perfectly natural.

"Thank you," she said.

"For what? Approving the way you're dressed?"

"For that and for saving my life."

He had forgotten. Sweet Lord, he had actually managed to put those desperate moments under water out of his mind, however briefly. She was so vividly alive, so real and so near to his hand that he could hardly believe she had come so close to death. Yet she had, and he had come near to following her.

"Next time," he said gruffly, "let the oxen take care of themselves."

She laughed and looked at him shyly. "I just might." Her eyes dropped. She stared at the sand. "It was very brave, what you did."

"It was nothing," he said firmly. "You're not the first person I've fished out of the drink."

Offhand he couldn't think of any others, but there must be some. People were always getting in over their heads. Not quite as drastically as she had done, but it happened.

"Still," she added stubbornly, "I'm very grateful to you."

He didn't want her gratitude. He wanted her naked in his arms in a large, cool bed locked away from the world.

And he had about as much likelihood of getting that as he did wings to fly to the moon. For one thing, there were no beds in this godforsaken, previously Pequot, now unnamed, settlement. There was nothing except sand, dirt, trees, streams and unrelenting work.

"What are you going to call this place?" he asked, not because he cared all that much, but simply to change the subject.

"We should all discuss it among ourselves. It should be something everyone likes."

He nodded perfunctorily. As master of a ship, he was accustomed to making decisions on his own. So far as he was concerned, that was the best way. "It was your idea. You must have something you'd like to call it."

"I was thinking of Belle Haven," she admitted.

His eyes widened. He thought of the wild land, the surging river, the Pequots of uncertain temperament. Surely, she was jesting. "Belle Haven?"

"It is beautiful," she said defiantly, "and it is a haven for those of us seeking freedom. I think the name fits."

He resisted the urge to tell her that in a century or two she might be right, presuming it could survive that long. She believed the name was deserved, and he supposed that was what mattered. Soon enough, she would have to come to terms with the reality.

"You need something to eat," he said bluntly. The white dress, plain as it was, made her look younger than ever. She seemed to have shucked off any pretense of maturity along with the mourning. He guessed the other good citizens of Belle Haven would be in for a shock when they saw her.

"We all do," she agreed. Her shoulders straightened. She lifted her chin, took a deep breath, and said, "I must go help."

"You nearly drowned. Do you think just this once you might let the others do the work?"

She looked surprised. "I'm fine now."

She took a step forward, teetered and stopped abruptly. "I will be in a few minutes, I'm sure."

He caught her around the waist, ignored her startled exclamation and said, "Amelia Daniels, for once in your life, you are going to be sensible."

She cast him a narrow look that spoke volumes for the notion that an inexperienced woman was not necessarily a dumb one. "Are you sure that's what you want me to be?"

He froze. Her body was warm and pliant against his. He smelled lavender again, the heady scent of full-blown summer. The rude canvas shelter, the beach and the hustle and bustle of the people coming and going from the ship, all faded to nothing. They might have been alone.

But they were not. As his head bent, toward Amelia, Lissy pushed back the canvas flap and announced— loudly—that supper was ready.

"Are you alright, mistress?" she asked as she eyed Amelia standing so very close to the tall, taut-faced man. The tension between them could have been cut with a knife. "Mistress?"

"I'm coming, Lissy."

"Supper..."

"I'll come and help," Amelia said, her eyes still locked on Garrick. She was hardly aware of what she said. She always helped. People depended on her. She had responsibilities. But all she wanted to do was stay there, with him, and let the strange currents of desire follow their predestined course.

"Now," she added, and moved away from him. Breaking that physical contact was almost painful. She felt as though she had left a part of herself behind. The imprint of his hand remained firm on her waist as she walked quickly from the shelter.

On the beach, the air was cooler. She was glad of the shawl she had pulled around her. The settlers and the sailors alike were gathered around a freshly lit bonfire. Brush and dry wood gathered from the edges of the nearby forest sufficed to give them light and heat and to cook the simple meal the women had prepared.

Westward, over the gently rolling hills, the sun was going down in glory. *Lady Star* rode at anchor on water gilded by the rising moon. The bonfire leaped high as the comforting scent of wood smoke filled the air.

One of the crew brought out a flute, one of the farmers a fiddle. It wasn't planned, for no one spoke of it, yet for the first time on that alien beach, an English tune filled the air.

Somewhere nearby, Amelia supposed, the Pequot were present. Listening, perhaps; thinking, certainly, about whether or not they had done the right thing. Did their doubts ease as they listened to the fast, lilting tune or did they deepen?

A child laughed. The sound brought a smile to the faces of the adults. Several of the older couples came out to dance. They did it well, with an oddly dignified grace that showed they were not strangers to the exercise, despite how the Puritans frowned on it.

A little girl squealed with delight. Her father laughed, scooped her up and carried her out onto the impromptu dance floor. The women tipped their heads together indulgently as they tended the food in bubbling pots over the smaller cook fires.

Amelia breathed deeply, taking in the night and the smoke, the music and the laughter. Pleasure filled her. It was so intense that it came perilously close to joy. Had she been able to, she would not have chosen anywhere else on earth to be other than that narrow beach hard by the forest, surrounded by friends and on the brink of what was surely her life's greatest adventure.

The life that had so nearly been lost in the chill, dark deeps only a short time before. She turned her head and saw Garrick standing not far away. A daring smile curved her lips.

Eyes bright, she walked toward him, unaware of how her hips swayed beneath the pure white dress or how her hair gleamed in the high-leaping fire. "Do you dance, Captain?" she asked. Oh, she dared greatly now, so much so, that her breath almost stopped in anticipation of his response. Never in her life had she done such a thing. But, now, on this beach, life was beginning again. Old rules no longer applied.

"I've been known to," he said gruffly, and took her in his arms.

Time fled. The music soared, the laughter grew bolder and the wilderness, with all its unknown dangers, sank back behind the wall of light and joy. In his arms she was free. There were no barriers. She fairly flew, following his steps, for he danced as well as he seemed to do all else.

She had learned in secret, not that her father disapproved but because he would not have understood the waste of time. Never before had she danced in public, nor with so able a partner.

The experience was exhilarating. To the clapping, cheering accompaniment of their audience, they circled the impromptu floor, faster, ever faster, until at last, breathless and laughing, she begged to stop.

"Enough, I'm spent. Truly, Captain, you hide your light under a bushel. You might be a courtier, so well do you prance."

"Faint praise," he said, grinning. They drew off to the side as others took their place. His arm was still around her. She knew she should draw away but could not seem to remember how to do it.

"In consideration of all that has occurred today," he said with mock gravity, "do you think you might manage to call me Garrick?"

"I might," she agreed, "provided you didn't think me too forward." She stepped back a pace as she spoke and regarded him seriously.

He didn't want to understand her, indeed he tried telling himself that she was just a young girl caught in circumstances beyond her. But her meaning was all too clear.

She would call him Garrick, dance with him and thank him for saving her life. But he must not forget that she was bound by ties of honor and prudence that could not be lightly set aside.

The ladies at court, the women of the brothel—those were the company he chose. This woman—proud, honorable, defiant—could be in his arms and yet still be removed from him. She was always just beyond the reach of his hand. Or was she?

Lissy called them to the fragrant stew and the stone-baked bread. Cider was poured and a libation drunk to their first night in their new home.

Garrick noticed his sailors seated now, not so much in their own group but scattered among the settlers. One held a sleepy child who belonged to some farmer, another was talking gently with a seemingly pleased young girl.

How many of them would sail with him to England? he wondered. He had combined the crews of *Venturer* and *Lady Star,* giving due chance to anyone who did not relish the thought of months spent in the wilderness carving out a new settlement. The men with him were there because they had chosen to be. Some might well choose to stay.

But not him. He was for the sea and the wind, for the fortune he meant to build and the future he meant to seize. This lonely place on the edge of the world had no attraction for him.

Amelia moved away. She went to help Lissy and the other women ladle stew into rough-hewn bowls and pass them around. She was smiling and looked very happy. He wanted to seize that image of her and put it away somewhere safe so that it might always be his. But she moved too quickly, and the moment was lost.

He took a bowl of the stew and sat down a little distance from the others. Someone passed him a mug of cider and he drank deeply. On the beach, he heard the sea crashing against the sand, but the laughter and talk almost drowned it out.

Belle Haven, he thought grimly. A dream. The reality would be very different, he was sure of that. It would be hard, unrelenting work and disappointment. But in the end . . .

Neat houses, neat lives—a neat, orderly world. Not for him. He would go and he would forget. Please God.

She came and sat beside him, so naturally as though it had always been thus. They ate in silence and when they were done, she reached out her hand and touched his gently.

Chapter Ten

Amelia turned over on the sand, seeking a position that might be slightly comfortable. She had no success. The sand was lumpy, the air was cold, her blanket was thin and she was thoroughly miserable.

All around her, the settlers were sleeping in couples, their children snuggled against them. The sailors had gone back to the ship and were undoubtedly snug in their hammocks. Only she was alone and awake.

She judged it to be after midnight. The moon had passed its apex and was settling westward in the sky.

What few clouds there had been earlier had vanished. It was almost light as day. She could clearly see every bundle and barrel gathered around them.

Slowly, she unwound the blanket and stood up. The cattle rustled softly in the enclosure nearby. A few of the ducks fluttered their wings, but most had their heads tucked into them, fast asleep.

Beneath the blanket, she still had on the simple white dress, but before settling down to try to rest, she had also donned a sturdy wool cloak.

When she left the Lowlands, she thought her father had insisted she bring along far too many clothes. Now she was glad that he had, for there was no telling when she would be able to add to her wardrobe.

Hesitantly, she took a few steps down the beach and stood poised, listening to the sounds of the night. The more attentive she became to them, the louder they seemed. The surf pounding against the shore could not mute the rustles and cheeps, the slithers and murmurs of the night forest.

Something swooped over her head. She ducked and instinctively put her arm over her head. But it was only an owl, out hunting. It landed on a branch of a nearby tree and studied her with slow-blinking curiosity.

Smiling at her own fright, she continued a little farther. A heady sense of daring filled her. She was a visitor here in this alien world, delighted to feel as welcome as she did.

Not that she was foolish. She had no intention of going too far from the others. The night and the nearby forest might well hold dangers she knew nothing about. Hadn't Garrick been at some pains to point that out?

She had not meant to think of him, but once begun it seemed she had no choice. For the first time since it had happened, she allowed herself to remember those terrifying moments in the sea.

A tremor ran through her. She clasped her arms around herself and gave a silent prayer of thanks that she was here, on the moon-drenched beach, rather than lying cold and dead beneath the waves.

In a sense, her life had begun again when he pulled her from the waters. She was deeply indebted to him, and wished there was some way to show her gratitude. But the one thing she was sure he wanted—clear title to *Lady Star* and a swift return to England—was beyond her to grant.

She and the others needed his help and the help of the crew too much for that. The agreement was that they would stay through the first harvest and so it would have to remain.

There were other ways in which a woman might show her gratitude, and for just a moment she dared to contemplate them. Not that there was much to think about. She was woefully ignorant of such things.

Latin she had, and the keeping of accounts, music and domestic skills, as well. But of the ways of a man with a maid, she knew almost nothing.

Not that she wasn't willing to learn. She touched a fingertip to her lips and smiled faintly. How very bold she had become, alone in the moonlight, where there was no one to observe her. It was as though a secret self she had never before acknowledged was stirring within her.

She walked a little farther before stopping again. Reason told her she should go back. Morning would come soon enough, and there would be much to do.

The area immediately inland had to be scouted and a suitable place found for a more substantial shelter. Fields had to be laid out and prepared for seed. Fodder had to be found for the animals. There was no end to the tasks ahead of them.

Yet the night beckoned.

She had no intention of going as far as the copse, yet she found herself turning in that direction. Sooner than she would have thought possible, she had reached it.

The small cluster of people was far down the beach now. She was more alone than ever before. She paused near the river and stood watching as it poured out into the sea.

Even at this hour, she could see the glint of fish moving just below the surface. Truly, this was a rich land. The means for survival and far more were close at hand. They only had to be strong enough to make the most of them.

The stand of ancient trees drew her. Here, the land twisted outward, reaching for the sea in the same way the river did. She bent and lifted a handful of the pine-scented earth, letting it trickle through her fingers.

"Daniels Neck is your name now," she said softly, "and may it please you." She supposed she should have felt self-conscious, but the impulse came naturally enough. The land stirred around her, as though listening.

She straightened, brushed off her hand and looked around. There, at the break in the trees, she would build her house.

It would be a fine, strong building with neatly notched planks, a stone chimney and flagstones before the front door. There would be two stories with windows on each. The roof would be low, for this close to the shore there were bound to be storms with high winds.

She would plant her garden to the south where it would catch the most sun. And later there would be an orchard, even if that meant dirt for it had to be brought from inland.

What fine plans she had. Her smile deepened. The farther she came, the more she did and the greater she dared.

Perhaps it was the air in this new land, or the heady sense of space reaching out on all sides of her. The old confinements of Europe slipped away so easily. All things seemed possible.

Here, she would have a shed for poultry, and over there, a milking barn. Sam had already said he would build her a loom when there was time, and Lissy had of-

fered to teach her to weave. She would sit in the sun and
spin fine wool with her children around her skirts.

Children. The very word trembled through her. She
had always liked children, been happy to be among them,
even sought excuses for their company. But now, for the
first time, she really thought about what it would mean
to have some of her own.

And not merely to have them, but to be able to raise
them, here, in this place in freedom.

She sighed and tried to shake the thought away. To do
that, she would need a husband. There were no single
men among the settlers, for families gave greater stabil-
ity to any such venture.

In time, Belle Haven would draw such men. Already,
she had heard some of the sailors murmuring that it was
a good place, that a man could do far worse. There would
be others. They would come for the land and the freedom, for the chance to make a life that seemed impossible anywhere else.

Should she choose to marry, it would not be difficult.
There was no vanity in knowing that. Women were in
short supply in this new world and would undoubtedly
remain that way for some time to come.

But the thought of that faceless, unknown man caused
her to shake her head in rejection. She did not want him,
whoever he may be. She wanted—

Oh, no, she thought fiercely. She wasn't going to do
this to herself. Standing there in the moonlight thinking
of Garrick Marlowe was the height of folly. She should
turn around, march right back to the camp and get some
much-needed sleep.

She remained where she was. The pine-scented air
brushed her face gently. The copse shimmered in moon-

light and the river with it. Great power, the chief had said.

She felt it through the soles of her shoes, tingling up her body bringing her alive in ways she had never been before. It should have frightened her, for this was something ancient and powerful, far removed from the plain speech and rational notions of her faith. Yet it was oddly familiar to her, as though she had known it in some other self.

She had to go back. Yet she stayed, trembling on the brink of something she could not name.

The air shimmered and the earth seemed to grow warmer beneath her feet. For the merest instant, she thought she smelled the heady fragrances of a summer yet to come, ripe with life and promise.

Then it was gone and she smelled something altogether different: tobacco.

Garrick tossed the cheroot away, ground it carefully under his foot to put out the small ember, and straightened away from the tree he had been leaning against. Not more than ten yards separated them. He crossed it purposefully.

"What are you doing here?" Amelia asked faintly. The shock of his sudden presence was so great that for a moment she thought she was imagining it. But this was no figment of a dream. This was a real, strong, compelling man who seemed to have sprung directly from her deepest yearnings.

"I might ask you the same," he said. He stopped in front of her, close enough to touch but not touching.

He had changed after returning to *Lady Star* and wore a fresh shirt and breeches. His thick ebony hair was brushed back from his forehead and secured at the nape of his neck. He looked very big—almost intimidating—and completely male.

She swallowed hard and said, "I couldn't sleep."

He smiled ruefully. "Neither could I. I took the longboat and came back. Jacob is resting well."

She nodded, glad that they had something else to speak of besides the most dangerous subject—themselves. "He is very strong."

"And very lucky. If you hadn't been there, he would have died. How did you learn such skill?"

"My father had me taught when he saw that I was interested and had some small ability." Taking a chance, she smiled in turn. "But perhaps I shouldn't tell you that. I know your opinion about educating women."

"Do you?" he asked. "What was it I said about that?"

"That most men steer clear of the notion."

He laughed, a deeply masculine sound that reverberated through her. "I could have said worse. Actually, I'm beginning to think it isn't such a bad idea."

Surprised, she asked, "Are you really?"

"It does seem to lead to all sorts of interesting encounters."

Moonlight paled her skin, but even so, she knew she was blushing. The propriety that had shielded her all her life was gone. Just then she missed it.

"Did you follow me?" she asked suddenly.

He nodded. "I saw you leave the camp. You really have to get over this habit of wandering off alone. It's dangerous."

"Have you appointed yourself my guardian then?" Odd, she hadn't noticed how close they were. She could see the flecks of silver in his eyes and the slow, steady rise and fall of his broad chest. So very close.

"It seems someone has to," he said roughly. "Why can't you sleep? The others are fast in dreams. You should be, too."

She sighed and surreptitiously rubbed the small of her back where a dull ache still lingered. "I suspect they've led less pampered lives than I have. Sleeping on sand seems a contradiction."

He laughed, remembering the times he'd tried it himself. "Is that the reason for all the ducks and geese? Do you fancy a fine, down-filled mattress?"

"I fancy any sort of mattress at all." Which was true enough, but this was definitely not the time to discuss it, she surmised. There had to be a safer topic. "I've been thinking about my house."

His eyebrows rose. "Your what?"

"My house. I'll have to have one, of course. We all will." Mischievously, she added, "People do that, you know. They build houses in a new place. It's called settling down."

"People do all sorts of foolish things. But I suppose you're right. What kind do you have in mind?"

She was surprised that he seemed genuinely interested, and she felt suddenly embarrassed about telling him. "Just a house. Something that will last."

He nodded, for this he understood. Ships were meant to last. There were vessels afloat that had seen the previous century. Not many, to be sure, for the sea took its toll. But he recognized the need to create something that would endure.

"For how long?" he asked.

"A hundred years, two, perhaps longer. We had a house in Amsterdam that old and there were some older still. It can be done."

He shook his head bemusedly. A hundred years in this place? He could not imagine it. But she could. He saw that in her eyes. She could look at the wild land and see something altogether different from anything that had ever been. It was what had brought her here.

"Alright then," he said. "A house to stand a hundred years or more. Here on the neck, I suppose?"

She nodded and pointed a little shyly to the clearing amid the trees. "There, I think."

Garrick frowned. The clearing looked old. There were no tree stumps or other rubble to be seen. And it was the right size for a proud house, almost as though it had been waiting for just that. She would build the house and here she would stay. While he—

"And then what will you do, Mistress Daniels, when your house is done?"

She met his eyes, there in the moonlit, shimmering night. "I was thinking of that earlier, Captain Marlowe." Amelia was very proper now, very careful when she continued for the ground was suddenly very thin. "Our house in Amsterdam was too quiet. I would like this one to be different. I want to fill it with laughter and with life."

His body hardened. It happened in an instant, and with such fierceness that his breath was sucked away. A bone-deep ache seized him. He wanted this woman as he had never wanted anyone or anything. He wanted to take her there on the pine-scented ground, to fill her completely, to give in to the life she spoke of with such strength and tenderness.

And he might have, for all that he clung to honor, had it not been for the sudden shout raised from *Lady Star* and the sight over the water of another vessel fast approaching.

Chapter Eleven

The ship was a small, fast-moving galleon called the *Beacon* out of Boston town. She was Puritan built, one of the first such vessels constructed in the New World, and there was no doubt as to her purpose. She came with gun ports open and her crew on deck.

The full moon had lit their way to where *Lady Star* rode at anchor, sleeping but not completely unprotected. As usual, discipline was strict on Garrick's ship. He had checked the watch himself before returning to the beach. The sailors' shouts awakened the people on shore. Men and women were running about, uncertain what to do, and the children were crying when Garrick and Amelia reached the camp.

"Get into the trees," he shouted above the din. "Take what weapons you have and leave the rest."

"The animals," Sam protested. "If they kill them, we'll be lost."

"There's no time," Garrick insisted. He pointed out over the water. Already, a longboat was setting off from the *Beacon*. She carried armed men toward the shore.

Sam needed no further persuading. He seized his musket with one hand, Lissy with the other, and raced for the trees. The rest of the settlers did the same. Within moments, the beach was almost deserted.

"Go with them," Garrick said giving Amelia a small push in the right direction. A terrible urgency filled him. Whatever shelter the trees offered, it would not last long. They had to stop the men on the beach.

The only weapon he had with him was the knife sheathed along his boot. But his men knew what was needed. Already, a half dozen of them were rowing madly for the shore, while the rest took their positions on board *Lady Star.* Those who had come from *Venturer* had already lost one ship. They were determined not to lose another.

They had a few minutes to make a beachhead behind the barrels and crates. Barely were they in place when the *Beacon*'s longboat rammed up on the shore and her crew spilled out.

First among them was Peter Harkness, his black coat flapping around his legs and a musket lodged firmly under his arm. He strode up the beach like a dark, avenging angel, drawing the others in his wake.

Behind him, Master Barton stumbled. The lawyer looked pale and anxious. There were a dozen others, all equally unenthused but lacking the will to challenge the madman who had decreed that only pursuit and punishment were the rightful end for those who dared to flee fair Boston. He had dragged them out in a fury, sailing through the night, determined to catch those he called renegades, upon whose heads he called down all the vengeance of his angry god.

Garrick guessed the council had not argued very hard. He had worried that they would see the danger inherent in letting Amelia and her stalwart band go peacefully. They would recognize it for the slight to their authority that it was, and fear that it would inspire too many others to the same spirit of independence.

And then where would they be, these fine, upstanding gentlemen who depended on the subservience of lesser men to secure their own place in heaven?

Here they were on the beach, ready to wreak mayhem in the name of what they considered to be theirs alone—the right to decide how men and women should live.

There were more of them, and they were better armed than the men from *Lady Star*. Unless Garrick acted very quickly, they would have the advantage.

He didn't hesitate. He picked up one of the muskets his crewmen had brought, put it to his shoulder and fired. The mighty blast reverberated up and down the beach.

Behind him, he heard the people in the trees scream. His own men appeared shaken but they, too, shouldered their weapons and prepared to fire.

Peter Harkness might be mad—of that Garrick had little doubt—but the Puritan had not sailed the seas for a decade fending off every sort of brigand and pirate who happened by. He expected men to stand and wait while he attacked. It was time he learned of another way.

Garrick's first shot had been aimed short on purpose. It exploded the sand several feet ahead of where Master Harkness stood. Garrick still hoped to end this without bloodshed, but if it came down to it, he would do whatever he had to.

"Devil's spawn!" Harkness shouted. "Surrender the good men and women of Boston you stole or the Almighty will smite you seven times seven and drive you into the eternal fires!"

The men with Harkness glanced at each other nervously. Such fanaticism was a bit much—even for them.

Among Garrick's men, it prompted looks of disbelief and scorn. Several hooted sarcastically.

Resentment bubbled just below the surface, anger at all those who presumed to know best and looked down on others. It would take very little to bring it bursting into the open.

Before a full-fledged brawl broke out, Garrick reached a decision. He shouted a single order to his men, rearmed his musket and raised it again. At his command, a dozen muskets roared out over the heads of the Puritans.

"Reload," he directed loudly enough for all to hear. To the startled group on the beach, some with their arms over their heads and other fumbling for their weapons, he said, "The next time, they'll be aiming square for your middles and they won't miss. You've to the count of ten to show me the back of you."

The men from Boston town were not precisely cowards—most had dared great dangers to come to the new land—but they weren't stupid, either. They had followed Harkness reluctantly, and they were not prepared to die in his cause.

But he was, or at least he was prepared to make others die for him. His eyes were filled with hate as he took aim directly at Garrick.

"Ten," Garrick said, and fired. Alone among his men, he had held back and so had not needed to rearm. Harkness had not realized that. He was not prepared for the sudden burst of shot that ripped past him. The small, deadly musket ball struck his weapon and knocked it clean from his hands.

Harkness stared at it with disbelief that was equaled only by Garrick's. He had aimed at the Puritan's musket, true enough, but he hadn't really counted on hitting it. Anything in the immediate vicinity, including Harkness himself, would have done as well.

Still, the musket was where he wanted it to be, and the Puritans were turning in flight. Several stayed long enough to tug at Harkness, trying to get him to come with them, but he shook them off like flies. Roaring, he charged up the beach straight at Garrick.

And straight into the stock of the musket. Garrick had flipped it around and just held it, not even trying all that hard. Harkness went right into it. Garrick sighed, handed the musket to one of his men and hauled the elder upright.

Harkness had turned an interesting shade of green, except for his eyes. They were rolling up so that the whites showed starkly.

"If you hurry," Garrick said nicely, "you can catch your friends before they leave without you."

Harkness gurgled something—probably more about hellfire and damnation. Garrick didn't understand it and didn't try. He gestured to two of his men. "Make sure he gets back on board the *Beacon.* If he stays here, I'm going to gut him and serve him for dinner."

To Harkness, he added, "I know you aren't feeling real good right about now, but you listen hard and get what I'm saying. This is the second time we've gone at it, and you've lost both times. Get a little sense through that thick skull and keep your distance, otherwise the next time is going to be the last. Understand?"

Maybe Harkness did and maybe he didn't. The look he shot Garrick as he was dragged away by his men reeked of hatred and the urge to destroy. But there had to be some hope that he'd give up what was obviously a losing proposition. Didn't there?

With the men from the *Beacon* gone, the settlers emerged from the trees, shouting and whooping in relief. The sudden victory emboldened them.

Whereas before they had felt merely relieved to be away from Boston, now they felt vindicated. They had faced the enemy—or at least Garrick and his men had faced them—and had come away triumphant. Beside that, not much else mattered.

Under the moon, they danced and capered on the beach, pounding the men of *Lady Star* on their backs and sending the *Beacon* on its way with hoots and threats.

"By God," Sam Whitler declared, "let them come at us again. We'll teach them a thing or two, won't we?"

All agreed that indeed they would. They had won, they were safe.

"For the time being," Garrick said under his breath.

"You think they may be back?" Amelia asked.

They were standing close together, neither quite sure why, but it seemed natural enough. While all about them celebrated, they remained aloof, watching the *Beacon* fade into the distance.

"They may," Garrick agreed. It did not escape his notice that she had armed herself. Not with a musket, for the settlers had few of them, but with a nasty-looking fireplace poker that he, personally, wouldn't have wanted to go up against.

"Were you really planning on using that?" he asked.

She looked surprised that he would doubt it. "Of course. If they tried to take us by force, we would have to defend ourselves."

"It could have gotten very rough."

She shrugged as though any child knew that. "This is our land. As short a time as we have been here, I think it's fair to say that it is already our home. Wouldn't you shed blood to protect what is yours?"

"Of course I would, but that's different. I'm a—"

He got no further. She turned on him, her hazel eyes glinting, and said, "A man? Good captain, I'll have you know that women are every bit as valiant as men. Have you ever seen a child born?"

"No," he admitted. "That's—"

"Women's work? It is *life's* work, captain, plain and simple. Without some woman having suffered all the agonies of hell, you wouldn't be here now. Nor would any of us. Men have this illusion that women are somehow weaker. Our strength is different, but it is no less. Believe me, we will fight to protect our hearths. God help the man who forgets that."

Despite himself, Garrick smiled. He suspected she was telling him a truth he wasn't entirely ready to hear. But at the moment, he was more interested in the way her eyes flashed and the becoming color stained her cheeks.

Halfheartedly, he said, "We should get some sleep."

She laughed. "No one is going to sleep anymore tonight, except perhaps the children, and I wouldn't count on that."

"Then what do you propose we do, Mistress Daniels?"

There was a great deal she could have said to that, but none of it was remotely proper. She took a deep breath, straightened her shoulders and said, "I suppose we had better get to work."

So it was that the valiant band of Belle Haven settlers set off from the beach by the light of the moon. Following the trail laid down long ago by the local Pequot, they trekked inland. The trail ran near the river. It flowed between gently rolling hills to emerge amid cleared fields set on a rock ledge sufficiently elevated to provide a view of the shore from which they had come.

"Cleared land," Amelia said with awe. She had not even dared to hope they would find anything of the like.

"The Pequot must have planted here in the past," Garrick said.

Which also meant that they had cut the trees, girdling them around the middle so that they died slowly and became gray, leafless wrecks that rotted away. Later, the underbrush would have been burned off and crops sown. Husks from the previous year's maize crop remained in the fields. They had only to be cleared and the earth turned to receive fresh seed.

"Truly, the Lord has blessed us," Lissy said fervently. No one had to explain to her that the presence of cleared land meant they had a far better chance of surviving than would otherwise have been the case. A strong-bodied man could not hope to clear more than an acre or two in a year. To create a prosperous farm, one needed at least a hundred acres, which required the work of several lifetimes.

The others stopped, dropped their bundles to the ground and stared around them in awe. Immediately, they began to calculate how much could be planted and what it should be, and beyond that, how much additional land could be cleared immediately.

They had been given a beginning that assured a real chance of prosperity for themselves and for their children. Belle Haven was suddenly far more than dream. It had become reality.

Chapter Twelve

The first house built in Belle Haven was the meeting-house. Work on it began the second day. It was made of notched logs brought from Boston, and it went up quickly.

Garrick was glad of that. He had taken over responsibility for erecting the building since shelter was a priority. Much of his crew and several of the settlers were part of the work team. They labored from sunup throughout the day and were rewarded when, still well before dusk, the last of the roof was lowered into place.

Barely had they finished when the planters began returning from the fields. Amelia was among them. She trudged back, shoulders bent and head down, more exhausted than she had ever been. Beside her, Sam Whitler tried to offer encouragement.

"We did very well. Two acres turned and half to seed already. With a bit of luck on the weather, there'll be no hunger this winter."

She nodded, knowing she should be cheery, but she was unable to muster the energy for it. Tales of the starving times were well-known throughout the colonies. Almost every new settlement had suffered them. Belle Haven might be the first to escape.

For that alone, she should rejoice. But her shoulders and back hurt so much. And her hands—she really didn't want to think of her hands at all.

She lifted her head reluctantly and glanced toward the clearing where they had pitched the canvas shelter. The sight that met her eyes caused her to blink once, twice, and again.

"You didn't—" she breathed, turning toward Garrick, who stood nearby.

He glanced at the ground modestly, as though he raised buildings every day and failed to see why she would be surprised. "Of course we did. How did it go in the fields?"

"Oh, fine... We..." She continued to stare at the building in a daze. The more she looked, the more obscurely proud he felt. It really wasn't much as buildings went, being small and plain. But it was the first one he'd ever had anything to do with, and he supposed that under the circumstances it wasn't too bad.

Not remotely comparable to a ship, of course, but still not bad.

Amelia reached out and touched the rough-hewn planks gently. She ran her fingers around the doorposts and over the window frame. Garrick watched as she breathed deeply, savoring the scent of freshly hewn wood. A smile spread over her face.

"This is wonderful."

"We've still the chimney to do," he said.

She nodded and turned to look around the clearing. "A green over there, don't you think?" she asked. Her smile deepened. "And on the other side, perhaps a tavern. A meetinghouse and a tavern in the same place should guarantee good business."

He shook his head bemusedly. She was tired, dirty and bedraggled, yet she looked thoroughly happy. He could hardly fathom such a woman.

"We should feast tonight," she said, "to celebrate our accomplishments."

The other settlers agreed. Weary though they were, they set about the preparations immediately. A large cooking fire was set up in front of the meetinghouse, several of the men went out to hunt while there was still light, and came back marveling at their swift success.

Water was drawn from the river and people went off to find what privacy they could so that they might bathe. Fresh clothes drawn from chests sparkled with color.

The previous night there had been relief and pleasure, but now there was more. No longer were they perched on the edge of their new home. They had come into the heart of it and had made it their own.

A farsighted soul—one Bernard Fletcher—had brought along a keg of ale. This was tapped and the mugs passed round as duck browned on the spits and the children raced madly about, taking advantage of their elders' indulgence.

Master Fletcher's health was drunk, as was his beaming wife's. They were among the older settlers but were no less stalwart for that. With them was their pretty daughter who, escaping no one's eyes, had already attracted the notice of a young seaman.

The music was brought out again, but this time no one had the energy to dance. They were content to sit quietly in the firelight and listen to the familiar tunes.

Amelia sat beside Garrick. Weary and yet exultant, she hardly knew that she leaned against him. The scent of her hair, uncovered and left in a long braid down her back, filled his breath. The night was cool and she was wrapped in her cape, but he could feel her warmth and was stirred by it.

Slowly, not wanting to startle her, he slipped his arm around her waist and settled her more comfortably in the curve of his body. She murmured softly and nestled closer.

He waited through the pace of several heartbeats as her eyelids drooped. Snug against him, she drifted into sleep as securely as a child would have.

They rested that night in the meetinghouse, their blankets and straw mattresses spread out on the dirt floor. The shelter was welcome, for away from the warmer offshore currents, the air grew chill. But the house itself was snug, and after midnight when it began to rain, the interior remained dry. Garrick lay awake long after the rest were asleep. He had considered going back to the ship, but decided against it. There was so much to be done that he preferred to save the time spent coming and going.

Of course, there was also the fact that he preferred to stay near Amelia, but he saw no reason to dwell on that.

Six months. That long until the first harvest would come in and his debt to her would be discharged. Ordinarily, he did not think of that as a long time, but now each day threatened to stretch out endlessly. And each night.

He sighed and turned over, seeking a more comfortable position. Amelia lay a short distance away, separate enough for what passed for propriety, but not so far that he couldn't watch the soft rise and fall of her breathing.

He smiled regretfully as he studied her. In a handful of days, she had survived a beating and a near-drowning, founded a colony and helped stand off those who would have destroyed it. She could be pardoned for sleeping so soundly.

He wished he could do the same, but rest remained elusive, and too soon the starlit night gave way to blazing day.

Amelia straightened slowly. Her back was stiff, her shoulders throbbed and the effort of straightening up made her feel slightly dizzy. But the sight that greeted her eyes made her smile.

The first fields were seeded in neat rows of corn kernels placed several feet apart. According to local wisdom, they were planting "when the white oak leaves reach the size of a mouse's ear." When the first green shoots appeared, they would scoop dirt in tiny hillocks to support them, fertilize them with herring and, in time, plant pumpkin and beans among the stalks.

She shaded her eyes and looked out over the fields to where several of the men were erecting a wooden fence. They planned on letting the pigs out to forage and wanted to make sure the crops were safe from them.

Farther away, near the meetinghouse, several women were dressing game. Sarah Fletcher was among them. Amelia had taken little notice of the young woman before, being far too busy to concern herself, but now she realized that Mistress Fletcher was only slightly younger than she, perhaps fifteen or sixteen to her own nineteen years.

She had light blond hair, a pretty round face, and eyes that even at a distance appeared to sparkle. She was also possessed of that half endearing, half annoying self-consciousness that comes to those who are both young and fair. As she worked she tossed her head, seemingly glad to be free of the restricting cap she had worn in Boston town.

Her laughter rose among the voices of the other women, prompting indulgent looks from most of them. But not all. One or two were more cautious, Lissy Whitler among them, and Amelia could see why.

The young sailor who had appeared so smitten with Sarah the previous evening was lingering nearby, ostensibly sharpening knives but keeping her close within his view. He was not alone.

Behind the meetinghouse, in the shelter of the trees, stood a young Indian. No one else appeared to have noticed him. As Amelia watched, he took several steps toward the clearing, hesitated, turned suddenly and disappeared back into the woods. It had all happened so suddenly that she might almost have imagined him.

Amelia thought about the incident as she returned to the seeding, and she was still thinking about it much later in the day as she followed the others in from the fields.

Amelia did not fool herself. Her fellow settlers were good and honorable people, but they were not paragons. They had their own share of the fears and doubts that seemed to plague people everywhere.

Left to themselves, they would do their best to be good neighbors to the Indians, provided the two ways of life did not clash. Should that happen, it would be impossible to tell the results, only that they were certain to bring harm.

But what could she do? All she had seen was a young Pequot who was drawn to Sarah Fletcher. Nothing might ever come of it. He could decide on his own that it would be imprudent to ever let his interest be known.

Or, if he did find a way to approach the girl, she might demur with enough grace to convince him to simply forget about her.

The problem was that both of those possibilities depended on more good sense and self-control than people usually seemed to have, especially young ones in the throes of untoward emotions.

Amelia sighed as she set her hoe among the rest of the tools and slipped the seed bag off by raising it over her head. She was a good one to be worrying over Sarah Fletcher and the brave when she had her own unwonted feelings to deal with, she thought.

Had she needed any reminder of that, it was amply provided by the sight of Garrick Marlowe returning to the settlement. He had gone out early in the day with a group of men to survey the surrounding area. They looked tired but pleased with their labors as they strode into the clearing.

"Mistress Daniels," Garrick said as he passed near her.

Amelia bit her lip, knowing she should keep her own counsel. Yet the need to seek his help proved overwhelming.

"May I speak with you for a moment?" she asked.

Her gravity told him this was no light matter. Nodding, he drew her aside. "What troubles you?"

Briefly, she told him what she had observed. For a moment, she feared he would dismiss her concerns, believing she had read too much into what might well mean nothing.

But instead, he nodded slowly and said, "I think I know the brave you saw. He is Owenoke's son, a good enough lad but more accustomed to his own way than he ought to be."

Amelia frowned. This was worse than she feared. The chief's son would not be easily discouraged. "You've noticed that your seaman—"

"Young Will? Aye, he's smitten with her, too. He's a good lad—out of Bristol originally, still has family there."

"Would he make trouble?"

Garrick looked at her skeptically. "In a dispute over a woman and with a man of another race? What do you think?"

"Then we may have a serious problem." Chagrined, she shook her head. "What is it about men that they desire what they should not have? I'm certain there are lovely Pequot maidens who would welcome his suit. Why should he seek something that promises to make such difficulties?"

Garrick smiled. Light danced in his pewter eyes. He leaned against the wall of the meetinghouse and looked at her indulgently. "Are you asking me as a man, or as one who helped—however unwillingly—a certain young woman go off into the wilderness to found a settlement in violation of all custom and good sense?"

"It is not the same," she insisted, but doubt underlaid her words. He was looking at her so very closely with something of the same expression in his eyes that she had seen in the Pequot brave's.

But Garrick was no untried boy. This was a man of experience and strength, well accustomed to wresting from the world whatever it was that he desired.

And he desired her.

She could no longer deny it. As inexperienced as she was, an ancient, hidden part of herself understood and responded to him. She swayed slightly and caught the side of the meeting hall to steady herself.

"What can we do?" she asked, and for a moment did not know whether she meant about the Fletcher girl or about themselves.

Garrick frowned. She looked very pale all of a sudden. Had there not been so many people nearby—

"Keep her busy here at the camp," he said flatly. "Meanwhile, I'll put a word in Passicham's ear. My guess is Owenoke wants no more trouble than we do."

"And young Will?"

"Keep him busy, as well. There's certainly enough to do."

"Will that work?" she asked, looking up at him through the thick fringe of her lashes. "If they are so occupied, so distracted and so weary at the end of each day, will they forget their feelings for each other?"

They? Their? Garrick was confused. Will and the Fletcher girl shared no feelings, as yet, at least not so far as anyone knew.

He sighed and resisted the urge to touch the damask, smooth curve of her cheek. "It'd be more convenient if they did, wouldn't it? Safer all around?"

She nodded and drew a shaky breath. "Life is rarely that accommodating."

The burnished skin around his eyes crinkled. "So I've observed."

Moments more, they stood in the shelter of the meetinghouse wall, close enough to touch, but not touching. Until the world intruded once again and they were drawn apart.

Chapter Thirteen

The days passed, blending together as the rhythm of the season seized them all. Amelia ceased to worry about Sarah Fletcher, but she did keep an occasional eye out to see if the chief's son returned. He did not, or if he did, she did not notice him. She supposed that as the settlers were busy on their own lands, the Pequot were busy on theirs.

The moon swelled and the time of planting hastened. On clear nights they worked into the wee hours, hoeing and seeding, weeding and raking, nurturing the tiny green sprouts that so tentatively emerged. First corn, then wheat, pumpkins, beans and all manner of kitchen vegetables were tended in their turn.

April faded, dwindling to a few scarce days that Amelia marked in the journal she had begun to keep. In it, she recorded the progress in the fields, the clearing of more land and the parceling out of grants to each family. On the last day of April, writing shortly before midnight, she was able to note exultantly: "The planting is complete. With fortune's favor, Belle Haven's first harvest will be bountiful."

She barely managed to slip the book into her chest before sleep overcame her. Exhausted, she slept dreamlessly and with no sense of passing time, awakening to brilliant day as though scant moments had passed. Bewildered she sat up and looked around her. Through the window left bare of oiled paper or shutters, she could see Sam Whitler and several of the others pointing at something and laughing. Slowly, she rose, straightened her clothes and stepped outside.

Just as she did, the morning quiet was punctured by the long high-pitched sound of a horn. It was followed swiftly by another. Amelia froze in place. The sound was not unknown to her—she had heard it before, but so long ago and so far away that she could hardly recognize it. From deep within the hidden chords of her memory, she recalled a sun-splashed day as a very young child.

The mummers! They came out of the wood, three in all, bobbing and weaving in their intricately woven wicker baskets, which covered them from head to toe. The baskets were entwined with holly and ivy drawn from the forest floor and the vines around the budding trees. Firstborn flowers—crocus and wild marigold—added bursts of color. Stalks of last year's corn festooned the headpieces. From them hung balls painted silver and gold to represent the moon and sun. They came, ancient figures of myth yet real as living memory. With them came their escorts, young men from *Lady Star* and a few from among the settlers, blowing on their antler horns. The settlers looked more hesitant than the others, well aware that they were not behaving as good Puritans should, yet daring anyone to challenge them for it.

Not that anyone looked disposed to do so. The crowd that gathered quickly clapped hands in delight. All knew of the ritual, however furtively the knowledge had been imparted in the bad old days of the protector Cromwell.

Some had seen it enacted before, as had Amelia. But none had ever before been free to participate.

Had it not been for the seamen, they would have been without the knowledge to weave the wicker cages and decorate them, to perform the simple steps of the dance and to call upon their horns for the awakening of the earth with blasts of music more ancient than any cared to contemplate.

Amelia stared, as wide-eyed with delight as any of the children. Catching her wonder, the wicker men danced and capered before her, drawing her and all the others into their revelry.

Ah, well, she thought as she was swept away, a day without work would do them all good. It was the first such rest they had gotten since *Lady Star* dropped anchor on Belle Haven's shore. Not even the Sabbath had brought a pause, being only a time for hastily murmured prayers said, more often than not, while already at work in the fields.

But not today. This sun-bright morning was for celebration and thanksgiving. The planting was done, the earth had received her bounty and in due course, would give it back. But now it was time for the horn and the tree, for the ancient wicker men and the joy of life sustained.

Turned round and round, laughing and dizzy, Amelia was at last released from the midst of the dance and stumbled, swaying, falling...no, caught and held upright by arms of steel.

"You look like a child," Garrick said. Tenderness shone in his eyes. His hair was ruffled, his shirt hanging loosely open to bare his chest to the warm May breeze. A night's growth of beard darkened his cheeks, but his smile was broad and his eyes were sweet with indulgence.

"And you look far from your formidable self, Captain," she teased.

His eyebrows rose. He wasn't used to her like this—laughing and free, twirling to the rhythm of the dance. She was only nineteen, he reminded himself. In another world, another time, she would be dressed in silk and lace, with flowers in her hair, not in a work-worn dress shorn of any adornment other than what the supple grace of her body gave to it.

"A garland gay we bring you here," the sailors sang, "and at your door we stand. It is a sprout well budded out, the work of our Lord's hand."

To the cheers of their audience the mummers bowed extravagantly.

"To the pole!" one shouted, buoyed up by their reception.

"To the May!" came another cry, and as one, sailors and settlers alike, the crowd surged forward. At the edge of the clearing, not far beyond the meetinghouse, a stately oak stood. There they gathered, joining hands and dancing round while the horns blew and the mummers pranced, all close by the seeded fields fertile with new life.

"Come dance," Garrick commanded, and she went, close to his hand and safe in his arms, turning, whirling, laughing and exulting. Had life ever been sweeter? she wondered. Had anyone ever been freer? There, in the clearing beneath the sun, she cast off the last of grief and gave herself up to the sheer joy of rebirth. The others danced and celebrated, food was brought out and drink provided, but Amelia knew little of all that. She knew only that Garrick enthralled her, especially this relaxed and playful side of him she had never really seen before.

He kept her close, that much did not escape her. Several times, other men approached her, only to be warned off with a look from Garrick. After a time, no more came and they were alone in the midst of the revelry.

It was midday. The sun at its zenith shone over field and clearing, wood and sea. The air was heavy with the scents of spring. Voices were raised in old, remembered songs—some hymns, some of less holy origin. People were drowsy with contentment. A few of the younger children were curled up on blankets, napping. Here and there, a face was missing. Sam and Lissy had slipped away. Others had gone as well.

"Where are we going?" Amelia asked as she realized Garrick was leading her from the clearing.

"To the copse. I want to show you something."

Testament to her dazzled state of mind, she could not quite remember why it was she ought not to go.

They walked in silence to the river's edge. A canoe lay on the bank. Garrick lifted it easily and lowered it into the water. He held out his hand to help Amelia in.

"This is yours?" she asked.

He nodded. "I traded with Passicham for it. Our longboat can negotiate some of the inland waters around here, but not all. Canoes like this will be more useful."

"I see," she said, marveling that he could think of such useful things when she seemed unable to think at all. She sat behind him in the canoe, her hands holding on to either side, for she had never ridden in such a craft before and found the experience unsettling. Swiftly, they moved beyond the bank and downriver. She tried not to stare at the powerful flexing of his muscles as he raised and lowered the paddle, but she had to look at something, after all, and that seemed most compelling.

Too quickly for her wayward self, they reached their destination. He pulled the canoe onto the shore even as she realized where they were.

"The copse! I had no idea it was so close."

"It takes several hours to reach overland," he said, "but the river puts you close to the clearing. Come," he added, helping her out of the canoe.

She set her foot on the velvety soft ground and felt again the warm stirring she had experienced before. The scents were heavier here and the air shimmering with softly filtered sunlight.

Briefly, she remembered what had passed between them the last time they had stood in this place. Only the sudden arrival of the *Beacon* had stopped them from ... What? Her mind whirled at the thought. So much strangeness, so much half known and half dreamed. So much yet to experience.

She gazed into the clearing where one day she hoped to build her house. At first glance, it looked the same as before but after a few minutes, she noticed something was different. She looked more closely and felt the sudden fluttering of her heart as she realized what it was she saw. "That stone..."

It was large, smoothly dressed and laid flat in the ground, well secured by the solid earth around it. It had been positioned exactly where she had thought to put her front door—within sight of her garden and orchard.

She walked closer, unaware of how she looked to the man who followed her. Slim and proud, Amelia held her head high, the sunlight gilding her fire-breathed hair. There was writing on the stone. Someone had inscribed words upon it. Someone. Garrick.

"Amelia Daniels's House," it said.

She knelt and, trembling, traced the incised letters with her fingertips. The chisel had bitten deeply.

"To last a hundred years and more," Garrick said quietly.

She nodded, blinking back tears. "You did this?"

He shrugged, suddenly embarrassed. "I had some free time."

Her laugh was shaky. "When? Deep in the night when the rest of us were asleep?"

In fact, he had done the work on such a night when the moon was so full that he could see almost as clearly as he could by day. Then he had come alone to Daniels Neck and the clearing in the copse, and found the stone. It lay in the riverbed, washed down some endless time ago. He had fished it out and patiently chiseled away the rough edges until it could lie true and flat. Then he had carved the words and, lastly put it in place, remembering where she wanted her house.

"It didn't take long," he claimed, although he had not counted the time. Time might as well have not existed.

"It's beautiful," she said. Turning, she looked at him with such fullness in her eyes that his breath caught.

"Amelia's house," he said, and knelt down beside her.

She turned to him? He turned to her? Neither knew which of them moved first. It didn't matter. She was in his arms, warm and alive. Far off, along the winding river, the mummers chanted and the maypole hung, festooned with promises of spring. Here, in this secret place, there was only a man and a woman, bound in their own sacred rites.

He shouldn't do this. He knew that as surely as he knew the curve of the earth beneath the stars and the deep-running currents that beckoned him on.

He should stop now, walk away, forget Amelia Daniels and go on with his life. But he might as well stop breathing and bid his heart to stop in its appointed course.

Still, he was an honorable man, and for the sake of honor, he hesitated. She looked into his eyes and smiled. Slowly, her hand cupped the back of his head, her fingers tangling in the thick, black hair.

"Come," she whispered, not Amelia now, but something eternal and everlasting, beyond them both.

"Come," the earth affirmed, and gathered them in blankets of scented pine and new-sown earth, spring born and bearing.

Chapter Fourteen

Her mouth enthralled him. It was infinitely sweet and endlessly soft. She tasted of the mulled wine they had drunk round the maypole and of some flavor intrinsically her own. Her lips parted, and he felt the warmth of her breath tantalizing him.

He had meant to go slowly. The decision taken, the corner turned, he had still presumed to be in proper control of the situation. He, the man of experience and sophistication, she, the green girl.

It wasn't happening that way. Barely had he touched her than the bonds of his self-control stretched near to breaking. Raw, primal desire roared through him. He had no thought but for possession.

Swiftly, he lowered her to the moss-covered ground. Above her, braced on his powerful arms, he stared down into her eyes and saw there the heat of his own desire. Far from seeming hesitant or afraid, she smiled.

"A new world, Garrick," she whispered as her cool, slender hands reached for him.

He was not used to this. Women in his experience were compliant when they had something to gain apart from the pleasure of the moment, be it the straightforward payment of money, or a favor done, or perhaps merely the conquest of a man others desired. It was never this simple, this sweetly pure.

Not until now, in this place, with this woman. Her russet hair spilled like fire over the green, green ground. Her hazel eyes were as deep and mysterious as the surrounding wood. Her lips were slightly parted and her breasts rose and fell with each breath. He touched a finger to her cheek and traced the smooth, soft skin.

"Amelia," he whispered huskily, "there is no going back from this. Are you sure?"

She hesitated and he waited, tremors moving deep within him through seemingly endless time, until slowly, so slowly, she tilted her head.

"I'm sure," she said, and her smile deepened.

The tautness of his features, the pulse beating in his jaw, the stunning difference of him, so overwhelmingly male, all drove the breath from her. She hovered out of herself, watching the strangely beautiful scene almost as though she was not really part of it.

The man and woman, the primal forest, the sunlight filtering through the branches overhead and the world all so distant, surely this was not her? And yet it was, undeniably. She could no more explain to him why she wanted this than she could explain it to herself.

In England, in the Lowlands, in Boston town, it would have been impossible. She would not even have considered it.

But here, in Belle Haven, everything was different. She called it a new world, and that she truly believed. They had escaped, they were free, the future was their own to make.

She would lose him. The certainty of that pain twisted within her. The months would pass, the harvest would be gathered, and he would sail away. She could no more prevent that than she could stop the turning of the stars in the heavens above.

But she could create a memory and save it away like the rare and precious jewel it would be.

Her hands traced the muscled contours of his chest through the loose linen shirt. She felt the overpowering strength of him, the burnished skin stretched tight over bone and sinew and the heat shimmering deep within.

He was so strong that he could easily overpower her. Yet he held back, giving her the liberty to learn to know him, and in that, to lessen in some measure the strangeness he represented.

Her hands shook and her breath quickened, but still she persevered. Dimly, in the back of her mind, she realized that he was being extraordinarily patient. Her heart warmed with gratitude even as her need for him heightened. Still, she could go only so far before maidenly confusion overwhelmed her.

He laughed softly at her plight and cupped her face between his hands. Lightly, he kissed her, once, twice, again. Her lips parted on a sigh, admitting the slow thrust of his tongue. She stiffened for an instant but soon relaxed again and joined him in the playful stroking.

Had it not been for the hunger racking his body, he might have gone on like that for some time, indulging to the full the passion of his senses. Everything about her delighted him—the alabaster glow of her skin lightly warmed by the sun, the sweet scent of lavender, the delicate line of her throat to her finely curved shoulders. The soft swell of her breasts touching his chest and the gentle ripeness of her hips filled him with deep, shuddering heat.

Swiftly, he undid the buttons down her back and slid the dress down her arms. For a moment, she clutched at it, covering her breasts. Their eyes met. She drew a long breath and let the dress go.

He inhaled sharply. Her high, rounded breasts, tipped by large pink aureoles, were perfection. Beneath them, faint shadows accentuated the delicate line of her rib cage tapering to her slim waist.

He put his hands around that waist, so small that his fingers almost touched, and he raised her to him. Her head fell back as a soft, urgent moan escaped her.

His mouth closed on her nipples, first one and then the other, laving gently with his tongue before suckling her. He felt her tighten within his mouth as rippling shudders coursed through her. Her fingers moved desperately through his hair and down his muscled back to clutch at his hips.

When he raised his head at last, his eyes were smoky gray with lambent fires. A dark flush stained his high-boned cheeks. His chest shuddered, straining to breathe.

The effort to go slowly for her sake was almost more than he could bear. The thrumming of his blood, the pounding of his heart and the heat soaring through him, all urged him to haste. But still he held back. Carefully, he removed the rest of her garments, one by one, until there, in the shadowed copse, she was bared to him.

The warm spring breeze caressed her body as he drew back just long enough to hastily remove his own clothes. A slight smile touched his mouth when it occurred to him that he hadn't always bothered to be so thorough.

Many couplings he had known had been far hastier, stolen moments in a lady's chamber, a carriage, or even, on one particularly memorable occasion, a closed market stall. He had enjoyed each and every one of them, but now they seemed to have no more significance than a satisfying meal or a long, hot bath—merely one more sensual pleasure to be taken and done with.

Not this, not here, not with Amelia. He felt as a bridegroom gone to his wedding bed and could not find the strength to mock so delicate a notion. Ruefully, he acknowledged that the gentle but strong-willed lady brought out the best in him, even as she lured him to unbearable temptation.

Naked, he came to her with soft words of reassurance. Her eyes widened at the sight of his erect manhood, but she did not flinch. When he moved against her, she welcomed him with all the generous warmth of her body and spirit.

Aching with need, he yet restrained himself to draw out her pleasure to the fullest. When at last she was gasping his name and writhing beneath him, he gently moved his fingers between her legs to assure her readiness to receive him. Only then did he penetrate within her, very slightly at first. She was small and tight, and he was desperate not to hurt her.

With her features taut and her eyes locked on his, her lips shaped his name again as she struggled to adjust to his possession. He bent his head, his dark hair falling over her breasts, and drew her nipple deep within his mouth. She cried out softly, arching against him, as pleasure filled her.

At the same moment, he moved decisively, hips plunging, and filled her completely. She gasped and stiffened, her hands flat against his shoulders as though to push him away. But so quickly, her touch altered, becoming gentle.

He waited, jaw clenched, waited until her body moved around him, drawing him deeper. Only then did he at last give way to the hot, pounding ecstasy moving within him, bringing them both to shattering release.

The following day, Jacob Dykler came ashore. He was carried first in the longboat and then by stretcher inland to the camp—all the while grumbling that he was well enough to walk. Despite the bandages that still swathed his head and arms, he was doing remarkably well.

When he was settled on a bed made up in front of the meetinghouse where he could observe all the comings and goings, Amelia sat beside him for a time. She made herself comfortable on the ground beside him, her knees drawn up and her head resting pensively on them.

With a smile, she said, "You surprised us all, Master Dykler. We feared we might lose you."

He shook his head. "Not likely, mistress. Your good care gave me the edge I needed. But to tell you truth, it was thoughts of home that carried me through."

"You miss Holland that much?"

"I do miss it," he affirmed, "but when I think of home, it is my Vilma I mean." His smile deepened and became soft as he fumbled in the pocket of his breeches for something.

Fearing he might hurt himself, Amelia sprang up to help. At his direction, she eased a small, gold locket from the neatly stitched velvet pouch that held it.

"Look inside," Jacob directed.

She snapped the locket open carefully and turned it to the light. Inside were two tiny portraits, both of the same woman.

In the first picture, the woman could not have been even as old as Amelia. The other showed her several decades later when maturity had added weight and solidness but had taken nothing from her girlish smile and the bright light of her eyes.

"My wife," Jacob said with quiet fierceness, "and my friend—the best ever a man could have. I met her when I was twenty-five and she but a lass of fifteen."

He chuckled as he remembered. "Her father, Master Vilhelme DeVries, was a grand merchant, if only in his own estimation, and he wanted nothing to do with a water rat like me. But I persevered, and to be fair, I won some favor in Vilma's eyes. She worked to make her father see that I had some worth."

"I'm sure you did the same," Amelia said gently. She looked at the woman in the pictures thoughtfully. How happy she looked, how supremely content despite the fact that her husband must have been away through so much of their marriage.

Was the pose mere pretense? Amelia pondered. Or was it perhaps the look a truly loving wife would naturally adopt for a portrait she meant to send with her husband on his far journeys so that he would remember her pleasantly and without the burden of her own loneliness?

"Aye," Jacob murmured, "I worked harder than ever in my life. Five voyages the first year after I met Vilma, and six the next. My feet hardly touched land except to see her. And all that time, she never forgot me or gave heed to the young bucks who were closer to hand, eager to win her. She had pledged herself to me, and she kept that vow."

"Until at last even her father saw that you should be together?"

Jacob sighed. He took the locket from her and gave it a last, tender look before carefully putting it away.

"No, he never did. He caught a chill and died while I was at sea. Vilma was devastated, for she had truly loved him even though he wouldn't give her what her heart desired. For a while it looked as though we might never be together. But then Vilma's mother, bless her, said enough was enough, and that we should do what was right."

He slipped the pouch into his pocket with Amelia's help and settled himself more comfortably on the bed. "Just in time she was, too, for in God's truth, I was ready to carry Vilma away. Had a deal struck with my captain to give us passage and all. I was that desperate, I was."

"Would you have really?" Amelia asked, her eyes wide. Jacob Dykler seemed like such a quiet and reasonable man. Would he truly have absconded with a woman against all the censure of society simply because he believed they should be as one?

"Without a doubt," he said, and the firmness in his voice made it clear he meant exactly that. He cast her a wry look as he said, "Such matters are as deep waters, lass. No one can ever really be sure where they will lead, but it is for certain that they'll sweep you away before you know what's happened."

"Not always," she whispered.

He stroked his beard and looked up at the bright blue sky. "It's always the young ones who think they know what love can do, and always them who are overwhelmed by it."

She turned slightly so that he could not see what was in her eyes. Men and women were moving along the neat rows in the fields, checking closely for weeds.

Nearby, trees were being felled to extend the clearing. Several faces were missing, couples having gone off to examine their own lands and decided what needed to be done there.

"Love?" she asked softly. "As to that, I know nothing. You are to be envied, Master Dykler."

"Do you not, mistress? I'd have thought—"

She glanced at him cautiously. "What?"

"Nothing really, only that one as fair and brave as yourself might have had a passing acquaintance with the phenomenon."

"Not I," she insisted, "unless you mean the love I felt for my father or the love I bear God. But I don't think either of those are what you have in mind."

"True enough," he agreed. "Still, love goes by many names. It isn't always recognized for what it is."

Her startled look seemed to give him some satisfaction, for he chuckled gently. "Didn't you know that, lass? Love is like that funny little lizard they have down in the Caribbees—chameleon they call it. Changes color so quickly that if you blink, you miss it. Always hiding itself as something else. Popping up all of a sudden when you least expect it."

"I don't expect it at all," she said stoutly. "Love is a fantasy invented by poets. Not," she added hastily, "that I don't believe it can exist in cases such as you and Vilma. It is simply very rare. Few ever encounter it for themselves."

"If you say so," Jacob murmured, his tone making it plain that he did not agree. His amusement deepened, and he said gently, "One thing I learned all those long days and nights away from Vilma is that however love comes, it's never to be regretted. It's the Lord's greatest gift, and as such, it should always be held precious."

Amelia touched his hand lightly. "You're a lucky man, Master Dykler. I don't ever expect to be as fortunate."

For some reason she could not fathom, he laughed. When he stopped, he said, "Forgive me, mistress, but if there's one thing old Eros likes the best, it's to pop up visiting someone who doesn't even believe he exists. Nothing tickles the old devil's fancy more.''

Despite herself, Amelia grinned. "One moment you say it is a gift from God and the next you warn of pagan deities. Which is it, master?''

"Both, mistress," he said gravely, "for truly, love's as old as human imagination. It's what sets us apart from the beasts of the field and the lilies of the valley. I'll go to my reward believing love is what makes us pleasing in God's sight.''

"And Eros's?" she asked lightly.

"Aye, his, too, for give him his due. This old world wouldn't be anywhere near as interesting as it is without him dropping by every now and again.''

"I'll be sure to keep an eye out," Amelia said dryly.

"You do that, mistress," Jacob said as she took her leave. He glanced around at the verdant surroundings and smiled again. "For truly, I vow this is just the sort of place the old gentleman wouldn't mind finding himself.''

He chuckled softly and closed his eyes as his hand slipped into his pocket. His fingers closed gently around the velvet pouch, and he took the touch of it with him into healing sleep.

Chapter Fifteen

Amelia was deep in thought as she left Jacob. She desperately wanted to dismiss all the talk of love as meaningless to her, yet it lingered at the edge of her mind like a shimmering light she could not quite hide from her eyes. She could not love Garrick. What they had found together was beautiful, wonderful, filled with delight. She refused to have any regrets about it. He had given her a window on the wonder of God's creation that she had never so much as suspected might exist. With all else, she was grateful for that. But not all the pleasure or passion in the world was love. Love was something altogether different. Quieter and gentler, patient and kind. Love was what Jacob felt for his Vilma, what enabled him to struggle against death and hold her firmly in his heart despite all the miles that separated them.

That was love. Not the powerful, overwhelming, incandescent coupling she had shared with Garrick. She could not—would not—love him. For as surely as the trees above her were now coming into the first tender bud, the season would pass, the year age, and all things turn round once again.

He would leave. She had to keep that thought before her at all times. If she forgot for even a moment, she would be lost.

Even so deep in thought, she felt the skin at the back of her neck prickling. Shading her eyes, she looked across the fields to the path that led toward the shore. Garrick was coming through the trees.

He carried a sack of provisions in one hand and had a musket slung over his back. His black hair shown in the sunlight and his burnished skin glowed like molten bronze. The shirt he wore was open down much of his chest, exposing dark whorls of hair and rippling muscle. Breeches clung snugly to his taut hips and sinewy thighs. He paused to speak briefly with Sam Whitler, laughed at something the younger man said and continued on his way.

Amelia did not move. To be fair, she couldn't have if she had wanted to. Memory swept over her. Her knees trembled, and she could feel her skin flushing hotly. Part of her wanted to flee, but the impulse passed quickly. She lifted her head high and faced him squarely.

"Good morn, Captain," she said. Her voice was slightly husky. She cleared her throat self-consciously.

He gave her a long, level stare that ended with a smile no less than shattering. "And good morn to you, mistress. May I say it is very fair you're looking?"

Her flush deepened. Another moment and she would burst into flames.

"I suppose you can if you must," she murmured, a shade tartly. They had stayed in the copse until the spreading cold of night at last drove them back to the meetinghouse. There, they separated with regrets, both feeling the need to preserve the slim fragments of propriety.

She had spent the hours of darkness in a half-sleeping daze, wandering between dreams and reality. Her body had felt almost a stranger's, but with morning that had changed. She rose strong and reassured, determined to face whatever the future brought with grace.

Bold thoughts—and she meant to live by them. But this first moment of meeting him again almost robbed her of composure. Somewhere in the back of her mind, she had feared he might condemn her for her licentiousness. Far from that, this playful, teasing Garrick took her breath away.

"Fair indeed," he said, and cupped her chin in his hand. So softly that no passing whisper of wind could have picked up his words, he asked, "Are you well?"

She nodded mutely. His touch caressed her briefly, and both recalled the familiar feeling before he dropped his hand.

"How is Jacob?" he asked.

"Sleeping now. He gains in strength."

Garrick nodded, relieved. "He expects to resume his duties shortly. That isn't actually possible, is it?"

"It might be good for him if he doesn't overdo. He will be in pain, there's no avoiding that, but the pain will exist whether he is active or not. If he feels busy and useful, he may be better able to overcome it."

"He wouldn't have survived without you," Garrick said quietly.

She shrugged, embarrassed by the praise. "It is as God wills it."

They stood in silence a moment longer, their bodies naturally inclining toward one another. Abruptly, Amelia straightened. "I must go."

"Where?" he asked, reluctant to part from her.

She smiled and shook out her skirts. "To search for sassafras."

His eyes gleamed. "By odd coincidence, I happened to spot several bushes not far from here."

"Oh, good, you can tell me where to find them."

"Alas, the directions are most complex. It would be better if I showed you the way."

"Better for whom?" she asked on a breath.

He laughed and took her hand. "For us both, mistress, I assure you."

She should not do this, Amelia thought. The soft, secret hours after the May festival were one thing. Full morning on a working day was quite another. Still, she did most sincerely need the sassafras.

"This is no light folly," she warned. "I have work to do."

"And so you shall," he promised. "Truly, it is the finest sassafras I have ever seen."

So persuaded, she came away and, truth be told, walked gladly at his side.

An hour later, in the full heat of midday, Amelia wiped the dampness from her brow and frowned at Garrick. She was no longer sure how far they had gone from the camp. Although she couldn't be certain, she thought they might have been turning in wide circles.

"The finest sassafras you have ever seen?" she muttered as she paused to remove a bur from her shoe. "*Never* seen would be closer to it. Or have these marvelous bushes simply vanished?"

"I can't understand it," Garrick said complacently. He leaned against a tree and watched her as she brushed the bur from the bottom of her stockings and wiggled her toes to ease the cramps in them. "They were right around here when last I looked."

Amelia put her shoe on and looked around at the woods. Oak and maple there were aplenty, also pine and hemlock. Many early flowers were in bud, and she could see several wild herbs she could use. But no sassafras. Most definitely.

"Garrick," she asked with dangerous softness, "do you have any idea what sassafras actually looks like?"

He sighed, and made an effort to appear repentant. "A vile brown tea?"

"I knew it," she exclaimed. Hands on her hips, she glared at him. "It is a species of laurel, valued for its bark, which can be steeped to make a useful tonic, or tea if you will, which most definitely does not taste vile. It invigorates the blood, especially after the rigors of winter."

Amusement played around the corners of his mouth. "Yes, teacher."

Her exasperation grew. "You lured me out here under false pretenses."

"Guilty," he admitted, and walked toward her.

Holding firm to her annoyance, she took a step back, only to find that a tree prevented her from going farther. Most emphatically not a laurel tree.

"Garrick—"

"Yes, Amelia?"

"You behaved badly."

"I did indeed, but never fear, I mean to make amends."

That was exactly what she was afraid of, she realized. Her heart beat more swiftly and she could feel again the strange tightening in her most secret places.

"That really isn't necessary," she assured him weakly.

"Oh, but it is. I can hardly forgive myself for misleading so sterling a person as yourself. Surely, you wouldn't deny me a chance to win back your favor?"

"Actually, I'm not sure you've lost it," she admitted.

He put his head back and laughed. She watched the ripple of muscles in the thick column of his throat with unabashed fascination.

"Ah, Amelia, truly you are no glib court lady to keep a man dangling at the end of a string."

"I should hope not," she said with asperity. "I've never had the time or inclination for such nonsense."

"Neither have I," he said. Belatedly, she realized that the humor was gone from his voice. He was suddenly very serious. The distance still remaining between them evaporated as though it had never been. He was close to her, so very close. She breathed in the crisp, clean scent of his skin and for a head-swimming moment closed her eyes.

His hands grasped her waist. He drew her into his arms, into his strength, into the shattering, delightful world of difference between them. She leaned her head on his shoulder and sent to flight the last of her hesitation.

He gathered her to him, holding her high against his chest, and found a hidden place deep within the trees. There he laid her, and then laid down beside her. With infinite care, he removed her clothes. Before the cool air could touch her, he covered her with his body.

His hands cupped her breasts, drawing her nipples into his mouth. Hair-roughened thighs moved against her softness. He slipped a knee between her legs, opening her to him. She felt the surging power of his manhood against her, matching the surging hunger of her womb, and moaned helplessly.

Slowly, drawing out their passion to the fullest, he moved down her body. His hot, seeking mouth traced a line of fire between her breasts, over the pale shadows of her ribs, across her flat abdomen. He licked lightly around her navel as his fingers found her. With infinite gentleness, he stroked the heart of her womanhood, making her writhe beneath him.

She gasped his name and tried to draw him to her, but he stopped her. Again, she gasped, this time in shock as his caresses grew infinitely bolder. Never had she imagined that any man would touch her in such a way, much less use his mouth to...

Thought ceased. Reason vanished. She cried out, and the sound echoed high among the leafy trees. When he moved at last to enter her, she almost sobbed with relief. With long, hard thrusts, he drove them both ever upward, until at last the fiery tension shattered and she was left, spent and safe, in his arms.

Much later, when she was at last able to do so, Amelia raised her head from his chest and glanced around her. A moment passed before she broke out in peals of laughter.

Garrick opened his eyes slowly, almost as though the weight of the lids was too much for him. Sweet heaven! Why had no one ever warned him that such women existed? he wondered. And worse yet, behind prim and proper skirts?

"What is it?" he asked thickly.

"Look," she said, not satisfied until he managed to pick his head up and glance in the direction she indicated.

He fell back with a sigh. "What is it?"

"A laurel bush," she said, and laughed again. "Although truth be told, I'm not so sure anymore that it's a tonic we need."

Chapter Sixteen

May aged, and the pattern of work continued. Garrick and Amelia found what stolen moments together they could. Each was precious to them.

Jacob rose from his sickbed and insisted on assuming responsibility for the construction of a forge. It was a major undertaking, and critical to the survival of the settlement.

Sam Whitler helped him as Lissy continued to clear the plot where they would build their house. The forced intimacy of the meetinghouse was wearing thin. As the weather warmed, most people moved outside to the privacy found under the stars.

Garrick and Amelia were among them. With each passing day, they grew less cautious. The sight of them returning of a morning to the settlement, walking hand in hand with their blankets over their shoulders, raised no eyebrows. People accorded them the freedom they were so swiftly coming to relish for themselves.

The rhythm of love and labor was interrupted at last on a bright morning in early June when Passicham came to call. He appeared out of nowhere, standing at the edge of the clearing just as they were finishing breakfast. Garrick went to meet him. They walked back together to join Amelia.

"You prosper, mistress?" the Pequot emissary inquired pleasantly.

"The land is bounteous," she replied with a smile. "Will you eat with us?"

"Thank you, but I have already done so, and I see that you are finished." He raised his voice so that the others could hear him. "I come bearing an invitation. Our planting is done. At the next fullness of the moon, we will gather to celebrate. Owenoke bids our new neighbors to join with us."

Amelia cast a quick glance at Garrick. She was unsure how to respond. The way the invitation was phrased, they seemed to have little choice. But was it wise to go?

At length, because she could think of no courteous refusal, she said, "We would be happy to come."

Passicham gave her an approving smile. He seemed to find nothing odd in her accepting the invitation for all the settlers, she noticed. Her negotiation with him had established her as Belle Haven's leader. The realization, however, was at least a little unsettling to Amelia. It clashed with the freedom she had lately begun to so appreciate. Already she could foresee a time when her personal wishes might be at odds with her responsibilities.

Rather than think of that, she offered to show Passicham around the settlement. He accepted, and they spent a pleasant hour examining all that the residents had accomplished so far. Before taking his leave, he proclaimed himself to be impressed.

"Did I do right?" Amelia asked Garrick when the Pequot was gone. "We've seen no more of the chief's son, but I'm still concerned about his interest in Sarah and how she might respond. Also, to be honest, I do wonder if the Indians have any regrets about allowing us to settle here.''

"Why would they?" he asked. "We've caused them no trouble."

"Not yet, but they must be aware that the *Beacon* came. I've no idea of what they make of that, but it can't be anything good."

"Aye," he agreed, "they'll see the way of it. But remember, lass, we're pledged to help one another. You swore to that yourself." He looked at her closely. "I only hope you really understand what that means."

"If the Mohawk attack, we must go to the aid of our neighbors," she said.

"So it is, but there's another side. If we are attacked again, you can expect the Pequot to help us."

Her eyes widened. "I hadn't thought of that. Do you think we will be attacked again?"

He hesitated, not wanting to burden her unduly. At length, he said, "A sane man would trouble us not further. The problem is that Elder Harkness seems moon-touched."

She paled slightly. In a whisper, she said, "Aye, there is that."

Garrick touched her arm gently, imparting comfort while also reminding her of his strength so close at hand. "Don't be worrying about him. It's a far notion. All I mean is that our dealings with the Pequot could get complicated. We should get to know them better while we can."

"So we go?"

"Didn't you already say we would, lass?" he asked, smiling.

The moon swelled. Oats were sown and wheat with them. The beans began to climb up their long poles, and the flowers on the pumpkin vines gave way to tiny gourds that grew with each passing day. The weather was fair— just enough rain and ample sun.

One of the women, Bette Marbury shyly announced a new life would be coming before the turning of the year. Elijah Williams, a carpenter, promised the best-made cradle she had ever seen.

Lissy Whitler walked away from the rejoicing with sorrow in her eyes, but came back with a smile and the offer of small garments she had hidden away in her trunk. Bette thanked her, but refused. She pressed Lissy's hand to her belly and said, "So shall you be, Mistress Whitler, before this season dies, for truly there is life for all in this land."

Amelia thought of her vision, children dancing round her own hearthstone and said nothing. But she thought much and even dared to dream in the long, sweet nights when she lay with Garrick. By now, she had learned his ways and knew how he tried to protect her. But on a night when clouds drifted over the moon and owls hooted overhead, she stopped him from withdrawing with the sudden touch of her hands on his hips and took his seed into herself.

Afterward, he said she shouldn't have done it, but she only smiled in the manner of women and went on with her work. Mayhap nothing would come of it. The dream alone might have to be enough. But whatever the case, there would be no regrets. On that she was determined.

The evening came when they gathered together and, with torches gleaming high, made their way up the long and winding track to the Pequot settlement. It was to the north and east of their own land in a fair place well watered by several creeks. While they were still on the outskirts of the village, they passed broad, lush fields slumbering green and gold in the fading sun.

The fields were empty, everyone having gone to the village. Before they got much farther, they heard the music of drums and voices chanting. A child darted out from among the trees, a small brown sprite who eyed them winsomely before vanishing like the wind.

Still, they came, three dozen in all with men from *Lady Star* who had chosen to accompany them. With them they brought the offerings of friendship—bread fresh baked that morning, a wheel of good Holland cheese, a bolt of cloth, and, this last for Passicham especially, a book of poems Garrick had donated.

On the outskirts of the village, they were met by a contingent of young men and greeted with grave courtesy. They were dressed in buckskin breeches and moccasins, their chests bare to the warm air but for the elaborate necklaces of shells they wore. Their hair was long and braided, tied at the tips with leather thongs decorated with vividly colored feathers. They looked excited, despite their best efforts to appear grave. The arriva' of so many strange people among them—and people who undoubtedly had been the subject of much speculation—was a break from routine they could not help but appreciate.

With this gallant escort, they were led to the center of the village. Walking close beside Garrick, Amelia whispered, "I had no idea it was so large."

He nodded. "We call it a village but that's a mistake. Think of it more as a good-sized town and you'll have the right idea."

She looked out over the neat rows of longhouses stretching a goodly distance away, many with family cook fires before them and tools neatly stacked. Everywhere, the impression of great cleanliness and order.

"How many people live here, do you think?" Amelia asked.

"Two hundred certainly, perhaps more," Garrick said. "They move within a radius of a few miles every few years. If the population grows too large, a young couple of strength and promise will be chosen to begin a new settlement. This way, the land is kept fertile and protected from over-farming."

"In Boston town, the elders said they were savages and referred to them as children in need of guidance from those wiser than themselves."

Garrick snorted under his breath. "You hear a great deal of foolishness in Boston these days. Passicham and his brethren have survived in this place for uncounted time. They have their problems, true enough, chiefly war with the other tribes. But they live with dignity and honor."

"Yet they do not know God," she said, repeating what she had been told so often, yet doubting it all the same. How could anyone fail to know God in such a place as this?

"For people who are supposedly ignorant of Him, they seem to be doing well enough. Besides, they have their own gods. They believe all the world is alive, the dwelling place of spirits and that we are only one small part of an eternal order. Hence, man does not become too much above himself or too anxious to inflict his ways on others."

"Yet they make war."

Regretfully, Garrick nodded. "Passicham speaks of a time when it wasn't so, but I gather that was long before his birth. The tribes grow in numbers yearly. Despite their best efforts, they encroach upon one another. This brings them into competition for the best hunting and fishing territories, and the best lands. So they fight, but in small bands and with relatively few deaths compared to what we in civilized Europe manage."

Amelia thought of what she had seen in the Lowlands, and before then, in England. The cities teemed with the poor and hungry. Each man's hand could be set against his neighbor in an instant. An undercurrent of dissatisfaction and yearning rippled constantly just below the surface.

Did the Pequot and the other tribes have any idea how many more would willingly seize the chance to cross the ocean and begin a new life here? The few thousand who had so far done it were only the first, faint glimmer of what could easily become a ravenous horde.

"That could change," she said.

Garrick's hand tightened on her own. "Don't fret over it, Melly—not tonight. This is a time for rejoicing."

She nodded, but her heart was far from light. Ahead, she saw Passicham coming to welcome them and behind him the chieftain, Owenoke and the old sachem, Amogerone. For Amogerone, Amelia had brought a stone bottle containing her sassafras tonic. She offered it with the humble comment that she was certain he had far better but thought he might find it of some small interest.

He took it, removed the cork stopper and sniffed cautiously. A deep frown furrowed his brow. The others remained hushed until, abruptly, he smiled.

"He says you are a healing woman," Passicham interpreted, "and that he suspected this when he met you before. He also says you are welcome here. Later, he has several things he would like to show you, which you, too, might find of interest."

Amelia nodded eagerly. She was always delighted to add to her collection of medicinals.

Owenoke came forth then to formally welcome them. By the dancing light of the torches, he appeared even larger and more solidly built than Amelia remembered. Equally impressive was the young man at his side who stood, chin tilted proudly, arms folded over his broad chest, and eyed each of them challengingly.

"My son," Owenoke said with obvious pride, "Mayano."

The younger man spoke briefly in a voice of great authority bordering on, if not crossing over into, arrogance. Passicham frowned and said something. Mayano bristled and said something more that caused the emissary to answer with obvious anger. As the settlers watched, Owenoke stepped in hastily to put a stop to the matter.

"What happened?" Amelia whispered.

"The young buck says we should have brought more tribute," Garrick replied under his breath. "Passicham is reminding him that we are guests, and were required to bring nothing but ourselves."

"He doesn't seem satisfied with that," she said as she watched the play of anger over the younger man's face. He was a handsome lad only a few years older than herself, but his air of discontent and barely bridled temper sent a shiver through her.

"Let us all hope that Owenoke lives a long and healthy life," Garrick whispered as they followed their host into the center of the camp.

Chapter Seventeen

They sat in a circle around the fire. Women passed around small carved wooden bowls filled with corn samp that was ladled into the mouth using two fingers. Children vied for their turn at the spit, where a thick haunch of venison was roasting. Choice bits of it were hacked off and divided among the guests.

Smoked fish and raw oysters followed. Duck, wrapped in green leaves and roasted in embers was served, and with it, fiddlehead greens, which Amelia had never tasted before but found delicious.

All the while, drums beat, the fire crackled and groups rose one by one to dance in celebration, portraying the struggle to win favor from the earth and the joy that followed when it was given.

The guests were generously served, but there was little conversation, all attention being given to the food. When they at last sat back replete, Owenoke put aside his dignity long enough to permit a slow smile of satisfaction.

Through Passicham, he said, "In this England we hear so much about, they have many great festivals, do they not?"

"They do," Garrick agreed. "But none greater than this, noble chieftain. What could bring more honor than to gather your people under the sky, with guests at hand, and enjoy what your wisdom and endeavor have brought to you?''

''You speak well,'' Owenoke said graciously, and Passicham translated. His manner grew more stern. ''Unfortunately, many of your people do not behave as properly. They have the manner—'' here Passicham hesitated, as though grappling for the words ''—of those raised in caves and other wild places.''

''There are some,'' Garrick said, ''who dwell in ignorance. They do not understand that if the spirits wanted us to be all alike, we would not have been created different.''

Owenoke nodded at the truth of this, but beside him, Mayano bristled. He spoke rapidly and gestured at Garrick with what was obviously contempt. Passicham made no attempt to translate, nor did he reply to the chief's son, but merely looked away from him disdainfully. Owenoke was not so constrained. He spoke in a low tone that nonetheless reverberated with anger. Mayano heard him out in silence. When the tongue-lashing was over, he stood up without asking for leave and stomped away into the darkness.

''My son is hot-tempered,'' Owenoke said, the closest he could bring himself to come to an apology. ''It is best he seek the solitude of the night to cool him.''

''He should seek the solitude of the far mountains,'' Passicham muttered. He took a long draught of cool spring water as though to wash away the taste of unsaid words.

''Not all men are fortunate in their children,'' Garrick murmured.

Passicham nodded. Quietly, he said, ''There was another before Mayano, older and far wiser in his spirit. But he died a year ago. Now Mayano holds first place. Owenoke wishes him to be chief after him."

"Will this happen?" Amelia asked softly. The possibility worried her. The peace they so badly needed to maintain with the Pequot would be threatened if Mayano came to power, she thought.

"It should not," Passicham said. "Most of the old ones are opposed to him. But the bucks like his spirit. In time, Mayano might be able to win enough to his side to fulfill his father's hope."

"Then we shall have to hope that he grows in wisdom," Garrick said in a tone that suggested there was little likelihood of that coming to pass.

Passicham shrugged. "Such men make too many mistakes. If the first one is not fatal, the hundredth will be. The only question is how much damage is done to others in between."

Amelia frowned and looked in the direction Mayano had gone. Darkness had swallowed him. A log snapped in the fire just then, drawing her back into the circle. She gazed at the flames for several minutes until she realized that her eyelids were growing heavy.

The unaccustomedly sumptuous meal made her drowsy. She leaned her head against Garrick's shoulder and let her eyes close.

A long time later—she wasn't sure exactly how much time had passed—she stirred from sleep to hear him speaking with Passicham.

"The man in the long black coat has much hatred in him," the Pequot was saying. "I was one of those who watched him from the woods and I saw that for myself." His voice changed slightly, making it clear that he was smiling. "You fought well, my friend. Almost as well as a Pequot."

Garrick laughed softly. "High praise. I thank you. But you are right about the man. His name is Peter Harkness. He is from the settlement at Boston."

"What brings him to this place?"

Garrick hesitated. His arm tightened around Amelia. "He desires this woman."

"Why? Surely she would be much trouble to one such as him."

Garrick laughed again, making Amelia frown, seemingly in her sleep. "True," he said. More seriously, he added, "But I fear that before she could free herself, he would hurt her badly."

"You are wise to think so," Passicham said. "Men with such evil in them enjoy hurting. Do you believe he will return?"

"I don't know," Garrick admitted. "Reasonably, he should not, but he is not a reasonable man. Anything is possible."

"Then I will tell the others to keep watch for him. If he comes within our lands, we will know of it and warn you."

"I thank you. It is good to have friends."

"Always, and if I might be frank, *my friend,* it seems that you and the others could use more friends than you have."

"Whom do you speak of?" Garrick asked.

"The men to the south in the lands of the Manhates."

"The Dutch? Surely you know they have long been enemies of the English?"

"What matters that? You have a Dutchman second in your command, do you not? And unless I am very much mistaken, you trade with them."

"I have been known to," Garrick agreed without compunction. "Still, you must understand, the English see the Dutch as a serious threat to them. They will stop at nothing to push them from their lands. The Dutch know that and are naturally suspicious of all English. Why would they seek friendship with us?"

"Because of Peter Harkness, perhaps," Passicham suggested. "He and his kind are their enemy *and* yours. Is it truly impossible for you to make common cause?"

"Not so far as I am concerned," Garrick said. "But I cannot speak for the others. Still, it is a provoking thought."

"Isn't it?" Passicham asked. Amelia could tell that he was smiling again. Shortly thereafter, he got up and moved away. She waited a discreet space of time before apparently awakening.

"I must have dozed off," she said apologetically as she made a show of rubbing her eyes.

"You did," Garrick said absently. His thoughts were clearly far away. Southward, perhaps, toward Nieuw Amsterdam and the lands of the Dutch.

Around them, several of the settlers were beginning to nod off. With their stomachs full and the long walk from Belle Haven behind them, they had trouble staying awake. Fortunately, many of the Pequot were also relaxed and seemed to take no offense.

Amelia smiled and snuggled closer against Garrick. She had no desire to leave, and neither did anyone else. The woods were deep, the night dark and the walk back too long to contemplate just then. Morning would be time enough.

Several of the settlers had unrolled blankets. Some had exchanged their own for the tanned deer hides the Pequot used—in a simple barter that bridged the gap of alien languages. Both sides looked pleased with their trade.

Elijah Williams and his wife were curled up together a short distance away, talking softly. So, too, Bette Marbury and her husband were in comfortable companionship. The Fletchers had just shared a jest with Sam Whitler, and all three were laughing. Lissy was already asleep, and the others looked likely to follow soon.

Of Sarah Fletcher, there was no sign.

Slowly, Amelia straightened. She had almost been asleep herself, feeling drowsier by the moment as she glanced contentedly around the fire. Now that contentment was gone. Where was the girl?

She sat up, fully alert and looked again. One by one, she found each of those she had come with, some from Belle Haven and some from the ship. But not Sarah.

Perhaps the girl had merely gone off to relieve herself and would return at any moment. Amelia waited. A cloud moved across the moon, paused and moved on. Still no sign of Sarah.

Softly, she touched Garrick's arm. "The Fletcher girl is missing."

She did not need to say anything more. His mouth tightened. Swiftly, he stood. "Stay here."

Amelia got to her feet. She had no intention of remaining behind. "Sarah is as much my problem as yours."

"This is better handled without you," he insisted.

Despite the quelling look he gave her, she stood her ground. Head high, she demanded, "What if something has happened to her? Something . . . personal? Do you want to have to deal with that?"

He grimaced and reluctantly shook his head. "I suppose you have a point. But you stay behind me, woman, and don't speak unless you're spoken to, understand?"

"Perfectly well," she retorted. He strode off in the direction of the wood. She followed.

The moon lit their way. They got a short distance from the camp when the sounds of rustling stopped them. Garrick gestured Amelia back. Instead, she edged closer.

There was a narrow creek ahead. Two people sat beside it. One was small and delicately built, with hair that, in the moonlight, looked almost silver. A woman. The other was larger, far more muscular, unmistakably male.

As they watched, the man put his arm around the woman's shoulders and drew her close. She giggled nervously and made a halfhearted effort to fend him off. He ignored it and pressed her onto the ground. His hand reached for the hem of her skirt.

A twig snapped beneath Amelia's foot. She put a hand to her mouth, but it was too late. The man heard the sound. He raised his head quickly and stared into the wood. In the clear light, they could see every detail of his face. Mayano. And Sarah Fletcher. Exactly as Amelia had feared.

At the same time, the girl took advantage of his preoccupation to twist away from him. She stood up hastily and started away.

He said something in Pequot and gripped her wrist. She protested and tried to pull loose, but without success.

Garrick cursed under his breath. Amelia did not have to ask what he thought of the situation. It was only too obvious from the look of extreme annoyance that tightened his hard features. He rose, tall and powerful, out of the underbrush and faced Mayano bluntly.

Amelia could not understand what he said. She gathered it was in Pequot. But whatever it meant, Mayano did not take it well. He shook his head emphatically and answered with words that sounded suspiciously like an insult.

"What is he saying?" she demanded.

"Essentially, that we should mind our own business. But if we insist on skulking around in the bushes, we shouldn't be too surprised by anything we see."

Amelia flushed. She put her hands on her hips and glared at the chieftain's son. "What gall. If your father were not the noble Owenoke, you would not dare to behave this way."

"He can't understand you," Garrick murmured.

Mayano's lips curved in a sneer. "You think only Passicham speaks your tongue? Many of us have learned it, but keep silent, listening to the intent behind your words." His face darkened as he tightened his grip on Sarah's wrist so much that she cried out.

"My father is a fool to let you come here. The day is fast approaching when we will have to cleanse our land with the strangers' blood. On that day, the leadership of the tribes will pass away from old men to those strong enough to lead."

"To you?" Garrick asked softly. "Your father has guided your people through difficult times. What makes you think you can do better?"

"Because I see the truth," Mayano replied. "First, only a few whites came. They were weak and bewildered, and no one feared them. But soon more arrived, and more after them. Now the winged ships come without cease. My father and the other old men think it will stop soon. I believe otherwise."

Garrick and Amelia exchanged a glance. They disliked Mayano, but he was right. More clearly than his father, he saw the danger the white man represented.

Unfortunately, his remedy was not negotiation or peaceful coexistence. It was war.

"Let the woman go," Garrick said, taking a step toward Sarah.

Mayano laughed unpleasantly. "Soon we will take everything that belongs to you. She is only the beginning. Besides, she was willing enough when she came away with me."

"She isn't willing now," Garrick said. His fist clenched at his sides. He did not want to fight Mayano. But he wasn't about to let him walk off with Sarah Fletcher, either. If that happened, it would guarantee a swift end to anything resembling peace. His mouth twisted. How often, in how many far places, had men believed they must fight in order to preserve peace? The fundamental illogic never changed, yet remained inescapable.

Mayano straightened. He looked pleased by the prospect of conflict.

But before either he or Garrick could move, Amelia stepped forward. Speaking quietly, even humbly, she said, "This is no woman worthy of a chieftain's son, only a foolish girl. You would quickly regret taking her. She would bring you no honor."

Mayano frowned. "What do you know of such things?"

Garrick wondered the same. She had spoken with a man's wisdom about matters he wouldn't have thought she understood at all.

Amelia bit back the impatient words that rose to her tongue. Did all men truly believe women were daft? Women were always trophies of one kind or another. It was the same in England, in the Lowlands, in Boston town and in the camp of the Pequot, hard by the edge of the endless wilderness.

"Such a great noise you make about the differences between you," she said, to Mayano and Garrick, "white and red, 'savage' and enlightened European, pagan and God-fearing Christian. But for true you are all brothers under the skin."

She did not mean that kindly, and each man sensed it. Enemies they might be, but they shared an uneasy glance that spoke volumes of the difficulties their common gender faced when confronted by an irate female in high dudgeon.

Still, Mayano was far from ready to back down. "Perhaps you are right," he said. "For a chieftain's son, a woman such as yourself would be more appropriate."

If he had expected her to quail in fear at the thought, he was in for a disappointment. She merely looked him up and down with insolent slowness and said, "I doubt it. There would be little enough of you left for the Pequot maidens by the time I was finished. Now let us end this. The hour grows late and my patience thins."

With a glare that could have withered the fair green leaves above their heads, she said, "You're trouble, Sarah Fletcher. No settlement needs that, not even one as free thinking as Belle Haven. You'll mend your ways, or I will personally see to it that you return to Boston town in disgrace. Do you understand me?"

Sarah nodded frantically. She tried again to pull free and this time was amazed to discover she could do so. Mayano had loosened his hold at the same moment he seemed to lose all interest in her. Instead, he gazed at Amelia so intently she had to look away lest her flush betray how very frightened she really was.

"Come along then," she said briskly. "With luck, we can return to camp before anyone else misses you."

The younger woman ran quickly to Amelia's side. Almost incoherently, she spilled her gratitude. Amelia ignored her. She was so worried about what the young woman had almost precipitated, that she could not bring herself to speak to her directly. Later, perhaps, but not before her nerves settled and her temper cooled.

Garrick felt no such compunction. He waited until the women had disappeared in the direction of the camp. When he was sure they were alone, he faced Mayano squarely.

"Just so you don't go off with any wrong impressions, mate, Amelia Daniels is spoken for. Come near her and I'll rip you apart piece by piece. That plain enough for you?"

Mayano bared his teeth in what did not remotely resemble a smile. "Perfectly," he said. He moved almost imperceptibly, blending into the woods. The wind carried his parting words.

"I shall enjoy taking her from you."

Chapter Eighteen

Amelia straightened beside the stream. She pushed damp strands of hair away from her eyes and rubbed her back slowly.

Her shoulders ached and her fingers were so stiff she could barely feel them, but the washing was done. Now all she had to do was spread it out on the nearby bushes and let the sun take care of the rest.

Not a moment too soon. She'd been up a good part of the night with one of the older settlers, Benjamin Potter, a gruff but kindly man who had worked as a tanner most of his life in England and was hoping to eventually do the same in the new land.

In his eagerness to get settled, he had worked ferociously hard, often going without sleep as he labored in the fields while he also built the drying barn he would need. Mistress Potter had finally come to Amelia because she was worried about her husband.

She had reason to be. The once and future tanner was worn to a shadow of himself, having developed a constant pain in his stomach that had, at last, become unbearable.

Amelia counseled rest and insofar as it was possible, freedom from worry. She prescribed a tonic of comfrey and sweet fern to relax him and help ease the burning in his stomach.

But she warned that the medicine could only accomplish so much. It would take time and the aid of Master Potter's own effort to heal himself.

He had fallen asleep at last, his brow still furrowed in discomfort, but at least able to rest. She wished she could do the same, but the day's chores had already waited too long.

Nor could she ask anyone for help. Since returning from the Pequot camp, the pace of activity had increased even further.

Hour by hour, the women and children worked the fields, protecting the precious crops from weeds and pests. Some of the men hunted or continued the endless work of clearing land, but most were busy building a stockade around the area that included the meeting-house.

The decision to protect themselves had been prompted by news from Passicham that Peter Harkness had not forgotten them. At his urging, the Boston elders were sending emissaries to the other new settlements in Connecticut—these authorized by them—warning of the renegades.

Worse yet, a group handpicked by the Puritan council had appeared scant days before only a few miles up the coast from Belle Haven. There, on lands that belonged to a rival chieftain, they received permission to stay.

"They have told this foolish man," Passicham said of the neighboring chieftain, "that Owenoke has allowed dangerous and violent people in his midst and that they have been sent to 'bring you back to the fold.' I don't know that expression. What does it mean?"

"Trouble," Garrick had replied succinctly. Shortly thereafter, work began on the stockade.

Amelia finished spreading out the laundry. She planned to take her turn in the fields next, but first she wanted to pause for a few moments to watch the men's progress.

The entire area around the meetinghouse—including where she hoped someday a town green would stand—was hidden by timber.

Stately trees had been felled, one by one, and dragged into the clearing by the oxen. Stripped of their bark and branches, they were swiftly tapered at the top by a few ax blows.

As she watched, the men made ready to raise one of the stark, bare trunks.

"Together," Garrick shouted. He was working barechested in the sun, the powerful muscles and sinews of his chest rippling with strength.

A rope was attached to the top of the trunk. Several of the men pulled on it while the others pushed the limb upright.

It settled into the trench with an audible thunk and swayed dangerously. Garrick strained to hold it as the others rushed to shovel dirt around the base.

That done, they began lashing it to the stake next to it and hammering in long, hardwood pegs to hold it steady.

Already, two sides of the wall had been built and the third was underway. The resulting enclosure was small; no one would want to have to remain in it for very long. But in the case of attack, it could mean the difference between survival and disaster.

For the moment, what it meant was that little of ordinary life could take place near the meetinghouse. The cooking had to be moved elsewhere lest sawdust and de-

bris fall into everything. Children had to be shooed away
rather than be underfoot where they might be harmed.

The constant sound of saws and hammers was an inescapable reminder that the refuge they had sought could
be endangered. The noise seemed to follow Amelia into
her sleep, where she worried over whether she had done
these people more harm than good by helping them come
to such a place.

She shook her head and smiled ruefully. Her advice to
Benjamin Potter could as easily be to herself. Worry did
no good.

They were sensibly taking every precaution they possibly could. As for the rest, it was in God's hands.

Garrick paused to wipe the sweat from his arms and
chest. He saw her standing a little distance away and
came to speak with her. There had been little time for
them to be alone since the Pequot celebration, and no
opportunity at all for intimacy.

Standing close to him now, watching the rapid rise and
fall of his chest as he recovered from his exertions, she
had to remind herself that there was stern business to be
done. Yet for all that, she flushed warmly and was help-
less to control the rapid beat of her heart.

"The work goes well?" she asked.

"Tolerably." He studied her closely. "You look tired."

A husky laugh broke from her. "Which of us
doesn't?"

"Everyone is working hard," he acknowledged, "but
to good cause. The stockade will be finished by the end
of the week."

"That soon?" She was surprised. To her, it seemed like
such a huge undertaking.

He shrugged, making light of it. "The plan is simple enough and everyone recognizes the importance. Until this is done, all other building must wait."

She nodded, understanding how anxious many were to begin their own houses. Even with the threat of trouble—or perhaps because of it—the need to put their roots down ever more deeply was irresistible.

"I, too, have been thinking about that," she admitted.

"I know how anxious you are," he said softly, "but there is another matter you need to consider."

She frowned, hoping this was not yet more trouble. Since the episode at the Pequot village, Sarah Fletcher had been a model of decorum and hard work. Apparently, the fright she had received was enough to make her appreciate how serious careless behavior could be.

Aside from Benjamin Potter, the other settlers seemed well. Bette was flourishing in her pregnancy, there were no fevers, and with the addition of fresh vegetables to their diet, all felt healthier.

Garrick smiled slightly and touched a finger to her brow, smoothing it. "Nothing so terrible," he assured her, "only a suggestion, but one I think you must take seriously. When we were at the Pequot village, Passicham mentioned that it would be useful for us to speak with the Dutch in Nieuw Amsterdam."

Before Amelia could object, he went on. "The Dutch are rightly concerned to have English settlers encroaching ever closer to their own territories. They must know about us by now and may be deciding how we should be viewed. Our peculiar status could make them inclined to deal with us favorably."

"Perhaps so," Amelia agreed, "but there are no Dutch hereabouts. Even if we did want to talk with them, how could we manage it?"

He stooped to ladle water from a bucket and pour it over his head. Straightening, he shook droplets from his hair and laughed as she darted back.

"You came all the way from the Lowlands and then from Boston, and you cannot imagine how to solve that problem?"

"I don't...."

"We'll go to Nieuw Amsterdam. It isn't far from here, only a few miles along the coast. The main settlement lies at the point of the Manhates Island, between two rivers. It's easily reachable."

"Maybe to you," Amelia grumbled. He seemed to think any place near water was but a stone's throw away, while she considered any journey that involved a boat of whatever sort to be a major undertaking.

"Besides," she added, "there is far too much to do here."

"Whatever we do," he pointed out reasonably, "won't amount to much if we find ourselves outflanked by Master Harkness and his like. We need allies, Amelia, it's that plain and simple. Right now we can count on Passicham and Owenoke so far as it goes. But there's no guarantee that will last. You saw Mayano for yourself and you heard his views on the subject."

Reluctantly, she nodded. "But there is another reason we cannot go. The situation is too uncertain here. What if Mayano were to suddenly pose a problem again?"

"Passicham tells me the chieftain has sent his son on a mission inland to visit another tribe. I gather the chieftain there is an old friend of Owenoke's. The idea seems to be to keep Mayano out of trouble and possibly find a wife for him.''

''Do you think that can work?''

''I doubt it, but it does buy us some time. We should make the best use of it.''

Her concerns remained, but she realized he was right. Slowly, she asked, ''Would you mean to sail there?''

He nodded. ''But not on *Lady Star.* I want to keep her—and her guns—here, in case of trouble. I can rig a sail on the longboat. Allowing time to finish the stockade, we could be in Nieuw Amsterdam within a fortnight.''

''I see....'' Matters were closing in on her, Amelia thought. The notion of a visit to the Dutch, so seemingly farfetched at first, was appearing more and more achievable.

''Do you intend to go alone?'' she asked, tacitly acknowledging that the trip would take place, while still leaving open the possibility that her presence would not be necessary. The thought of traveling alone with Garrick pleased her, but not to the extent that she would leave her settlement in what seemed to be a vulnerable state.

Garrick quashed that hope without a twinge of misgiving. ''To what point? I have no authority to negotiate for Belle Haven. Only the founder can do that.''

With each of her arguments falling away one by one, Amelia still hesitated. To go to the Dutch? To possibly come to terms with them? She had never imagined attempting any such thing. A deep sigh escaped her.

''What is it?'' Garrick asked, instantly concerned.

''Only that I feel rather foolish,'' she said wryly. ''I set out only to find a place to live in greater freedom. It never occurred to me that it would be this complicated.''

"It hasn't been so far," Garrick agreed. "But we've been unusually fortunate. If we want that to last, we must take steps to protect ourselves now."

Amelia could not disagree with him. What he said made too much sense. Like it or not, the answer to their problems might well lie in the direction of the Dutch.

"Alright," she said softly, "I will go."

He nodded, his gray eyes scrutinizing her briefly before he drew another ladleful of water from the bucket and drank. "I must get back to work," he said, putting the ladle down.

"And I," she added. She did not move, but watched as he walked away, a tall, powerful man, long-limbed, graceful, tanned by the sun and honed to ruthless strength by a lifetime of struggle. A man who held her with tender passion and raised her to heights of ecstasy.

A man who would walk away again, in only a few months, and sail out of her life forever.

And yet, the same man who, whether he realized it or not, was coming to closely identify himself with Belle Haven. "*We've* been unusually fortunate," he said. "*We* must take steps to protect ourselves."

A small subtlety, to be sure, yet even as she told herself not to put too much store in it, a tremulous hope stirred within her.

Chapter Nineteen

They left the week after the stockade was completed and Passicham confirmed that Mayano was still away. By common consent, Sam Whitler and Jacob Dykler were put in charge of the settlement.

"Now don't you be fretting over us," Lissy advised as she helped Amelia pack the belongings she was taking with her. "We'll manage fine. You concentrate on winning the Dutch to our side."

"I don't know how persuasive I'll be," Amelia said doubtfully. "I've never done anything like this before."

Lissy laughed. Despite all the work she'd been doing, she looked younger somehow. Her skin glowed, and there was a becoming color in her cheeks.

"You'd never founded a colony before, either, and you didn't do badly at that. Just relax and follow your instincts. Besides," she added with a grin, "Captain Marlowe will be along to help you."

Amelia murmured something indistinct, and turned away. She could feel herself blushing.

As she bent over her small bundle, securing it, she asked, "Lissy, has anyone... that is, do people think it odd about us going together?"

"Odd? That a man and a woman should go off by themselves, away from everyone else? Faith, mistress, what's odd about that?"

"We're going on a matter of business," Amelia insisted. She really was blushing now. In another moment, they'd be able to light tinder from the heat of her cheeks.

Seeing her discomfort, Lissy relented, if only slightly. "No one thinks it's wrong, if that's what worries you." Softly, she added, "We all came to Belle Haven to get away from people thinking this or that, always passing judgment and making everyone's life miserable in the process. No one's about to criticize you or the captain just because you've found a bit of happiness together."

Amelia's eyes were moist. She blinked quickly to clear them and pressed the other woman's hand. "Thank you," she said huskily.

Lissy nodded but said nothing more. Some things were simply too important for words.

A few minutes later, her bundle in hand, Amelia walked down the path to meet Garrick. There was no leave-taking with the other settlers. She wanted no farewells.

Everyone knew where they were going and why. No one cared to dwell on the fact that the fate of the settlement might depend on what they accomplished. But it was well understood all the same.

Garrick was finishing work on the longboat. It bobbed gently on the slight chop kicked up by a steady offshore breeze. The mast was raised and the sail furled around it.

As she came onto the beach, he was loading the last of their provisions. While it was likely they would find fresh water without difficulty, they were carrying their own supply, along with several days' worth of food, as well as blankets and weapons.

He straightened and stood as she approached, a hand shading his eyes, watching her. The water lapped around his legs. His chest was bare. His breeches, dampened by the waves, clung snugly.

She swallowed hard, told herself she was a grown woman and could take all this in stride, and called good morning.

"The day looks fair," she said. Weather was always a safe topic.

He nodded and came up onto the beach. "The wind's against us, but with a bit of luck, we'll reach Nieuw Amsterdam tomorrow."

She glanced at the supplies and smiled. "All this for a single day's journey?"

"That's if the weather holds," he cautioned. "There's never any guarantee that it will." He gestured at her bundle. "Have you everything you'll need, then?"

When she nodded, he wasted no time in scooping her up and carrying her high against his broad chest while he waded into the water.

"No sense in both of us getting wet," he said with a grin.

She nodded again, shakily this time, and said nothing until she was settled in the boat. Only then did the smallness of the longboat really strike her. On the few trips she had made on it back and forth from the shore to *Lady Star* she hadn't really thought about it.

But now she was confronting a far longer journey. Instinctively, her hands closed around the edges of the narrow wooden seat.

Garrick was preparing to cast off when he noticed her discomfort. "What's wrong, lass?"

"Nothing," she said hastily. "I'm fine. I'm just not used to little boats, that's all."

His eyebrows rose. "Little? This fine vessel seats twelve in a pinch. It's far from little."

"It isn't big," she muttered, and tightened her hold further. Garrick pulled the anchor up and then stood in the prow and pushed one of the oars into the sandy bottom, gently nudging them away. The outgoing tide did the rest.

Garrick laughed. He took his seat facing her and began smoothly rowing them into deeper water.

"Relax, Melly, you're as safe as a babe in arms. We won't be out of sight of shore once."

Feeling a fool, she loosened her fingers and tried to relax. The sight of rippling muscles beneath taut, burnished skin did little to help her.

With a sigh, she forced herself to look out over the water. In the distance, she could see the low hills of Laang Eylaadt, the long island south of Belle Haven. Seabirds circled overhead. The day was clear as crystal and almost balmy. Her plain cotton dress, new when she left Amsterdam the previous year but now well-worn, felt uncomfortably restricting. The high collar itched, and she had a sudden, impulsive wish to take off her stiff leather boots and discard her thickly woven stockings.

"Go ahead," Garrick said.

Her eyes flew to his face. "What did you say?"

"Go ahead and get yourself more comfortable." At her stunned expression, he laughed. "Sweet lord, lass, do you think you're so hard to read? You're sitting there looking for all the world like a three-pound hen cooped up in a one-pound box, and no wonder. In case you hadn't noticed, this isn't the Strand in London. No one's going to care what you wear—certainly not me."

"How reassuring," Amelia muttered. She had to concede that he had a point. All things considered, there seemed little reason to preserve proprieties that, when you got right down to it, didn't make any sense to begin with.

Averting her eyes, she quickly undid the ties at the top of her dress by her throat and opened it. The relief was instantaneous, but not enough. More quickly, she unfastened her cap, took it off and stuck it in her pocket. Treating it so cavalierly wrinkled it badly, but she didn't care. She decided right then and there that she wouldn't put it on again, not even once they reached Nieuw Amsterdam.

Beneath the cap, she had bound her hair up with bone pins that pressed into her scalp. She pulled them loose, added them to her pocket, and shook her hair free.

A smile danced over her lips. This really wasn't so bad at all, this skimming over the water with a freshening breeze and the warm sun. She felt free, unrestricted, filled with strength and youthful optimism.

Except for her feet. They itched. Forgetting how very much she had wanted to hold on to the bench, she let go, bent over and made short work of her boots. Wiggling her toes was luxury. It was even better when she'd reached up under her skirt and unpeeled her thick flaxen stockings. Fortunately, her pockets were deep.

"Better?" Garrick asked. His voice sounded unexpectedly husky. Odd that such a fit man should raise such color with just a little rowing, she thought. Her grin deepened.

"Much, thank you," she said demurely, and returned to her contemplation of the sea and sky.

He sighed, an utterly male sound of mingled desire and frustration. A few months before, she wouldn't have recognized it for what it was. Now she understood it perfectly.

With shaded eyes, she looked toward the sun. Hours of daylight remained, but darkness would finally come. They would have to put into shore for the night. And then . . .

Garrick lifted the oars from the water and lowered them into the boat. "It's time you learned a bit about sailing," he said. "This is the mast, and this the jib. We'll raise the sheet now, catch us a bit of wind and tack around to the southwest. Follow?"

She didn't, but not for a moment was she about to exhibit the full extent of her ignorance. She had grown up in port towns, daughter to a merchant whose ventures spanned much of the world. Yet she couldn't swim, and she knew next to nothing about sailing.

"It seems simple enough," she braved. "Surely you can handle it yourself."

"I can," he agreed. Wickedly, he added, "But I thought it'd be more fun watching you do it."

That was a dare if she'd ever heard one, and she wasn't about to turn away from it. "Fine," she said, and stood up, wavering just a little as she got her sea legs.

Garrick watched closely as she untied the canvas, freed the small jib and carefully raised the sail. The wind filled it immediately. The sudden surge of the longboat caught her unawares. She stumbled and would have fallen, possibly straight into the water, had not Garrick swiftly caught her.

With a sinewy arm wrapped around her slim waist, he sat down and settled her onto his lap. Her irate look did nothing to quell him. He merely laughed and held her closer.

"Not bad, sweetling. A few more tries and you'll be a regular old salt."

The sunshine bouncing off the water blinded her for an instant. She blinked, felt tears behind her lids, and laughed. After all, what could she do sitting there with the rising hardness of his manhood so close beneath her and her own body stirring in response? Waves lapped gently against the longboat and wind filled the sail, carrying them far away from all else.

"I'll wager you gave your mother a terrible time," she said with a look that was unabashedly fond.

"I did," he admitted. With a wicked gleam in his eye, he added, "But she loved me anyway."

"Aye," Amelia murmured, "I suppose she did." For an instant, she saw him as he must have been, black-haired, red-cheeked and devil-eyed running over fields, arms waving, dashing into the sun. Until he grew old enough and angry enough to turn his back on hearth and home and go seeking a better way.

"Is she still alive?" she asked softly.

He shook his head. "She died ten years ago and more, while I was still at sea."

"I'm sure she knew you'd done what was right."

His eyes widened slightly, reflecting in their silvery depths the azure helmet of the sky.

"She left me a letter that said just that—but how did you know of it?"

Amelia shrugged. She turned away, before looking at him could become too painful.

"If you love someone," she said softly, "you want him to do what's best for himself."

His arms tightened around her. For a moment, he thought of women he had known. "You would never have survived at court, sweetling, let alone another place or two I've visited."

"Then it's a good thing I'm here, isn't it?" she asked. A smile danced in her eyes. "Learning to be an old salt."

He shifted her slightly on his lap. "Aye, well, as to that, you've other talents I'm more interested in."

She widened her eyes in exaggerated innocence. "Why, Captain Marlowe, I've no notion what you mean."

"Don't you now, lass? Then I'll have to remind you. Once we've landed this tub, I'll—"

"Tub? What do you mean tub? I thought this was a perfectly substantial boat. Too small, of course, but not anything to be called a tub."

"It's a term of affection," he said patiently, but even as he spoke a suspicion was dawning. "You're not really fond of sailing, are you?"

"It's fine."

"No, now I'm serious. You've no love of the sea to speak of?"

"It's pleasant enough to look at," she admitted, then wrecked it by adding, "from a nice beach."

"Before you left England, had you ever been to sea?"

She shivered. "Once, on a voyage across the Channel to Brittany. We were caught in a terrible storm. Everyone on board thought we were going to die."

He nodded slowly. "The Channel can be like that. Clear one moment, raging like all the devils in creation the next. How old were you then?"

"Six," she said softly. "My father did his best, but I can still remember how terrified I was."

"A fright like that will take a child hard. How did you manage on the voyage to the Lowlands?"

"I didn't think twice about it until we were actually on board. It was only as we were leaving the harbor that I began to feel afraid again. Fortunately, the weather was perfectly clear and we had no problem at all."

She tried to sound brave and thought she succeeded, but Garrick was not fooled.

"Your hands are cold," he said quietly as he closed his own around them. They both knew that the day was warm. Any chill she felt came from remembered terror.

"I felt so foolish," she remembered, "that I never told my father. When he decided we should come to the New World, he was so excited. I couldn't dash his anticipation by letting him see how much I dreaded the voyage."

She was silent for several moments. Softly, she said, "As it was, I had little time to worry. He was taken sick halfway across, and from then on I did nothing but nurse him—to no avail."

"You sailed from Boston."

"And I've come here with you. I won't be stopped from doing what I must just because I'm afraid."

He shook his head wryly. "Most people would be, lass. Has that ever occurred to you?"

"Oh, I know I'm odd that way," she admitted. "It's just that life is too short to be wasted. If I'd stopped where I was because I was afraid of going on, I'd never have gotten very far, would I?"

"No," he agreed, remembering how powerful the need had been in him to keep moving, to see what was over the next hill and beyond the next horizon. But he was a man. It was acceptable for him to feel that way. She was supposed to be content with hearth and home, husband and children—the narrow, restricted world reserved for women.

She wasn't supposed to challenge him at every turn, making him feel that, even as he held her close against him, some secret part of her spirit would always be flying free.

And drawing him with her, deeper and deeper into a world of wonder he had never before believed existed.

He shook himself slightly and slid her gently from his lap. "Wind's changing," he said, and turned his attention to the sail.

Chapter Twenty

The soft gray shadows of twilight were deepening over the land as the longboat pulled toward shore. They were somewhere west of Connecticut in the lands of the Dutch, called aptly enough New Netherland.

Late in the afternoon, they had seen smoke curling from the chimneys and cooking fires of a settlement a short distance from the shore behind a thick screen of pine, hemlock and fir trees.

Whether the inhabitants were Dutch or Indian they could not guess, nor did they see any further signs of human life. They might have been the sole rulers of an undiscovered paradise.

Garrick furled the sail and rowed the longboat into a sandy cove. As they scraped bottom, he jumped out and pulled the craft up onto the shore. Amelia jumped out to help.

She got wet in the process but didn't care. With bare feet and her skirt hiked up around her knees, it hardly seemed to matter.

By the time they had secured the boat, unloaded their supplies and got a small fire going, full night had fallen. Beyond the circle of the fire, only the stars could be seen.

They were in the phase of the new moon, adding further to the darkness. But out beyond the waves, a strange green luminescence glowed in the waters as though, Amelia thought, a city filled with inhabitants going about their business dwelled below.

Supper was a simple meal. They sipped cool water from one of the barrels they had brought, chewed bread and cheese and ate a handful of dried fruits saved over from the previous autumn.

It was enough. Before she was hardly aware of it, Amelia's eyelids were drooping.

She sighed regretfully. Here she was alone on an untouched beach with the man who was her lover, and all she could think of was sleep.

Garrick smiled indulgently. "You did well today," he said softly. "We'll make a sailor of you yet."

Her laughter was hushed in the night air. "In a hundred years perhaps. I did little, yet I ache in every muscle. Why?"

He could have told her it was fear, and the conquering of fear, that did that. He might have added that her courage won his admiration. Given the slightest encouragement, he might even have said that he . . . held her in the greatest esteem.

But she was already asleep, as suddenly as a child, curled on her side with her cheek resting in the palm of her hand.

He covered her gently and took a deep, steadying breath. It would be a long night. Ruefully, he poked the fire and watched the sparks leap high.

Give her the sail, by all means, he thought. Get her to confront her fear. Exhaust her in the process and spend this night alone, then tell yourself it was all for the best.

Like it or not, he was becoming all too close to Mistress Amelia Daniels. She filled his thoughts just as the smoky, salty scent of night filled his breath. And like the air, she was becoming essential to him.

He grimaced and stretched the kinks from his back. She was only a woman. Above all, he had to remember that.

And yet, sweet heaven, it was hard when his glance strayed her way and he saw her so beautiful and trusting, a dream of passion from which he longed never to wake.

June, he recited, July, August, September, October. Four months and part of one more. He would sail on All Sabbath's Eve, stop most likely at the same Nieuw Amsterdam to which he now made his way, take on cargo and then turn east. He would be home by Christmas.

Home to what? The rough-and-tumble of his sailing friends, a woman made warm and willing by his coin, and yet another time of promise made to be gotten through with little thought given to what it really meant.

Home.

Venturer was gone, but he would learn to know *Lady Star* as well. She would carry him far. Home was the sea, and the wealth he was determined to wrest from it. Nothing else mattered.

Amelia sighed in her sleep. Hardly conscious of what he did, he bent over her and pulled the blanket up more snugly. Russet hair drifted over her cheek. Gently, he moved it away.

Her skin was petal smooth, warm and living to the touch. She smelled of lavender, salt, sun and smoke. He watched the easy rise and fall of her bosom and traced the faint blue veins that throbbed lightly in her throat.

She was only a woman. Not a ship or a dream.

He would forget her.

He would learn to live with the memory. He was strong, he could do that.

But not yet. He could postpone it a little in these sweet months of summer fading into autumn. He didn't have to think of it right now.

All he had to do was lie down and draw her gently to him.

Amelia woke in the fullness of the night. She opened her eyes, the pupils reflecting the star-strewn sky.

For long moments, the sheer immensity of that endless sea engulfed her. She lay very still, breathing faintly, dwelling in the immensity.

The air beyond the blanket was warm and still scented by the fire. She raised her head slightly and saw, there on the sand among the glowing embers, another universe of tiny, shimmering fire. Softly, she sighed and laid back down again.

And felt then the man strong and protective against her. She was nestled in the curve of Garrick's body. Her buttocks pressed against his groin, his arm rested just below her breasts and his breath teased her cheek. The touch and warmth, the scent and sound of him, enveloped her.

She closed her eyes and for a dizzying instant felt herself rising . . . rising up into the infinity of stars. Dazzled, she curled her hand around his steadying arm, seeking the anchor that would hold her to the earth.

He moved slightly, murmuring her name.

"Hush," she whispered. "Go back to sleep."

The coming day would test them both. Ahead lay Nieuw Amsterdam, the Dutch, and a daring gamble that could be their hope or their despair. Sleep then, she thought, and gather the strength we both will need.

And, too, she believed he would, so quietly did he hold her. Only gradually, almost imperceptibly, did the awareness creep over her that she was no longer alone in her reverie of the starry night.

"Beautiful," he said into the silken warmth of her hair.

"The stars?"

"Oh, yes, those, too."

"Flatterer," she whispered, "I didn't mean to wake you."

He chuckled under his breath. "Sweetling, I could be a week in heaven, and the touch of you would draw me back."

"Oh, you in heaven, I can see that."

"Among the elect, for sure, gadded up in one of those black coats they favor, with a high crowned hat and a book of holy writ clutched to my chest. I'll make a fine sight, don't you think?"

"I think," she said, "there must be more than one heaven."

"Aye, that's what's needed. I'll take a fine tropical island such as I've seen in the southern seas, palm fronds waving in the breeze and dusky-skinned maidens.... Well, no, not the maidens actually, but their older sisters, doing one of those fine dances they've such a gift for."

She snorted. "That's how you want to spend eternity? Lolling on a beach with women tending to your every need."

"Not every one," he protested righteously. Only to ruin it by adding, "A man needs the companionship of his own kind from time to time, a pint or two, a game of draughts. But then right back to the beach and the former maidens. Wouldn't do to let them get lonely, would it?''

''Wouldn't do to let your foolish head get any more swelled than it already is. Go back to sleep.''

''Ah, well.'' He sighed. ''As to that, I seem to have developed a bit of a problem.''

His hand flattened over her abdomen as he drew her back so that her buttocks pressed even more intimately against him.

She swallowed a gasp. ''Oh, yes, that's a bit alright, no more. Take a few deep breaths, count to a hundred and I'm sure it'll go away.''

''You are, are you?'' he growled. ''Impudent baggage. Hasn't anyone told you a woman ought to have more respect?

Daring greatly and not knowing quite how she came to it, she laughed. ''For that *bit* of a thing?''

''For my poor, wounded soul feeling the sting of unappreciation.''

''Soul is it now? And here I was thinking it had another name.''

He shook his head in mock dismay even as he moved with sudden deftness to settle her under him. ''What sort of talk is this from a proper Puritan woman?''

''I thought we'd already dealt with the matter of my propriety.''

''True,'' he admitted. ''We did take care of that right enough. Are you sure it's in no danger of coming back?''

''Does it sound as though it is?''

''No, but still, it wouldn't do to be taking chances. Propriety's a funny thing. It can sneak up on you when you least expect it.''

''I'll have to keep that in mind,'' she said.

Her voice sounded high and far away. That might have
had something to do with the fact that his hands had
slipped beneath her back and were swiftly undoing the
buttons of her dress.

His fingers were strong and sure as they stroked her
bared skin. He murmured gently, soothing her sudden
nervousness, and slipped the dress from her arms.

She lay revealed in starlight, washed of color, alabaster bathed by silver. Above her, his eyes gleamed as his
mouth grew taut.

Braced on his knees, he grasped the cloth and slid it
down—down, over her waist and hips, along the slim line
of her thighs, until at last it lay discarded on the sand
beside them.

Below the dress she wore only a single linen petticoat
touched by ribands of lace set with tiny embroidered
rosebuds. Not a Puritan garment at all, but a secret indulgence she could never bring herself to regret.

Especially not now, as he growled deep in his throat
and ran his hands up under the lace to hungrily caress
her.

Fire tinged the night, coursing through her. She arched
her back, moaning. The blanket was rough beneath her
back, the earth warm and gently undulating.

She raised her slim, pale arms and welcomed him. His
mouth was hot and seeking over her throat, in the valley
between her breasts and across her abdomen. She twisted
wildly, wanting him, needing him—desperate to touch
him as he touched her.

His shirt fell away, a white sail billowing against the
night. He stood to remove his breeches. She followed
him, and rising, her russet hair fell to frame her nakedness. She tilted her head proudly and met his admiring
gaze.

As his hands went to the buttons at his waist, she pushed them aside gently and did the task herself. Her palm brushed the bulging hardness of his manhood, withdrew, returned and touched him again. He groaned thickly and reached for her.

She eluded him, shaking her head. Her eyes had gone slumberous, the lids heavy. Her mouth was slightly swollen and parted. Beneath the drifting wisps of her hair, her nipples were heavy and full.

"Let me," she said.

A long, surging tremor raced through him. He teetered on the brink of losing control, wanting only to lower her swiftly to the ground, press her satiny thighs open and bury himself deep within her.

Instead, he clenched his hands, gritted his teeth and slowly nodded.

Daring filled her. The secret self so long denied laughed now with delight and seized the moment.

His buttocks were muscular and taut as she slipped the breeches over them. Freed, his manhood surged, thick and long, the tip hot to her fleeting touch. She trembled, but went on, kneeling to draw the breeches down his rock-hard thighs.

He stepped out of them and reached for her, but she shook her head and stood again before him. There in the gilding moonlight, as the Creator had made him, he was almost inexpressibly beautiful.

Every plane and shadow of his body was perfectly formed. The broad sweep of his shoulders and chest tapered to a narrow waist and slim hips before thickening again at his powerfully muscled thighs.

Dark hair grew between his flat nipples, arching in a thin line down his torso to thicken again profusely at his groin. From that nest, his manhood sprung, thrusting into her hand.

"Melly," he said huskily, "I can't stand much more of this."

"Then you know," she whispered, "how I feel when you touch me. But you're bigger and stronger, and you can make me wait as you choose. I want the same freedom, Garrick Marlowe. I want to know you as you know me."

He looked at her for a long moment in disbelief. No woman—no bold court lady, no hardened whore—had ever been so clear with him. Nor had he ever been so challenged.

Truly, it wasn't only the world that was new here.

"Alright," he said, aware that his throat was thick. He'd withstood a great deal in his life. Surely he could stand this? "Do your worst, lass," he said, and took a deep breath.

Chapter Twenty-One

He tasted of salt and sun, sea and wind. His skin was hot, and beneath it his muscles tensed. She drew her hands down his chest, fascinated by the touch of him, and followed with her mouth.

So strong, so different and yet so compelling to her, as though without him she had never really been complete and simply hadn't known it.

The soft hair of his chest tickled her nose. She sighed with pleasure and licked each dark nipple, fascinated to discover that his, too, hardened. Beneath her cheek, she felt the strong throb of his heart, growing more urgent by the moment.

Much as she would have liked to take her time and luxuriate in him, she realized there was a limit to what he would, or could, stand. In all fairness, she could take little more herself. Her nipples were acutely sensitive, even to the touch of the air, and between her legs she was growing hot and moist.

Swiftly, while she still could, lest she grow to weak with passion, she lowered herself before him. Her hands stroked his bulging thighs as she breathed softly on his manhood.

He groaned and reached for her, his hands like steel on her shoulders.

"Wait," she entreated, and touched him lightly, one finger tracing the long, thick length. How precariously men were made in this regard. So exposed and vulnerable, and yet filled with an undeniable power that found its answer within women.

He fascinated her, so much so that all caution, all doubt, all hesitation went sailing off in the night wind as though they had never been.

The tip of her tongue touched her lips. He caressed her boldly, driving her to a frenzy. Surely, she could....

A harsh groan broke from Garrick. He threw his head back and beseeched whatever deities there might be, or ever had been, to come to his aid. Without it, he would surely break.

Her mouth was infinitely sweet. Sweet, too, was her unfeigned pleasure in his body. Never had he felt so desired, so loved—

No, he would not think of that. Indeed, thought was beyond him. "Enough," he growled deep in his throat, and this time there was no mistaking that he meant it.

She complied, overwhelmed by her own audacity and by the hot currents of need it had unleashed. The blanket was beneath her back. Her legs fell open. He was above and over her, around and within, thrusting deep and hard.

She moaned and twisted beneath him, her aching nipples brushing the soft hair of his chest. His hands grasped her hips, holding her to his will as he thrust again and again.

Control was almost beyond him now, but not quite. Despite the red-hot pulse within him, he managed to go slowly and deliberately. With each thrust, he withdrew almost entirely before returning, deeply and steadily, again and again, all the while whispering to her of her beauty and her passion and of exactly how she made him feel.

Frenzied, Amelia gasped and cried out his name. She could bear no more. Again and again, he brought her to the brink, only to hold back just enough to keep them both from tipping over it. His breath was labored, his chest rising and falling like a mighty bellows. Deep within her, he grew even harder and thicker. The soft, inner folds of her body stretched to hold him.

Again, he moved, and the shattering pleasure built yet further. She felt the first convulsions seize her as he bent his head, took her nipple deep within his mouth and suckled her urgently.

Amelia shattered. There on the night-draped beach, beneath the surging man, she screamed a raw sound of feminine fulfillment. The stars took the sound and thrust it at her, back and again, drawing her further and further.

She felt him then, lost in his own completion yet with her all the same, both together under the stars, linked in far more than body. Instinctively, her arms went around him almost protectively. They lay still, intimately entwined as night wrapped itself around them gently.

Morning came and with it came the realization that no matter what happened now, she would never be quite the same. As she moved about their small campsite, helping Garrick to pack up their belongings, she kept her eyes averted from him.

It wasn't so much that she felt embarrassed, for that was far too weak and commonplace an emotion. The earlier experience of giving up her virginity was not so different from what many women did, although she readily acknowledged her own initiation had been both more gentle and more fulfilling than what she suspected was usually the case.

But the daring, unbridled siren of the night before was a different matter. This hidden self was someone completely beyond her expectations. She simply did not know what to make of her.

Better then to keep her thoughts to herself and go about her work, exactly as she had done for so much of her life.

Except that Garrick was having none of it. As she began to lift a bundle, his hand closed over hers. Gently, he took the bundle from her, set it on the sand and turned her into his arms.

"Melly," he said gently, "there's little heavier in this world than regrets, or more foolish to go about carrying."

"I'm not," she insisted, for that truly wasn't it. "I'm just . . . confused."

He laughed a little at that. "So am I. But know this, you're a rare delight and a joy, lass. Don't let me catch you thinking otherwise."

She swallowed hard and impulsively hugged him. With a minimum of words, he had given her exactly the reassurance she needed.

"And you're a good man, Garrick, for all you deny it."

He sighed and reluctantly put her from him. "It's not goodness I'm feeling right now, lass. But if we tarry here much longer, I'll be tempted to stay forever. The tide's going out. We can make Nieuw Amsterdam before evening."

She nodded, stilling her regrets and even managed a smile. He was right, of course. They had to go on. Behind them lay duty and responsibility; ahead, more of the same. This golden beach was no more than a stolen interval out of time and place. Inevitably, the world drew them back into it.

They made good time. The wind was full and the longboat skimmed easily over the waves. Accustomed by now to the motion, Amelia was able to relax and even enjoy herself.

As they entered the river that ran east of the Manhates Island, she stared around her in fascination. To the north lay the thick, fertile lands belonging to one Jonas Bronck. His name was well-known to her, for he was reputed to have the largest library in the New World. To the east were the densely forested regions of Laang Eylaadt, where only a few of the most daring settlers had begun to carve out farms.

But it was to the island itself that she looked with greatest fascination. So far, she could see no sign of habitation until suddenly, where the river narrowed, she saw signs of a neatly tended farm.

Cleared fields rolled down almost to the shore. Neat stone walls had been built, and cattle grazed within them. She caught sight of a small but well-made house of wooden planks surmounted by a chimney from which smoke curled.

Her eyes widened slightly as she caught sight of the windmill turning not far behind the house. For a moment, she could almost have believed herself back in the Lowlands.

They continued on, and swiftly the wilderness appeared again. She glanced back over her shoulder to confirm that the farm was really there.

Seeing her interest, Garrick said, "That's the Kuyter family settlement. They call it Zeegendal. Do you know what that means?"

Slowly, Amelia nodded. "Valley of blessing. I can see why they would call it that. It is a beautiful place."

Garrick shifted the rudder slightly to take them around a sandbank. "When I last came this way, the Kuyters had been burned out. They were living down in the town until they could rebuild and begin again."

"The Indians?" Amelia asked softly.

He nodded. "The first leaders of the colony preferred violence over negotiation. They made a great many enemies very quickly. The local Algonquins went on a rampage and burned out almost everyone. The town itself was severely damaged. For a time it looked as though the colony might fail. But this new man, Stuyvesant's his name, has done more than anyone thought possible. He's tough but fair and he's turned this place around."

"You know him then?"

He nodded. "We've met a time or two."

Teasingly, she said, "I thought English captains weren't suppose to do business with the Dutch."

"They're not," he acknowledged. "But as it happens, I'm Irish and Welsh. Now I know the good gentlemen in London presume that makes me English, or at least think that when it suits them. So I do the same. I'm English when there's a reason to be. Otherwise, I use my own judgment and go my own way, provided it hurts no one."

"I always found the Dutch to be remarkably tolerant," Amelia said. "They gave us sanctuary when no one else would. If Master Stuyvesant is of like mind, we should do well enough."

"Don't expect too much of him," Garrick warned. "This isn't civilized Amsterdam. Stuyvesant believes in survival, plain and simple. That, and profits for the Dutch West India Company. Little else concerns him."

"I can't believe that," Amelia protested. "Not if he is a true Dutchman. They appreciate order and honest endeavor."

"They appreciate success," Garrick corrected. Quietly, he added, "What we need to do is convince Stuyvesant that our success will help his own. Without that, we will not interest him."

We again, Amelia thought, and wondered if he, too, noticed how his mind was tending.

A cluster of islands lay to port. Garrick tacked between them and the main island. A wide inlet ran down to the river. Beyond it they could see signs of another settlement and, shortly beyond that, a cluster of neat houses that seemed to form a small village surrounded by well-cultivated fields.

"What is that?" Amelia asked.

Garrick smiled. "Ah, well, that's a story. When the settlement was just getting started, the Dutch tried bringing slaves to do the heavy work. They imported a few from down Curaçao way, but they didn't work out too well."

Amelia grimaced. She couldn't see why he would be amused. For all that she knew, slavery existed, and people even pointed to passages of Holy Writ to justify it. Something in her shriveled at the thought.

"The Africans helped build the fort right enough," he went on, "but after that they just seemed to slip between the white man's fingers. Started going off on their own, carving out a farm here and a farm there for themselves. Every once in a while, the Dutch West India Company would complain they were property that was being wasted, but nothing was ever done about it. Finally, a few years back, they were all freed and given that piece of land over there."

"That's good," Amelia said softly.

"Aye," Garrick murmured, "for them at least. Too bad it doesn't often work out that way."

The tidy settlement faded behind them and they moved on, past a long stretch of uninhabited land. Finally, as they neared the tip of the island, the coastline swelled as though coming out to meet them. Signs of habitation grew more frequent until at last Amelia saw in the distance the rooftops of Nieuw Amsterdam.

Her heart quickened. Here might lie some measure of safety and security for Belle Haven. Or they might find only disappointment. She clenched her hands and hardly drew breath as they came up beside the pier.

It was the only such structure in sight and appeared fairly new. As Garrick helped her from the longboat, she took a long look around.

Directly in front of them was a narrow road and on the other side of it a cluster of sheds that appeared to belong to fishermen. Small but neat houses were on either side. Farther down to the left was a larger stone building facing the river. Several men in rough-spun breeches and linen shirts were coming and going as she watched.

"The tavern," Garrick explained. "We'll leave our belongings aboard." He gestured to their left where most of the town seemed to lie. "Stuyvesant could be anywhere at this hour but we might as well stop at his house first."

"Is it safe to leave everything?"

"It is now," he said with a grin. "The good governor is a fiend for order. He's stopped the smuggling, ended public drunkenness, made knife fights too expensive even for the wealthiest and even gone so far as to get the streets swept regularly. Thieving isn't tolerated. It's no accident the gallows are within view of his windows."

"You don't think he'll find it a little irregular for the two of us to suddenly appear like this?"

Garrick shrugged and took her hand reassuringly. "We're not his problem, he's not going to care much what we do. Besides, we know each other."

And with that, it seemed, she had to be content, for he wasted no more time but led the way toward a broad, three-story house.

Chapter Twenty-Two

The governor was out. So they were informed by his wife, a tall, slender woman in her late thirties with plentiful dark hair beneath a neat, white cap, and an air of quiet strength.

She needed that strength, Amelia decided, for old as she was, Mistress Stuyvesant was the mother of two young sons, one still an infant and the other only just toddling about. The older boy clutched her skirt and stared at the visitors solemnly as the governor's wife apologized for her husband's absence.

"He's gone over to Stadden Eylaadt, to inspect the Hendricksen distillery, but he should be back shortly," she explained. "You're welcome to wait."

"That's kind of you," Amelia said softly, "but..." Looking at the governor's wife, she was suddenly aware of her own disheveled state.

Although she had put on her stockings and boots again, her cap was sadly wrinkled from the cavalier treatment it had received on the journey, and the sea air had wilted the starch from her apron. In addition, she felt sandy in uncomfortable places, her nose was sunburned, and she was acutely conscious that she did not present at all the picture she would have liked to.

Judith Stuyvesant smiled sympathetically. "Travel is always a trial," she said gently. "When I first came here, I thought I would never recover. We have a spare room you are welcome to use. My girl will bring you up water to bathe and will iron any of your clothes."

Amelia could hardly have been more tempted had Mistress Stuyvesant offered her diamonds. Her longing shone in her eyes.

Garrick shook his head ruefully. She would strike out for the wilderness, dare any danger, reject the narrow bonds of propriety, conquer every fear. But dangle a warm bath in front of her, and she all but melts.

"There are some people I need to see," he said. "If you don't mind, Mistress Stuyvesant, I'll return later."

"That will be fine," their hostess said with a smile. "We'll sit down to eat at four. The governor said he would be back by then."

"Then so shall I," Garrick said.

When he was gone, Judith lifted the baby from his cradle and, with her other son toddling along at her heels, led the way upstairs. The house was substantial, set off from the road by a low fence and surrounded by a pretty garden.

It was not unlike many of the houses Amelia had seen in Amsterdam. Indeed, she even caught a glimpse of two tall windmills through a window.

Everything was immaculately clean, smelling of soap and lemon oil. The furnishings were not extravagant but were all well made, clearly brought from home and in keeping with the status of a colonial governor.

Yet for all its tidy formality, there was also something very happy about the house. Judith Stuyvesant smiled often, and her children looked the picture of contentment. It was almost impossible to believe that she lived on the edge of a largely unknown continent, in a settlement that only a few years before had been almost destroyed by war.

Amelia straightened her shoulders. "It's very good of you to take us in like this," she said politely.

Judith's eyes twinkled. "I've heard Petrus speak of Captain Marlowe. He has great admiration for him— even if they aren't always in complete agreement on every matter."

"They disagree?" Amelia asked worriedly. She had hoped Garrick would be able to influence the governor favorably.

"Only occasionally," Judith assured her. "Right after the Indian war ended, Garrick was one of the few captains willing to bring goods here. Even many of our own Dutch captains refused because they felt the danger was still too great. Without the help of Garrick and a handful of men like him, the settlement might well have had to be abandoned."

"He does have great courage," Amelia said.

"My mother used to say there were men for the tavern, men for the countinghouse and men for the world. Garrick is one of those last, as is Petrus."

She glanced over her shoulder at Amelia as she added, "It isn't always easy to live with such a man, but it's never boring either."

Mercifully, she turned her attention back to the stairs they were climbing, allowing Amelia's cheeks to warm unobserved.

The room to which Amelia was shown was on the second floor of the house, in the back where the windows looked out over the water. It was small, but brightly furnished with white lace curtains and a good wool rug in shades of green and blue. In many ways, the room reminded Amelia of the one she'd had in Amsterdam.

Gracious hostess that she was, Mistress Stuyvesant left her alone to rest, with promises that the maids would be up shortly with hot water. Grateful, Amelia lay down on the bed and closed her eyes. She was not so much tired as simply overwhelmed by all that had happened in such a short time.

Her mind pleasantly blank, she listened to the soft murmur of the wind around the house and the call of seabirds in the harbor. Only gradually did she become aware that time was passing. Still there was no sign of the maids.

In Amsterdam, good manners would have required her to remain where she was. To do otherwise would somehow hint that she thought it possible her hostess did not have the full ordering of her household.

But here on the edge of the wilderness, life was happily more practical. She rose, put her boots back on, and went swiftly downstairs.

Judith Stuyvesant was in the kitchen. Her two-year-old sat on the stone floor nearby amusing himself with a top.

The baby had been popped into a cradle which did not seem to please him. He was crying lustily. Meanwhile, his harried mother was filling the big iron kettle over the fire with water.

"You shouldn't be doing this," Amelia said hastily. "I appreciate it very much but I certainly don't expect you, of all people, to be waiting on me."

"I wouldn't be normally," Judith said with disarming frankness. "But the maids have vanished again. I should warn you, you absolutely cannot get good help here. Everyone wants to be off farming their own holding or doing heaven only knows what. Not that I blame them.

The opportunities are so great as to be well nigh irresistible.''

Since acquiring good help was very low on Amelia's list of things she needed to do, this news did not perturb her. Instead, she smiled and took the bucket from Judith.

''I'll see to the water,'' Amelia said. ''That little fellow in the cradle wouldn't have it any other way.''

Judith rolled her eyes heavenward but did not disagree. Instead, she smiled gratefully as she went to soothe her frazzled son.

''Hush, Nicholas,'' she murmured as she sat down in a plain wooden chair and, without any great ado, unfastened the top buttons of her dress. At once, the child quieted as he began to suck.

The older boy, Balthasar, came to sit beside his mother where he continued playing with his top. Amelia stared at the tender scene, struck by how simple, yet powerful, it was. It reminded her forcibly of her own vision in the copse and caused her throat to tighten painfully.

It was as well that she had to pay attention to what she was doing or risk being scalded by the water. By the time it was ready, Nicholas had finished nursing and allowed his mother to return him to the cradle in a much improved mood.

Judith helped pull the tin hip tub from the cupboard where it was kept. She agreed with Amelia that in the absence of servants, the kitchen was the most sensible place to bathe. When the tub was filled, she gave Amelia a fresh cake of soap scented with rose hips and took the children out into the garden.

Barely had she slipped her toes into the water than Amelia sighed with delight. Bathing was one of her greatest pleasures, but she had been hard-pressed to indulge it since leaving Amsterdam. Most of the time, she'd had to be content with a basin bath that, while it did the job, was in no way satisfying.

This was altogether different. She tipped her head back against the padded rim of the tub, closed her eyes, and luxuriated in the silken softness of the water caressing her skin.

She sighed deeply. Never had she felt so aware of her woman's body. Every inch of her was exquisitely sensitive. She had only to think of Garrick to become instantly responsive.

She felt wrapped in a delightful haze of contentment. All her cares seemed wiped away, if only briefly.

When she was at last able to rouse herself, she vigorously washed her hair, rinsed it dry and reluctantly left the tub. The water was growing cool, but she would still have been inclined to linger had she not been mindful that the kitchen was needed for other things.

The day was wearing on. Master Stuyvesant would be returning soon and expect his supper. So, too, might the maids come back, although that seemed a good deal more doubtful.

She dried herself off with a length of toweling Judith had provided and slipped into the fresh clothes her hostess had also kindly lent her. That done, she carefully emptied the tub, bucket by bucket, pouring the water into the little brick-lined gully that led away from the kitchen door. She was just putting the tub back into the cupboard when Judith returned with the children.

"Feeling better?" Judith asked.

"Much. I can't thank you enough. There's just something about a bath that puts everything in perspective."

The older woman laughed. "I've said the same myself. Life is never so terrible that a good hot soak can't make it better. Nicholas is still napping, and I've taken

Balthasar over to the fort where the men make a fuss over him and he has a lovely time playing soldier. Heaven knows when the girls will return.''

"I'll be happy to help you fix supper," Amelia said. Under the circumstances, she thought it was the least she could do.

Judith gave her a long, level look. "You know, when I first heard that the Pequot had sold land to an English-woman bent on founding her own colony, I thought you'd be one of two things—either an idle dreamer with more money than sense, or a wild-eyed prophetess leading hapless followers into disaster. Curiously enough, you don't seem to be either."

"Odd about that, isn't it?" Amelia asked with a grin. She liked Judith Stuyvesant very much. Her forthright-ness was refreshing, and her good-natured approach to life was exactly what was most needed in her circum-stances.

"But you are really serious, aren't you?" Judith called as she disappeared into the still room beside the kitchen. She returned a moment later with an armload of sup-plies. "You really mean to make a go of it?"

Amelia nodded. "It's not as though there's any choice now. We certainly can't go back to Boston—we'd be persecuted unmercifully. Nor is a return to England pos-sible. We're all determined to make a go of it, no matter how difficult the task."

"I admire that," Judith said as she laid out a round of cheese, apples and a haunch of smoked ham wrapped in a tight string bag. With a housewifely eye, she scruti-nized her selections, darted back into the stillroom and returned with a jar of cream and a handful of greens.

"A pie, I think," she said. "Ham, cheese, a bit of this and that for flavor, and the apples on the side for sweet. Sound all right to you?"

"Sounds lovely," Amelia said. With the exception of celebrations, meals had been catch-as-catch-can at Belle Haven. She was exceedingly tired of day-old stew, and even fish had begun to pall.

"I'll make the pastry, if you like."

Judith accepted the offer and showed her where to find flour and fat. Soon they were working contentedly at the big pine table.

The baby dozed in the cradle, and from outside they could hear the happy shouts of children at play. Before long, the intertwining smells of wood smoke, spices and baking pie filled the cheerful kitchen.

Amelia dusted the last of the flour from her hands as wistfulness swept over her. If she had stayed in Amsterdam, this was the life that would have been hers—a husband coming home soon from his labors, contented children, the comfortable routines of domestic life.

For just a moment, a piercing sense of longing filled her. It was gone in an instant as the deep sound of men's voices came up the path and a sudden blast of masculine vigor pierced the kitchen peace.

Instinctively, Amelia's gaze went to Garrick. Wherever he had been, it seemed to have agreed with him. He had bathed and shaved and was cleanly garbed.

Her eyes widened as she realized he had donned a full-length coat that she hadn't even realized he'd brought along. Not only that, but a stock was neatly tied around his throat, his hair was brushed and secured at the nape of his neck and he had gone so far as to wear finely spun stockings and shoes with silver buckles.

There was still an unmistakable air of the swashbuckler about him, but he also looked like a prosperous merchant very much at home in the finest drawing rooms.

And in Mistress Stuyvesant's kitchen. He greeted Judith with a smile and a bow, gave Amelia an approving grin and promptly shocked her to the soles of her feet by relieving the governor of the particular burden he was carrying—his two-year-old son, Balthasar.

The child chortled merrily and made a grab for Garrick's stock. Garrick stopped him gently and diverted his attention to the dust motes dancing in the sunlight.

"How was your journey, husband?" Judith asked as the governor hung his hat on a peg near the door and limped over to greet his wife. One leg was gone, shot off below the knee. In its place, he wore a wooden stump that, Amelia was surprised to see, served him surprisingly well.

"Tolerable," he said with a grimace. "Master Hendricksen has expanded the distillery again. He neglected to get a license before he did so, but I've decided to overlook that. His quality remains good and he has always been cautious about who he sells to."

"The Indians will give almost anything for jenever and brandy," Judith said, "even for lager. But spirits have a terrible effect on them."

Her husband nodded. "I don't understand it myself, but they seem to be more susceptible than we are. The results can be horrific. They become violent and attack everyone in sight or simply fade into decline and die."

"Their leaders know the problem," Garrick said. "The wiser among them are forbidding their people to drink spirits."

"Without sufficient effect," Stuyvesant said grimly. "Forgive me, mistress," he added to Amelia. "I'm rattling on and neglected to welcome you. I knew your father. He was a godly man.''

"Thank you," Amelia said softly. "He always spoke well of you."

Stuyvesant nodded. He was not given to a great many words, nor did he appear at all susceptible to flattery. Save for the lack of part of a leg, he was a well-built man, solid and with an air of intelligence.

His eyes, when they fell on his wife, were gentle. So, too, for his children. But Amelia would have wagered that they could turn hard as stone should he become displeased.

"What smells so good?" he asked.

"The pie Mistress Daniels has made," Judith replied. "But come, we have guests and I am not about to loiter in the kitchen, worthless maids or not."

She took Balthasar from Garrick and led the way to a pleasant sitting room that looked out toward the road. A wagon was passing by, but otherwise there was less activity than Amelia had noted before. People were beginning to think of their supper and the chance to relax a little from their labors.

As the governor poured brandy for himself and Garrick and a glass of fine wine for Amelia, Judith excused herself. She went off with a determined look in her eye and returned a short time later, without Balthasar.

"Margarita has returned," she informed her husband. To Amelia, she explained, "She is the children's nurse. Fortunately, she genuinely cares for them and is as reliable as possible, all things considered."

"She's taken up with a Frenchman," Stuyvesant said. "Can you believe such a thing?" It was a question that required no answer, for he went right on. "Ah, well, this isn't Amsterdam, is it? Within certain bonds, we let people do as they wish. They seem to benefit from it.''

"We have the same idea at Belle Haven," Amelia said quietly. She saw the flare of interest in the governor's eyes and suspected its cause. He had heard of the settlement and would naturally be curious about it, but the name made it real.

"Is that what you call it?" he asked. "Then I hope it will live up to its name for you, mistress. But to be blunt, you've chosen a precarious place to settle."

"The Pequot seem peaceful enough," she said.

He shrugged. "For the moment. What I meant is that you're right smack between us and the English. You must know the land you hold is contested? The Dutch West India Company claims it. So does the Massachusetts Bay Colony. Now where do you suppose that leaves you?"

"In possession," Amelia said. She, too, could be blunt. But she was also compelled to honesty. Quietly, she added, "For the moment."

He gave her a long, level look before slowly nodding. "And that, I presume, is what you would like to talk about?"

"We both would," Amelia said, looking at Garrick.

"Where exactly do you come into this, my friend?" Stuyvesant asked him. "I had the impression you did your best to set foot on land no more often than you could avoid."

Garrick hesitated. He took a swallow of his brandy, set the glass down and said quietly, "I have pledged to help Amelia establish the settlement and see it through its first harvest. So far, everything is going well. But the Puritans remain a threat. As for the Pequot...Owenoke grows no younger, and his son, Mayano, has much anger in him."

Stuyvesant nodded thoughtfully. He limped around the table and drew out a chair. "Sit then, Mistress Daniels. In my experience, all talk goes better on a full stomach."

They sat. Supper appeared, served by one of the tardy maids, and for a time they talked of inconsequential things. But soon enough the conversation turned serious. There at the governor's table, over fine linen and good china, they spoke of Belle Haven, of dreams and reality.

And ultimately of survival.

Chapter Twenty-Three

"Read it again," Sam Whitler requested quietly. They were all seated around the fire just beyond the fortification. Amelia and Garrick had returned earlier in the day. Word had gone out to the families, many of them scattered over their new holdings. Everyone had come to the meetinghouse to hear the results of the trip to Nieuw Amsterdam.

Amelia leaned closer to the fire. She held an impressive piece of vellum in her hands, decorated at the bottom with wax seals. Softly, she read, "'I, Petrus Stuyvesant, Governor-General of the Colony of New Netherlands, do proclaim this day that the settlement known as Belle Haven founded by the 'Lady Star Company' in the lands of the Pequot between the Asmatuck River and the creek Patomuck is an authorized settlement under the protection of the Noble Lords States General, His Highness the Prince of Orange, the West India Company and their Governor-General of New Netherlands. Residents of said manor of Belle Haven shall henceforth enjoy the same privileges, rights and freedoms accorded to patroons of New Netherlands. Signed, this day in New Amsterdam, Petrus Stuyvesant,

Governor-General. Amelia Daniels for the 'Lady Star Company.' Captain Garrick Marlowe of the *Lady Star*.'"

"Why did the captain have to sign?" Lissy asked. She was snuggled against her husband, her head on his shoulder. One hand rested gently against her belly in a gesture that made the other women smile even as they guessed she was unaware of it.

"Unlike the Pequot," Garrick said, "the Dutch feel more satisfied with a man's name at the bottom of a document such as this. Although to give the governor credit, he insisted Amelia sign first."

"Actually, Mistress Stuyvesant insisted," Amelia corrected lightly, and laughed at the memory. The governor's wife seemed to like the notion of a woman being responsible for things. "I suspect they have some interesting discussions ahead of them."

"But what does it really mean?" Bette asked. "Will we be safe?"

Amelia hesitated. She would have liked for all the world to say yes but she wasn't about to lie.

"News of this proclamation will reach Boston, we can be sure of that. Also Passicham will see to it that Mayano hears of it. Anyone who is thinking of causing trouble for us will know that we are not alone."

"But we are so far from Nieuw Amsterdam," Lissy said. "They could not reach us in time if we were attacked."

"No," Garrick agreed gently. He tightened his arm around Amelia, drawing her closer against him. "But they could avenge us."

Around the circle lit by fire, people looked at one another. It was hardly what they would have liked to hear, but they were realistic. The ever-present promise of vengeance might be the best protection they could have.

"And in return?" Elijah asked. "What do they expect from us?"

"That we form a buffer between the Dutch and further encroachments by the English," Amelia said. "Our presence draws a line here and says the English must go no farther."

"I'd not lay money on them listening," Sam muttered.

Garrick had to agree with him. The proclamation was more than they might have hoped for, but at most it only bought them time. Their best defense was to prepare to protect themselves.

When he said as much, heads nodded. Their ready acceptance did not surprise him. Somewhere along the line, he had stopped thinking of them as hopeless idealists and accepted that they were strong, hard people willing to do whatever they had to in order to succeed.

People not entirely unlike himself.

He sighed and nestled Amelia closer. The journey back to Belle Haven had been too swift. He wanted to be free to carry her away again, farther this time, to a place where nothing could hurt or frighten her. Where she would be safe always, happy always, his always.

His arms tightened, so much so that she made a small sound of discomfort. Instantly, he loosened his hold but did not let go of her entirely. He needed to feel the slender warmth of her close to him the same way he needed food and water.

But it was only a passing thing. Men often became infatuated with women. Possession was the surest route to recovery. Soon now, his ardor would cool. He would always be fond of her, to be sure, but it would be the fondness of memory. The driving need to hold and protect her would give way to satiation.

And any moment now the oxen would spout poetry.

Either event seemed as likely. Whether he wanted to admit it or not—and he most certainly didn't—she had become essential to him in a way he could not fathom.

Beyond the circle of fire, corn and wheat drowsed in the fields, vines entwined their way among the stalks, flowers bloomed and gave way to fruits. Life moved in its inexorable cycle. Soon the time of reaping would come.

But before then, he meant to seize the passing days and turn them to his own will in a way that, for both of them, would stand the test of time.

He began before first light.

Amelia woke to find herself alone but thought nothing of it. Garrick seemed to need less sleep than she did and was frequently up and about before she could barely crack an eye.

Even so, she was no layabout herself. It was scarcely dawn when she poked the fire beyond the meetinghouse and set porridge to cooking in the big kettle.

The birds were chirping and most people were done with breakfast when she noticed that Garrick had yet to appear. Still, she thought little of it. He had probably gone back to *Lady Star* on some errand.

She had work to do in the fields. The weeding never seemed to end no matter how much mulch they used. But the crops were coming in well and there were few problems with bugs.

She picked a fuzzy caterpillar off a cornstalk, dropped it in her bucket with various other small lives she had collected, and carried them all some distance from the field. There she released them, shaking her head at her own foolishness.

Tomorrow, she might well be picking the same bug or its cousin from the same cornstalk. If she had half the wits any of the others had, she would have finished off every one she could find.

And had the crops actually been threatened, she would have. But the bugs were so few and little enough trouble. It seemed wrong to kill where there was no need, even when what was killed was only an insect.

By midday, she was done in the fields and glad to take a short rest. Those who could, gathered for a simple meal. Still no sign of Garrick.

Jacob had come over from the ship. She paused to speak with him after she had finished eating.

"Is there a problem on *Lady Star*" Amelia asked.

He looked surprised by the question. "Problem? Not that I know of. Why do you ask?"

She shrugged, embarrassed. "No reason really. It's only that Garrick has been off somewhere all day and I just presumed he was at the ship."

Jacob frowned. "I haven't seen him. Didn't he say where he was going?"

She shook her head. "It's probably not important. He certainly doesn't have to tell me what he's doing."

"Still," Jacob murmured, "it isn't like him."

He went off looking puzzled, which did nothing at all for her peace of mind. Afternoon came and went and still there was no hint of where Garrick had gone.

Finally, just when she was beginning to think that she would have to mention his absence to the others and see if anyone knew where he had gone, he returned.

She did not see which direction he came from, but wherever he had been, he had clearly been working hard. His clothes were streaked with dirt and sweat, and he had the relaxed air of a man well pleased by his labors.

"Where have you been?" she demanded, instantly wishing she could have held her tongue.

He looked down at her with mingled surprise and amusement. His laugh was deep-throated and, she suspected, at her expense.

"Miss me?" he asked.

She should say no, tell him what he did was of no consequence and go back to her chores. Any sensible woman would have known to do that.

But it had already been well established that she and sense were at best only remote acquaintances.

"Yes," she said simply. "I was worried about you."

His smile vanished. He reached out a hand to touch her cheek but let it drop when he saw how dirty he was.

"I need a bath," he said. The lambent fires in his eyes swept over her. "Care to join me?"

She shouldn't, she couldn't, she . . .

"Where?"

"The rock pool on Daniels Neck."

She glanced over her shoulder. The other people in the clearing were going about their own business, paying no attention to them at all. Even if their absence was noticed, no one would care.

"Alright," she said, and went with him.

It was very quiet along the stream. The evening song of robins and bluebirds surrounded them. They left the canoe on the bank and walked a short distance to where the rock pool bubbled up from the ground.

Garrick put down the bundle he was carrying, stretched luxuriantly and sighed. "I've been thinking about this all day."

"Have you indeed?" Amelia asked.

He nodded, and without further ado began pulling off his shirt. She glanced away, but only for a moment. Her gaze was drawn back to him irresistibly.

When he began to strip his breeches off, her cheeks warmed but she still couldn't quite seem to look anywhere else. Magnificently naked, he walked to the edge of the pool and dove cleanly into the water. Moments later, he surfaced, shaking droplets from his hair.

Grinning, he said, "I think I'll live. What about you, lass? Going to stand there all evening gawking?"

She tossed her head and shot him a sidelong glance of reprimand. "And what is there worth gawking at?"

"Nothing I can think of," he said with a laugh.

She put her hands to the buttons on the back of her dress—which not incidentally had the effect of pulling the fabric tight across her breasts. "Think again."

Her confident tone belied the tremors racing through her. It was still light enough for him to see her clearly. To strip like that right in front of him was something she could never have imagined herself doing.

Yet once begun, she could think of no good reason to stop. Especially not when the deliciously cool water—and the equally delicious man—awaited her.

Her nipples hardened as the evening air—and his gaze—touched her. Keeping her eyes averted from him, she stepped gingerly to the edge of the pool.

"How deep is it?" she asked.

"Not too much at the sides and it slopes slowly. You'll be fine."

She stepped into the water, finding it about knee deep, and waded in farther until it modestly covered her. The bottom was soft and sandy beneath her toes. She leaned her head back to the blue-gray sky and sighed with pure happiness.

And almost instantly squealed. Strong, warm hands grasped her, powerful arms surrounded her and a mouth made for possession came down hard on her own.

The deep, slow thrust of his tongue filled her with molten heat. Clinging to him, she yielded completely to the spiraling passion he unleashed.

Frantically, she aided him as he leaned her against the moss-draped rocks, positioned her, and spread her legs. She was completely ready for him when he penetrated, slowly at first until he was certain of her response, then deep and hard.

The sky whirled above her. Rushing sound filled her ears. Caught between the velvety rocks and the steel hardness of his body, she clutched his shoulders as he drove into her again and again.

His name was on her lips as she was drawn tighter and tighter until, at last, the unbearable pleasure shattered consciousness and hurled her into dark, star-splattered ecstasy.

When she was next aware, she was lying beside Garrick next to the pool. His arm was draped lightly over her and his eyes were closed. When she stirred, they opened.

"I can't understand why bathing isn't more popular," he whispered.

"People just don't bring enough imagination to it," she suggested drowsily.

He chuckled and snuggled her closer to him. They lay like that for a long, peaceful time, until the cooling air roused them to dress.

Garrick had brought clean clothes with him. He donned them, then ran his fingers through his dark, damp hair.

"Hungry?" he asked.

Before she could answer, her stomach growled. He laughed at her chagrin and held out a hand. "Come on."

"Where to?"

"Supper."

"We're going the wrong way," she said as he led her toward the copse. "The canoe is over there."

He smiled enigmatically, but did not change direction. They followed a path through the trees toward the clearing where he had set her stone. Absently, she noticed that the path looked better worn than she remembered it, as though something heavy had passed over it.

They came to the clearing as the light was fading. A large fire had been laid, ready to be lit. A blanket was unfolded on the ground and someone had set out pewter dishes. Beside them was a large basket.

But all that was as nothing compared to what else had happened in the clearing. Her eyes widened as she took in the neat piles of fieldstone set around a good-sized rectangle. Already one side was walled to a height of several feet and another was half completed.

"What is this?" she asked breathlessly.

"Your house," he replied as though it should have been obvious. "I asked some of the crew to help me. By the way, do you have any idea how many stones there are around here? You could build a palace with them if you had the mind to."

"You've started building my house?" she asked. Slowly, she stepped forward and ran her hands over the stones. They were still warm from the sun.

"Several of the settlers have started theirs," he pointed out. "You won't want to live in the meetinghouse forever."

"No," she murmured, still amazed. That he should think to do such a thing, and not a house only of wood, either, like the rest of the settlers were building, but a house with a solid stone foundation that looked as though nothing would ever unsettle it.

"The labor is far more this way," she said.

He shrugged. "You want it done rightly, don't you?"

"Yes, of course I do, but still I can't ask you to take this on when you've already done so much."

She meant what she said, but the light in her eyes belied her words. Already, she could see how it would be when it was finished. A good-sized house, three rooms at least, with plenty of room for more as they were needed.

He had planned a central hearth; she could see where the chimney was already begun. Above the first few feet, the house would be of wood. Freshly hewn planks were already being piled up nearby.

There would be windows with painted shutters—white perhaps, or if she could somehow manage it, green. And there would be flowers—many, many flowers growing in profusion all around Amelia Daniels's house.

"This is very nice of you," she said simply. If she tried to say anything more, she was going to cry. The man she would lose, the house she would have.

Why doubt that the bargain was fair? This was what she had always wanted, wasn't it?

"It will be done before fall," he said, and took her again into his arms.

They were kissing, lost in the pleasure that swelled all around them, when the first faint warning sounded deep within their minds.

Smoke.

Smoke hardly perceptible, yet curling around the far reaches of their consciousness, drawing them reluctantly back into the world, back into reality.

Back into the sudden and shattering danger that confronted Belle Haven.

Chapter Twenty-Four

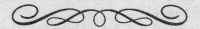

Mayano. He came out of the shadows of the night, brandishing fire and the sharp, deadly shock of arrows loosed from their bows by the braves who followed him.

There was no warning. Within minutes, the settlement was engulfed. People screamed, torn from the drowsy aftermath of supper. Seizing their children, they raced for the raw wood fortification around the meeting house.

Bette stumbled as she ran. Arms clutched to her belly to protect the babe who slept within, she almost fell. But her husband was there, just in time. He half carried, half dragged her through the gate. Scant seconds later, it slammed shut behind them.

The braves were all young, and hot in their blood from the exhortations that had brought them this far. They circled round the fortress, their war cries sending chilling fear through those trapped within.

Between them, the settlers possessed eight muskets. Sailors caught with them had three more. A quick calculation showed they had enough shot to fire perhaps a hundred rounds—if their weapons didn't overheat.

"We'll be all right," Sam Whitler said. "The walls are strong. No arrows can penetrate them. All we have to do is wait."

"Help will come from the ship," Elijah ventured.

"Passicham won't stand for this, nor will Owenoke," said another.

"We don't know where they stand on this," Lissy murmured. "And the ship may also be under attack. We could be on our own."

"Then so be it," her husband said. "We can hold out as long as we have to."

No one disagreed with him. There was no point. The children were sent into the meetinghouse along with several of the women.

Thanks to Garrick's insistence, water was stored there along with food. If necessary, they could withstand a siege of a week or more. Provided the fortress did not catch fire.

Beyond the walls, where torches now lit the night, Mayano studied the results of his first assault. They were exactly where he wanted them, trapped in the place the settlers imagined represented safety.

Fools, he thought, and smiled. They were just like his father. They would all die, and after them ...

He raised his fist at the silent sky and shouted his defiance. This was only the beginning. All the whites would die, from the northernmost reaches of the Massachusetts colony to the place they called Virginy. The land would be wiped clean with blood.

He would rise far, far above his status as a chief's son in a single clan. All the tribes would heed his call. He would unite them in one mighty confederation and, with their combined power, he would scourge the invaders until not a single one of them—not man, woman or babe in arms—was left alive within these lands.

Indeed, he would make their deaths so terrible that no more whites would journey across the great water to challenge what was meant to be his alone.

And those who opposed him, like Passicham—and his own father?—too would die, for he was right, he *knew* he was. Survival depended on the death of others—many, many deaths.

They would speak his name in terror, the whites *and* his own people. No one would dare to oppose him in even the slightest way. He would rule over all. But first, this lone, stark fortress had to die.

They thought they were safe, that death could not reach them. Odd, he thought, because from all he had learned of them, they should have known better.

Stupid Passicham. He thought they were interesting. He was excited by the prospect of different people coming together. He thought they could learn from each other.

No, Mayano knew better. Life was combat, struggle and merciless confrontation that only the mightiest could hope to win. He would prove that his way and his people were the greater, if only for being most willing to kill.

He shouted an order. The braves leaped to obey. He had been working with them in secret for a long time, having used words and imagery, the smoke of certain herbs and the twisting magic of sachem he had taught himself to win them to his way. They would die at his word.

But that was not his intention. He wanted them to live, to triumph, to sire many sons who would follow in their footsteps.

It was the strangers who would die, this great night— this beginning of his destiny.

The torches danced, leaping high. As one, they fell against the wooden walls of the fortress. Smoke rose, embers flew. The wood was fresh, still rich with sap. It did not catch easily as dry planks would have, but slowly, little by little, a spark here and there, it began to fire.

"Die!" Mayano screamed to the sky. Then he brandished his spear, thirsting for the blood it would soon drink.

Garrick launched himself straight at him.

He and Amelia had landed the canoe not far from the settlement, then raced the rest of the way back. She was still hidden by the trees, he hoped, for he couldn't be sure what she would do.

Nor was there time to worry about it. He saw the fortress walls beginning to catch and knew there was only one hope.

The braves, caught in the madness of Mayano's vision, did not see him. All attention was focused on the settlers trapped within the walls. No one expected anyone to come out of the woods.

But come Garrick did, swift as night, deadly and merciless as Mayano's darkest dreams.

He had been in battle too many times before. He knew it too well. Unlike the young braves and their leader, he was a man without illusions. He was beyond courage. For him, there was nothing—not life, love or dreams. There was only survival.

Not necessarily his.

He knew he could die. He had passed through that knowledge the moment the canoe touched shore and he saw what was happening. Death traveled with him. It sat on his shoulder like an old and well-known friend, urging him on.

He wanted to live. Life, and all it represented, was back there in the trees. It even had a name.

Amelia.

But if Mayano triumphed, Amelia would die, and then what?

Long years of anguished memory, regrets, recrimination. The endless tortured suffering of the soul that, by comparison, made death seem a friend.

So he would die.

But so would Mayano.

Now.

In an instant, in the fire and darkness he raised his knife high and plunged deep, endlessly. There was no hesitation, no thought, no mercy. Only an end to all the madness represented.

Mayano turned and saw what was coming. Shock lit his face.

He was, after all, the young and indulged son of a chief. By any standard he was brave, but he had never known defeat, much less this *thing* that was coming at him now. This end.

He screamed, but he did not retreat. Bravery and the conviction of his vision held him firm. Garrick went so far as to feel a moment's admiration for this man, young and untried as he was, for at least he did not give way when he saw the face of death.

Indeed, he fought and fought well. But he was face-to-face and hand-to-hand with a force he had not known existed, much less prepared to confront. He did not quite understand how far men would go to protect what was essential to them.

And by the time he did, it was too late.

He died with Garrick's knife in his chest, his blood flowing into the earth of Belle Haven, his voice still defiant, fading on the wind.

The braves were worthy of their name. Stunned though they were, they rallied to their dying leader. Garrick turned, weaponless, and faced those that rushed at him. The light in their eyes said he would be torn apart.

He had an instant to hope it would be over quickly. But that was before the night was torn by thunder.

One of the braves fell, another staggered away. The rest stood stunned for an instant before swiftly disappearing into the trees.

Garrick stood, arms at his side, Mayano's blood on his hands, and slowly absorbed the fact that he was alive. He looked toward the fortress.

The gate stood open. Sam Whitler stood there, a musket in his hands. He had been trying to load it, but he stopped now and looked dazedly ahead of him.

Garrick turned. Before the image reached his mind, he sensed what he would see. Some inner voice whispered to him of unspoken promises kept and unbroken vows preserved.

She stood just beyond the trees. Against the darkness, she looked very pale, almost like a wraith transported from a world beyond.

But the musket in her hands was real, as was the smoke rising from its barrel.

Somewhere—he would not even try to guess where—Mistress Amelia Daniels had learned how to load and fire a weapon. Perhaps she had done it once or twice in her life at the insistence of her careful father. By all that was holy, she had learned the lesson well.

This woman of beauty and passion, this creature of dreams trembling on the edge of reality, had learned to kill.

But she had not learned to bear it.

He reached her as her knees gave way. His arm caught her waist as his other hand took the musket from her. He laid it aside and pulled her hard against him, smoothing her hair, whispering words that needed no meaning save their soft, reassuring sound.

She whimpered and clutched him tightly. For a moment, he thought she would retch, but she controlled it. Slowly, still holding her, he lowered her to the ground.

A quick glance over his shoulder confirmed that the settlers were quickly getting the fire under control. The fortress would be damaged, but it could be repaired.

But Owenoke had lost a son, and not all the will in the world could change that.

The burning smell of illusion filled his lungs. He clung to what was real and gave himself up to the stark, simple pleasure of knowing he was still alive.

The village was wreathed in silence. Every man, woman and child stood watching as Mayano was carried home.

He came on a bark stretcher borne by the men of Belle Haven. Behind him, a dead brave was similarly conveyed.

The dead were not alone, for with them came the people they had sought to kill, all of them down to the very youngest. Come to witness an end. And, just perhaps, a beginning.

Owenoke looked very old. He stood against a length of hickory and, with his shoulders slumped, watched them come. The sachem was at his side. Passicham was nearby.

Slowly, they came, faces solemn. There was no gloating here, the pain for all was too intense. They stopped in front of Owenoke and gently lowered the stretchers to the ground.

Garrick stepped forward. Loudly enough for all to hear, he said, "They fought well."

Not justly—and certainly not wisely—but with courage, and for that they deserved acknowledgment, Garrick decided.

Besides, it was a kindness for Owenoke, who stood, devoured by grief, with his head bent and his eyes reddened by hours of mourning.

The chief said nothing, he only looked at his son for a long moment, as though remembering the child he had been and trying desperately to understand where so much had gone wrong.

Finally, the sachem reached forward and placed a covering of finely tanned deerskin over the young, dead face.

"It is good of you to do this," Passicham said quietly.

Garrick nodded once. "It is proper," he corrected.

"Owenoke wishes you to understand that his son attacked without his knowledge or approval. He was supposed to be on a mission to the other tribes. He returned secretly and summoned the foolish young braves who had been misled by his words. Had we known of his plans, we would have stopped him ourselves."

"I understand," Garrick said. "He was young and he believed, as many of the young do, that the world could be bent to his will. Perhaps he will find whatever he was seeking in the life beyond this."

"Perhaps," Passicham replied. He was silent for a moment before he said quietly, "Peace is the only way. Don't you agree, my friend?"

Garrick hesitated. He looked at the tall, somber Pequot as he said, "If all men were as you are, Passicham, peace would be all we know. Alas, the world is very far from that."

"But still we must try."

"Yes," Garrick agreed quietly, "we must."

Passicham turned to Amelia, who stood nearby. "The agreement between our peoples stands. Is that acceptable to you, Mistress Daniels?"

She inclined her head. "It is, and please tell Owenoke of our regret that he has suffered such a loss."

Passicham spoke softly to the chieftain. Owenoke did not reply, but he did raise his head slightly and look at each of them in turn. A long, shuddering sigh escaped him as he reached out a hand to bid his son farewell.

Chapter Twenty-Five

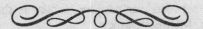

The sharp tang of raw wood filled the motionless air. Bees buzzed lazily among the lazy honeysuckle. Amelia opened her eyes and stirred reluctantly.

She had been dreaming, and the last, faint echoes of that dream still clung to her. The details were lost, but wherever she had been, she was very happy.

Around her, the copse of trees and the stone walls of her house took shape as the real world claimed her once again. She sat up slowly and looked around.

Garrick stood not far away, his hands on his lean hips and his brow furrowed in thought. He was scrutinizing his work.

Amelia smiled and got up. She went to stand behind him, slipping her arms around his waist. "It looks wonderful," she said.

He turned his head to look at her. His eyes were warm, still slumberous with the passion they had shared a short time before.

"I'm thinking it should be bigger," he said.

She shook her head. "No, no, it's perfect. Besides, it can always be expanded."

"Hmm," he murmured noncommittally. But a moment later, he laughed and scooped her into his arms. He whirled her around wildly, making her laugh with delight as a flock of startled blackbirds rose cloudlike over the house.

In the days since Mayano's funeral, a great deal had been accomplished. The charred walls of the fortress were replaced, and the relentless work of clearing land continued. So, too, progress was made on the several houses being built, including Amelia's.

The stone walls were finished and the chimney already towered over them. Almost all the planks were cut and ready. She was amazed at how quickly the structure was taking shape and didn't hesitate to tease Garrick about it.

"All those years at sea," she said, "while you were supposed to be building houses. Who would ever have guessed?"

"Not me," he admitted. "But there is something satisfying about it."

"Speaking of..." She laughed and twisted away from him.

He rolled his eyes and went after her. She got as far as the rock pool before he caught up.

"And what would you be thinking of, woman, when there's work to be done?"

She sighed and fanned herself with her hand. "It's awfully hot, don't you think?" Deliberately, she looked at the water.

He sighed, but truth be told, didn't resist. Still, he felt compelled to say, "Houses don't build themselves, you know."

Her eyes danced with merriment. "You're sounding more like a Puritan elder every day, going on about the work to be done and no time for pleasures."

His eyebrows rose. "Puritan...me? That's an insult, woman. Take it back."

She put her hands behind her back and assumed an expression of complete unconcern. "What will you do if I don't?"

He stopped halfway through stripping off his shirt, and said, "What I've been wanting to do for quite a while now."

Her eyes widened. "But didn't we just . . . ?"

"Shame on you, always thinking of one thing only."

"I do not," she sputtered, her cheeks flaming. "All I meant was . . ."

He tossed the shirt over his head and walked toward her deliberately. The corners of his mouth were lifting as he said, "What I meant, Amelia Daniels, is that it's high time and then some for you to learn to swim, and this is just the place to do it."

Her color waned. Instantly, she shook her head. "I don't want to. There's no need."

"There's every need," he corrected gently. Grasping her shoulders, he said, "Seriously, Melly, you could have drowned awhile back and you wouldn't have been anywhere near so scared when we went to Nieuw Amsterdam if you'd been able to swim. It isn't hard to learn. I did it as a child and scarcely remember it. Besides," he added, "once you've learned, you'll find out how much you enjoy it."

"No," she said again, more firmly than before. "I won't enjoy it, not ever, and I don't want to learn. Why should I? I'm right here where I'm going to stay."

A shadow flitted across his face. "You can't know that for certain," he said.

She sensed that much more lay behind those few words, but he did not expand on them. Instead, he ignored her protests and her attempts to ward him off, and boldly turned her around.

"Be still," he said sternly as he undid the buttons of her dress. "You *can* learn to swim wearing this, but you'll be more comfortable without it."

"I told you, I don't want to...ummpff..." The dress came off over her head and her petticoat followed swiftly. Without so much as a by-your-leave, he tumbled her onto the grass and pulled off her boots.

"There," he said, surveying her with purely male satisfaction, "that's much better."

Angry—and just a little frightened now—she crossed her arms over her breasts and glared at him. "I mean it, Garrick. If you dare to—"

"Sweetling," he said softly, "haven't you learned yet that there's just about nothing I won't dare?"

And with that, he picked her up and strode into the water.

"Lie back," he said and did not wait for her to obey but pressed his hand to her midsection so that she had no choice but to straighten out in the water. The sudden motion was disorienting. Her senses swam as she found herself looking up into the deep blue sky.

"You aren't in over your head," he told her reassuringly, "but it's deep enough for you to float. That's the first thing you need to learn. The water isn't your enemy, it's a friend. If you let it, it will do half the work for you."

"How nice," she muttered stiffly. Her body was rigid. She felt that any moment she would sink like a stone. Instinctively, she pushed her feet down, seeking the sandy bottom.

"Don't," Garrick ordered. He slipped his hand beneath her bottom, ignored her startled squeal and said, "Just relax."

Now why hadn't she thought of that? It was so obvious. What could possibly be preventing her from doing just as he said? Might it have anything to do with the fact that she was nude and being held most intimately by a half-naked male with whom she frankly had better things to do than learn to swim?

"I told you," she started to say, "I—"

Wrong move. Trying to sit up in order to make her point more firmly only succeeded in getting her dunked.

She came up sputtering, shaking water from her eyes and found Garrick looking at her in exasperation. "Satisfied?" he demanded.

"With what?" Satisfied? Of course she wasn't satisfied. Sweet heaven didn't the man know anything? If he wanted to talk about *satisfying,* she had other things in mind.

"That you're not going to drown. You can't—it's that simple. Now get on your back."

Under different circumstances, she might have responded with enthusiasm. But not here.

"I can't," she said simply.

"How do you know? You haven't tried."

"I did once, when I was a child. I saw people swimming and it looked wonderful. But when I tried it, I sank like a stone."

"Let me guess," Garrick said quietly, "you were all gadded up in some serious and very proper outfit."

"I was respectably garbed," she acknowledged, and she resisted the impulse to compare that to her present state.

"In other words, weighed down within an inch of your life. It's a wonder you didn't drown."

"And then there was that little episode when we first arrived." She shivered. Death had been so close, so real.

Even the memory of it was enough to terrify her. "I want to get out," she said, and turned toward the bank.

She was stopped by Garrick's gentle touch on her arm. "Amelia, trust me. I'm not going to let anything bad happen to you, I promise."

He waited, still holding her, but so lightly now that she could easily have freed herself. Their eyes met.

In his was a wealth of meaning far beyond his words, she sensed. *Trust me. Believe that I will not let you be harmed. Or walk away and make it clear that trust does not exist between us.*

She bit her lip. The water looked very dark. The child in her stirred fearfully.

But the woman held strong. "Alright," she said, and even managed a faint smile.

"Good," Garrick said. "That's better. You're getting the idea."

"I am?" Amelia sputtered. Her arms and legs were flailing, she felt like a complete dolt and she couldn't for the life of her figure out why she hadn't drowned. But Garrick seemed pleased.

She supposed she ought to be grateful for that. Maybe he'd let her stop soon.

"Just relax," he said again, for at least the twentieth time since they'd begun. "You don't have to kick that hard. Stretch your legs out a little farther and move them more under the water."

She tried it, only because she'd learned by now that if she didn't, he'd persist until she gave in. To her amazement, it worked. What had seemed awkward and clumsy was suddenly smooth and almost effortless.

But only for a moment. The instant she thought about it, she lost the rhythm and floundered again.

Fed up, she straightened, intending to tell him she was stopping whether he wanted her to or not. But as her feet went toward the bottom, the bottom wasn't there. It seemed to retreat below her.

She gasped, felt herself going down and instinctively moved her limbs. The terrible sinking sensation stopped. She leveled out and glided smoothly through the water.

"Not bad," Garrick said.

"Not bad?" she exclaimed incredulously. "Not bad! I can swim!"

"I said you would."

His bland complacency was more than she could bear. Laughing, she splashed water at him and paddled fiercely toward the bank.

He caught her, of course.

"Say thank you," he murmured as he slid his hands over her slick, smooth nakedness.

"For what?" she inquired innocently.

"Teaching you to swim, brat."

"Oh, that. Thank you very much, Captain Marlowe. You make a good teacher."

"So I've noticed," he muttered, his mouth grazing her cool, pale throat. "If I taught you any better, I'd be dead by now."

She laughed, as much with shock at his bluntness as with delight. Anticipation shimmered through her. "Lesson over?" she asked.

"Hmm, I suppose so."

He was distracted by her high, full breasts. By the time he thought of anything else they were up on the bank beside the pond. He stripped off his soaking breeches, draped them to dry over a convenient branch and swiftly covered her with his body.

For a very long time, the world was forgotten. Nothing existed except what they found together, close by the shadow of the fresh stone walls rising toward the sky.

But the world inevitably returned and they were drawn back to it. Before they reached the clearing beside the meetinghouse, they knew something had happened.

Garrick alighted from the canoe first and held out a hand to help Amelia. She stepped lightly onto the bank and looked around hastily.

"Where is everyone?"

"I don't know," he said. The words were automatic; he hardly knew he said them. Already, he was reaching for the musket lying in the canoe.

He checked the shot, slung it under his arm and started forward. Amelia followed. They had not gone far before they heard voices coming from the meetinghouse.

Voices raised in anger.

Swiftly, they moved forward and stepped into the building. Almost everyone was there. Only those busy on the far reaches of the settlement were missing.

But there was also a face neither of them had seen before.

The young man who was the center of all attention—and apparently of the angry comments—stood at the front of the meetinghouse. He was in his early twenties, tall and slender, with sandy hair and a calm, deliberate manner. Certainly, being the object of such censure did not seem to disturb him.

He smiled easily when he saw Garrick and Amelia and stepped forward to greet them.

"Mistress Daniels," he said and inclined his head politely. "Captain Marlowe. I hoped you would join us soon."

"Did you?" Garrick growled. Around them, the others grew silent, waiting to see what would happen next.

"And who would you happen to be?" Garrick demanded.

"Reverend Phineas Holling," the young man said readily. "I've been sent down from Boston to serve the settlement here."

At once, another fury of comment broke out, but it subsided quickly as Amelia stepped forward. Ignoring the sudden hammering of her heart, she said, "It is customary for a settlement to call a minister to serve in it, Reverend Holling. We did not call you."

That simple and irrefutable statement brought the young man up short for a moment. But he recovered quickly.

Spreading his hands in a conciliatory gesture, he said, "This is true, but it was thought, all the same, that in such wilderness, with ever-present danger to your souls, you should not go long without a spiritual counselor. Even if," he added pointedly, "the need for one has not yet occurred to you."

"It hadn't," Garrick said bluntly. "Who, exactly, sent you?"

"The council," Holling replied without hesitation, "acting out of their responsibility for the well-being of the colony."

"Which colony?" Amelia demanded. "We are no longer in Massachusetts, Reverend."

"Nonetheless," he answered smoothly, "you are in territory claimed by the Massachusetts Bay Colony on behalf of His Most August Majesty, the King."

"That will come as news to the Dutch," Garrick said, "who claimed it long ago."

The reverend shrugged, as though to say that what those gentlemen did was of no concern to him. "I don't see why you would object," he claimed. "Whatever differences you may have had with the elders, you are still all good, God-fearing people, are you not?"

Amelia shook her head in exasperation. "Our faith is a matter for our own consciences, Reverend. It was that conviction, as much as anything else, that led us here."

Around her, the others murmured their agreement. No one looked on the young pastor with favor, but here and there a few did seem more disposed to give him the benefit of the doubt.

He had done well to seem so nonthreatening, so unlike the blustery, sanctimonious pastors of Boston town.

"Still," Bette said softly, "with a minister, we can baptize our children."

"We can do that right enough ourselves," her husband protested. Defiantly, he added, "No one can convince me a decent, industrious man stands lower in the eyes of the Almighty than a whey-faced preacher who does nothing but live off the toil of others."

Holling flinched, but his response was measured. "I fear you have not seen the best of my calling, sir. Believe it or not, we are supposed to serve, and through that service, to contribute strength to a growing community."

There was some comment at this, not all of it negative.

"Still," Sam Whitler said thoughtfully, "we'll have the keeping of you. But then what? Just because we feed and house you doesn't mean you'll be looking out for our interests. How do we know you aren't here just to stir up trouble?"

"How do we know," Garrick added succinctly, "what part Elder Harkness played in your coming?"

At the mention of Harkness's name, the young reverend looked as though he had suddenly been confronted with something distasteful, rather embarrassing, and bad smelling to boot.

Quietly, he said, "Elder Harkness is not well."

"Indeed?" Amelia asked, her skepticism unhidden.

"He appears to have suffered a distortion of the mind. Hence his coming after you as he did. Upon his return to Boston, it was decided that he would do better kept close confined where he could not hurt himself or others."

"Who decided that?" Sam demanded, clearly astonished by the news. Harkness had seemed invulnerable in Boston, destined to always bend others to his will.

"The council," Holling said smoothly. "They thought it best. So you see," he added with a smile, "your fears about their motives are misplaced. They understand that certain—shall we say, injustices—caused you to strike off as you did. But that doesn't mean you must be permanently separated from your brethren."

He looked around at the gathering. Hostility was fading, replaced by slow but unmistakable interest.

"This is a wild land," he went on. "Surely we are all in need of comfort. That is all I bring. The chance to hear God's word and be strengthened by it here in your new home."

Amelia did not believe him. It was too easy, too pat. It ran contrary to everything she had seen and heard in Boston. Not even the news of Harkness's fate changed her mind about that.

But the others were not so sure, and the hunger on their faces showed that, like it or not, Holling was offering them something they needed.

He saw it, too. For a moment, his eyes met Amelia's. Hers were dark with doubt. But his held the bright sheen of righteousness, and deep within them, the growing assurance of victory.

Chapter Twenty-Six

Reverend Holling required little, he assured them all. A reasonable place to unroll his blankets, a simple meal or two each day and the pleasure of their company, no more.

Lest they think him lazy, he readily proved himself a handy man with a gun, bringing back his share of meat and more. Not only that, when it came to raising houses, he slung as good an ax as anyone had ever seen.

Also, to their astonishment, he made no secret that he had a sense of humor, going so far as to tease the safely married matrons with compliments that sent them into fits of giggles.

All before Amelia's disbelieving eyes.

Were these the same people who had risked their lives to free themselves from the tyranny of Boston?

They were, and she had to acknowledge it. The people themselves were unchanged. They simply wanted to believe that Holling was what he said he was and what he seemed—a simple, kindly man of God who had come only to help them.

There were even times when she wanted to believe it herself.

But then she would catch him looking at her with special scrutiny, or at Sarah Fletcher, who went around these days with her head down and a sad, frightened look in her eyes. Or at the men who, struggling to protect their families, worked through the Sabbath as though it was an ordinary day.

Or at Garrick, who seemed oblivious to the minister, but who was clearly—to Amelia, at least—a special source of interest to him.

"How long have you known Captain Marlowe?" the pastor asked her one day a fortnight or so after his arrival.

"A few months," Amelia replied. She would have thought he already had that information. Indeed, she was sure that he did and wondered why he chose to conceal it.

Surely, he had not left Boston without being well-informed as to all the circumstances of Belle Haven's founding, most particularly the scandalous departure of Amelia Daniels, an unmarried woman, with an irreverent sea captain.

"I see," Holling murmured. "I thought your acquaintance was longer than that."

"Why?" Amelia asked bluntly. She stopped stirring the stew she was tending and looked directly at him. "Why do you think that, pastor?"

"To trust him as you did, to put your life in his hands. I presumed there must be some strong connection between you for you to go so far."

"I see. You don't believe that it is possible for a person to want something so badly that she will take virtually any risk in order to obtain it?"

He hesitated, measuring his words. "I believe it is possible to be deluded by grief and misunderstanding, and in that state to make mistakes."

Her fingers tightened on the large wooden spoon. "Is that what you think this is, a delusion?"

"I don't quite know what to think of it," he admitted. He was genuinely perplexed as he glanced around the neat, bustling settlement, so filled with the order the Puritans valued.

It hardly looked like a place of depravity and evil, but then it could be hard to tell sometimes. Hadn't Eve beguiled Adam to destruction through her appearance of sweet domesticity?

And then there were the private goings-on the elders had warned him about in Boston but which he could still scarcely credit.

He was staring at the woman and knew he should not be, but he couldn't seem to turn away. She was younger than him by several years, but there was an air of wisdom about her that spoke of eternity.

Simply dressed as she was, her body stirred him powerfully. Being unmarried, he was naturally chaste—or so he thought it to be natural. But increasingly it tormented him. Of late, he had wakened from dreams to find himself shamed.

Had the beguiling creature of those dreams been only a phantasm sent to lure him into sin, it would have been bad enough. But she had a face and a name he knew too well.

Was it her doing? Did she come to him deliberately?

She looked so pure and strong, so hardworking and honest. So completely different from what they had told him in Boston. A woman he would never have suspected

of deceit, much less of evil, but for this queer insistence
on going off on her own in violation of all propriety.

The dreams were real, he could not deny them. He
shivered inwardly at the memory. She was close enough
for him to stretch out his hand and touch her. With hor-
ror, he realized that the impulse to do was almost irresistible.

In torment, he turned away, but not before she saw the
sudden fear in his eyes.

"Reverend?" she began, concerned for him.

"You must pardon me, mistress," he murmured, his
voice choked. "I fear the sun is too bright."

Instantly, she set the spoon down and went to his side.
"It is very warm today," she said sympathetically, "and
you were standing close to fire. Come, let me help you."

"No," he started to say, but her fingers brushed his
arm. That simple touch, so innocently meant, resonated
through him. He closed his eyes against the glare of truth
and knew himself lost.

She brought him a tea, which he only sniffed at gingerly. He was lying in the shade of an ancient oak where
she'd insisted he rest. It was much cooler there, but the
coiling tension deep within him had not eased. Indeed, it
was growing steadily worse.

"What is it?" he asked.

"Valerian and willow. The first will relax you, while
the second eases the pain too much sun brings."

"How do you know of such things?"

She looked surprised. "I was taught, of course, as
many women are."

That was true, women commonly had some knowledge of herbs to treat the sick. But since coming to Belle
Haven, he had seen people go to Mistress Daniels for
everything from a wound that would not heal, to stom-

ach troubles and matters—having to do with the women who were carrying—that he knew nothing about and did not wish to.

She was, he realized, more than merely lightly skilled at healing. She was what they called back in England a cunny woman, laden with ancient knowledge.

They burned such in England and in other civilized places.

"Here," she said softly as she knelt beside him. Her hand slipped beneath his neck, helping him to raise his head. "Drink."

He knew that he should not, but the woodsy, slightly sweet smell of the tea rose to tease his nostrils, mingling with the warm, perfumed scent of the woman herself. She was so close that he could feel the swell of her breasts against his arm. Instantly, his manhood stiffened.

He caught his breath, praying for protection from the strange, subtle temptation weaving itself about him. He was being drawn into something he did not understand and which frightened him greatly, for it spoke to all that was forbidden.

The edge of the cup brushed his lips. He closed his eyes and drank, seeking oblivion.

When Amelia came back to the clearing after tending to Reverend Holling, Garrick was waiting for her. He seemed to have been there for some time looking in the direction from which she returned.

"A problem?" he asked.

She set the cup down, checked on the stew and shook her head. "I don't think so. Master Holling has been overdoing and he seems a rather nervous sort to start. He just needs a little rest."

"And of course, Mistress Daniels sees to it that he gets it."

She frowned, uncertain what his tone meant. He sounded half amused, half angered.

"I was with him when he began to feel ill. It would hardly have been right not to help."

"Did you give him anything?"

She shrugged. "A tea, that's all. He'll sleep for a while and wake refreshed. Perhaps in time he'll settle down more."

"In time? How long do you imagine he will be here?"

"I don't know," she admitted. Reluctantly, she added, "The others seem to like him."

"They believe what they want to."

She didn't disagree with him, but neither did she like what he was suggesting. It made her people sound foolish.

"They have taken on a great challenge. It is understandable that they would want some comfort."

"Then they should find it within themselves, not from a spurious preacher sent to spy on us."

Her eyes widened. She turned away from the heat of the fire and stared at him. "Is that truly what you think?"

"What else? He comes just as it begins to look as though Belle Haven might actually survive, thanks to the agreement with the Dutch and our defeat of Mayano. He speaks calmly and persuasively, offering what he can be sure people want, but he watches everything very carefully. Haven't you noticed that?"

In truth, she had, but she had not wanted to dwell on it.

"It is only natural for him to be curious about us."

Garrick shook his head in exasperation. "You always want to think the best. There are times when it isn't justified."

"He's done no harm," she protested.

"Not yet. Mark my words, he will."

"I don't understand how you can be so sure. Certainly, he has done nothing to you."

"Of course he hasn't," Garrick said, looking at her in amazement. No man in his right senses dared to cross him, and none had in a very long time. Surely, she was not so naive that she didn't realize men chose their contests pitting themselves against those they believed they could defeat, not those who would obviously defeat them.

"He . . . watches you," she said hesitantly.

"He watches both of us," Garrick corrected gently. He touched her cheek with the back of his hand in a gesture of great tenderness.

She swayed slightly toward him. Around them, the bright day danced, filled with promise.

But not to the man beneath the ancient oak. Reverend Holling raised his head. The tea had left him faintly dazed. He blinked once, twice, unable to clear his mind.

In the middle distance, he saw a man and woman. Light seemed to shimmer behind them. The intimacy between them was unmistakable. It riveted him.

He should feel distaste. He knew that. But all he could muster was hollow envy so intense that his eyes grew moist. He was filled with a terrible sense of loss, something that had been missing from the very beginning of his life.

If he could not know that loving closeness, why should others? Especially, why should they know it outside the bonds of all propriety and the strictures of holy law?

It was, to his way of thinking, an ultimate injustice, and it filled him with loathing.

She had been so sweet, so kind to him, so womanly. Never mind for the moment the deep suspicions and fears she roused in him. He chose to pretend they didn't matter, that had she been willing to entrust herself to him, he could have saved her.

Instead, she chose the dark man. An unbeliever who followed no law but his own. A man who frightened the good reverend to the very core of his narrow, envious soul.

So be it. She had chosen her course. They both had. The reverend had no responsibility for anything that happened to them. He was only a vessel, the means by which justice could be done and holiness restored.

The peace of surrender filled him. He did not have to think or doubt or question. He had only to do as he had been charged and everything would follow as it should.

And yet, even as he laid his head down on the soft moss, he smelled again the lingering scent of her perfume. The regret was so piercing that he had to put his knuckles in his mouth and bite hard to keep himself from sobbing out loud.

Chapter Twenty-Seven

Summer ripened and the time of reaping came. Work in the settlement became unending.

Corn and beans, carrots and turnips all had to be gathered in and stored for the winter. Tangled mazes of raspberry and blackberry were invaded by eager children who filled their wooden buckets and their stomachs equally. In the broad meadows sloping down toward the water, wild strawberries rewarded the carefully seeking eye. Meanwhile, wheat matured in the fields and barley with it.

The air, when it moved at all, was constantly laden with the scents of life. Amelia delighted in it even as she went about in a haze of mingled anticipation and weariness.

They had done it! They had planted their first crops and survived to bring them in. Better yet, there would be no hunger in the coming winter. They would see their first year through in Belle Haven. And then...

Others would come, possibly. Already there were rumors that those dissatisfied by the harsh regime of other settlements were watching them with interest.

Garrick went down to Nieuw Amsterdam for a short time and returned with a hold filled with slate to roof the houses that were being rapidly built. The Whitlers had finished theirs, as had the Fletchers and half a dozen others. Sam Whitler had even managed to raise a barn complete with a floor for threshing.

The slate was a prize to be cherished, but equally important was the news Garrick brought. Petrus Stuyvesant sent word that the government in London was tightening its pressure on Dutch possessions in the New World. They had done nothing drastic so far, but there was a sense of tension building and danger moving nearer.

"Petrus believes they will try to make an example of Belle Haven," he said quietly. He and Amelia had gone off from the others to Daniels Neck. They sat outside her house, sharing a simple supper.

The chimney was done and the roof raised. Soon it would be done. The harvest would be finished and she would be alone.

"And you believe Holling is involved," she said.

Garrick shrugged. "I see no alternative."

"He's been very quiet of late, just going about his business and being helpful to people."

His eyebrows rose. "How much sleep have you had lately?"

"What has that to do with it?"

"There was a full moon last night. You were in the fields again as you have been many nights. You've slept little and you've had even less time to notice what is happening among the people here."

"You've been away," she reminded him. "Don't tell me you know better where matters stand."

"I know Holling goes about speaking privately in this ear and that. I know he vanishes every time he sees me.

And I know he watches you like a starving dog touched
not a little by the frothing sickness.''

"That's horrible," she exclaimed. "He has never said
or done anything to suggest that—"

"Fool," he said bluntly and reached for her.

She stiffened, unwilling to concede him so much. But,
as always, his touch weakened her best resolve. She
sighed and leaned back against him, giving herself up to
the joy they never failed to find together.

Above her, heavy leaves drooped in the still air. The
earth seemed to pause. She closed her eyes and willed
herself for this space of time to forget all else.

Amelia walked slowly toward the meetinghouse. It was
morning, and Garrick had gone off to the ship. Once
again, the endless round of work was about to begin.
Resistance stirred in her. She would have liked to idle
away this day with him. But the thought fled quickly. She
was grateful enough for the hours they did have together.

A slight flush warmed her cheeks as she remembered
the night. She was smiling faintly as she came around a
turn in the path. Without warning, she was pulled up
short.

Sarah Fletcher was there. She sat slumped on the
ground a little distance off the path. Laurel bushes
screened her, as though she had tried to conceal herself,
but without success. Even if she could not be seen, she
could be heard.

The sound of sickness brought an instinctive response
from Amelia. She rushed forward and held the girl as
Sarah retched again.

She was shaking convulsively and sobbing at the same
time. When she realized that someone was with her, she

tried to struggle away, but her strength was slight and she had no choice but to remain where she was.

At last, the worst of the sickness passed and she was able to raise her head.

"Don't move," Amelia said urgently. She hurried to a nearby stream, one of many that oozed from the mossy earth. Swiftly, she wet the edge of her apron and returned to Sarah.

With gentle hands, she washed the girl's face. The trembling had eased somewhat but not so the all-pervasive sense of despair. Sarah Fletcher looked as though she had been stripped of all hope, sunk into a despondency so severe that she would never be able to rise from it.

"When did this come upon you?" Amelia asked. Her thoughts were racing. There were plants that could cause retching, others could bring black moods. Then, too, there were illnesses that could do the same.

How long had she been sick? Amelia wondered. Had she told anyone or tried to do anything for it herself? With everyone so busy, Amelia blamed herself for not having paid closer attention. These were her people, she had brought them here. It was her responsibility to care for them.

Never mind that she was only a few years older than Sarah Fletcher and in the normal course of events would have been cared for herself. She did not even pause to consider that, but concentrated instead on the girl resting so limply against her.

"When?" she urged again.

"A w-week ago," Sarah murmured. "I think...I don't know." Her voice broke. Sobbing, she said, "Oh, God, I cannot bear this. Let me die!"

Amelia flinched. The girl was ill, there was no doubt of that. But to actually plead for death? Had there been any note of falseness in Sarah's voice, she would have put it down to a young girl's self-dramatizing. But her fervor was genuine. She truly was so burdened by despair as to not want to live.

"Sarah," she said urgently, "talk to me. Did you eat or drink anything unusual? A plant, perhaps. Something that looked attractive. Tell me."

"No, no," Sarah whispered. Her head drooped. Amelia could feel her hot tears running down her cheeks. "There is nothing you can do. No one can. This is my punishment, and I must accept it."

What ranting was this? "Illness is not punishment," Amelia said sharply. "It comes to the innocent as much as to the guilty. You have something wrong with you. If we can determine what it is, you can be helped."

She slipped her hand under Sarah's chin, trying to get her to raise her head so she could look into her face. Were the whites of her eyes yellowing? Was her skin unnaturally dry? Did her gums bleed?

All these and many more signs were well-known to Amelia. She could deal with them, and devise a remedy to fight the darkness she sensed coiling within Sarah.

But the younger girl had to help her. She had to take the first step.

"Look at me," Amelia said. Unconsciously, she adopted the tone Garrick used when he would brook no nonsense. It worked with her well enough, proud and independent though she was. Sarah had no resistance to it at all.

Her head shot up and she stared at Amelia.

"W-what do you want?"

"To help you. I will do anything I can. But you must trust me, Sarah. If you won't tell me what's happened, I can do nothing."

Pale blue eyes were suddenly narrowed as Sarah looked at her. Hoarsely, she asked, "You would help me?"

"Of course, I will. I have some small skill in healing."

"More than that," Sarah said. She sounded steadier now. Breathing deeply, she straightened and again looked deeply at Amelia. "You could help me."

Amelia nodded. Slight color had returned to the girl's cheeks. Her eyes were not yellow nor her skin unusually dry. There was no sign of bleeding.

Perhaps she really wasn't that ill after all. Amelia's mind raced, considering what would be most helpful. She had been lucky in collecting herbs and had a good selection of everything she might need.

But still she had to be sure. "Did you eat or drink anything unusual?"

Sarah laughed, a short, harsh sound. "I've been sick like this for a week, mistress, and before that I had scant appetite."

She stirred restlessly and wiped the corner of her mouth with her hand. As she did, her eyes shot to Amelia. "Reverend Holling says he fears there is a shadow over you, something born of grief perhaps, but opening the way for you to be taken," Sarah said out of nowhere.

Amelia's lips parted in shock. "What do you say?"

"You heard me. He hints at things about you. Dark things. He says you could be taken by evil without even realizing it."

"That is absurd," Amelia exclaimed. "I can't believe he is saying such things."

Yet she did believe it, or half so. Hadn't Garrick warned her? She had refused to listen, even knowing that he was vastly more experienced than herself. Now her pride cracked and she felt a sudden spurt of fear.

"You had best believe it," Sarah advised. She smiled coldly. "I heard him talking to my pa. He says we can all be taken if we follow those we shouldn't."

"He said that about me? But that's—"

"Not straight out. He's too clever for that. No, he just hints of bad things. He sighs and touches his brow, as though he is deep in regret. He speaks of your beauty, your courage, your intelligence. But he says all that breeds pride, and pride opens the Devil's way."

Amelia's stomach clenched. But hard on the fear came good, healthy anger. She would see Sarah safely back to the settlement and give her whatever care was needed. Then she would seek Holling out and—by God—they would clear the air between them. It might be air that would have to be scorched in the process, but she didn't care. She would not have anyone going about stirring up such trouble amid her people.

"Let's go," she said, and stood, drawing Sarah with her.

The girl complied but once on her feet, she resisted taking a single step. "Wait," she said. "We've not finished talking. I only told you about Holling to warn you. I did it as a favor. Now I want you to do me one."

"You need do no favor for me to help you," Amelia said, trying to urge the girl on.

Still, Sarah resisted. Her voice was very low as she said, "Oh, but I do, and if you think about it, you'll understand." Again, she smiled with that edge of nastiness that shrieked warning in Amelia's mind.

"I've seen you and the captain," she said, "going off together. Oh, not that I'm blaming you," she added hastily. "A man like that . . . any woman would be hard-pressed to resist. And why should you? You aren't married, you belong to no one. You should be able to make your own decisions."

"I don't want to talk about this," Amelia said firmly. No matter what the girl had in mind, she wasn't going to discuss such a private subject with her.

"You'd better," Sarah said. "We're two of a kind, you and me. Sisters under the skin, you could say. You like the captain, so you go with him. I . . . I liked another. I couldn't see the harm." She hesitated, her feigned confidence fading fast. Huskily, she asked, "How could I know what would happen?"

"I don't understand," Amelia said. "What are you—"

"Mayano, for God's sake! Are you daft that you don't see? I laid with him, and his seed is in me." Angrily, she shoved Amelia away and glared at her. "Don't look so shocked, mistress. You've done the same with a man not your husband. What matters that he was Pequot? He wanted me and I . . . I had not the wit to resist. But now he's gone, and I'm left to pay the price."

Amelia's thoughts reeled. In an instant, she realized the girl was telling the truth. It would profit her nothing to lie about such a thing, but beyond that, all the signs were there.

Her modest dress strained over breasts that were suddenly larger and a waist that was no longer slim. Her hair and eyes glowed, but she could not contain her stomach.

Seeing it all now, Amelia had to wonder how she had not known from the start. Only her own lingering innocence had prevented her.

"I am sorry," she said softly, thinking that this was a great burden for the girl to bear. "But you are here with your family and people who will not judge you. This is a new settlement, ripe to grow. All children will be welcome."

Sarah looked at her as though Amelia had taken leave of her senses. "Are you mad? It's bad enough that I carry a bastard, but a Pequot's get? No one will accept such spawn. My own parents will condemn me, and I will be driven away."

"No," Amelia said quickly. She grasped the girl by the shoulders, trying to still her near hysteria. "None of that will happen. Your parents love you, and this is not Boston. We left there to find a place of greater tolerance. Women have borne children alone before and not always by men of their own race. We will find a way."

"We?" Sarah repeated scathingly. "'Tis not your belly he filled, mistress. Oh, no, you lie with the fine captain and if you get by him, well then, I suppose you'll handle it in your own way."

She dug her fingers into Amelia's arms, suddenly filled with terrifying strength. "All I want is for you to do the same for me. You said you would help. Do it! Take this unwanted bastard from me!"

Amelia turned ashen. Belatedly, the full import of what Sarah wanted roared through her. Hard on it came a deep, piercing sadness.

She was right, of course. Amelia did know the way. She had learned it as she had learned so much else, in the dark, in secret—in the event that it might someday be needed.

But not like this, not this way.

"You are not old," she said quietly, ignoring the pain in her arms. "Nor are you too young. You have not already borne many children. You are healthy and you have the means to care for this baby. Think then, truly, of what you are asking me.''

Sarah's face crumbled. She laid her head against Amelia's shoulder and sobbed piteously. ''I made a mistake,'' she said. ''Before God, I repent of it. But must I pay forever? I will suffer childbirth, but it will not end there. I will have to raise a child no one will truly accept no matter what you say. No man will ever want to wed me. What chance will I ever have, or the child? I am sorry. I swear it! But for the love of God, help me!''

Amelia put her arms around her and held her tight. She felt Sarah's pain and grief in all its intensity. The girl was angry and terrified, but she was also sincere. She truly did not want to have this child and her reasons for feeling that way could not be easily dismissed.

Softly, Amelia asked, ''Tell me true, Sarah Fletcher. Did Mayano force you?''

She took a deep, sobbing breath and shook her head. ''He did not have to, such a lack wit am I. But before God, he was a man; for all, he was not one of us. I will not deny that. But it was only once—'' Her voice broke again. ''*Once* and I must bear it forever. It is not right!''

Amelia closed her eyes for a moment, praying for strength. She drew Sarah into her arms, murmuring soothingly even as she tried frantically to decide what to do.

Chapter Twenty-Eight

Garrick found Amelia sitting near the river that ran down to Daniels Neck. She sat with her knees drawn up and her head resting on them. Her shoulders were slumped. She looked weary and dispirited.

He had come looking for her when he did not find her in the fields. It wasn't like her to shirk her duties. Indeed, he thought wryly, he couldn't remember her ever doing it before.

Softly, he sat down beside her. She did not stir, and for a moment he thought she was unaware of his presence. But then, without looking at him, she said, "It would be better to leave me alone."

"Why?" he asked.

"I am very heavy in my mind. I need time to think."

Fear darted through him. Was she ill? Had something happened to her? His hands clenched as his throat went dry suddenly. "You..."

"Not me," she said hastily. She smiled at him reassuringly. The fear had not escaped her. That he should feel such a thing was very revealing but she did not want to assign too much importance to it.

"I have a problem I must solve," she said, "that's all."

"Perhaps we can solve it together," he suggested.

She shook her head. "I don't think so, but thank you."

She turned away again, looking out over the water. He was supposed to leave, she had made that clear. But he could not bring himself to do so. Instead, he reached over and took her hands in his.

"Don't do this, Amelia."

"Do what?"

"Close yourself off from me. It's too late for that, lass. We started this together and, like it or not, I'm bound to help you. Now what's the trouble?"

Amelia hesitated. She did not want to betray Sarah's confidence. But she did need help, and more than that, she trusted Garrick.

Trusted him with anything, as she had never trusted anyone before. Heaven help her.

She took a deep, shuddering breath. "Sarah Fletcher is with child."

He did not react at all. There was no flicker of surprise as he said, "Mayano."

It wasn't a question but she nodded anyway. "She doesn't want to have it."

He sighed. "There isn't much she can do about it now."

Amelia did not respond. The silence drew out between them until it became a kind of response itself.

Slowly, he asked, "There isn't, is there?"

When still she said nothing, he went on, "I have heard ... that is, people say ..."

"What do they say?" she asked quietly. "What do people whisper of, Garrick? That women—some of them, at least—know how to keep from bearing a child they do not want. But such knowledge is forbidden, isn't it? Women are not allowed to know such things, nor are we supposed to know how to keep from becoming pregnant. We are supposed to bear and bear and bear, until finally we die from it. Isn't that right?''

"I didn't say it was right," he objected. "There are things a man can do to protect a woman. I—"

"I know," she broke in, "but all that is too late for Sarah. Right or not, she is pregnant and she doesn't want to be."

He thought suddenly of all the herbs and the healing, of the way she had saved Jacob's life and tended all the settlers since their arrival. She knew how to heal. Did she then also know how to...

"She came to you," he said.

Slowly, Amelia nodded. "She asked for my help."

"Will you give it?"

So blunt, so unrelenting. There was never any escape from him, nor did she necessarily want there to be. A long sigh escaped her. "I've helped to bring children into the world and I've seen women die from the bearing. Sometimes they die because something goes wrong that there's simply no way to fix. But sometimes it's different. They may be too young or too old. They may have already borne ten, twelve children and are exhausted. They may have been raped, or have pleaded with their husbands to leave them alone, and were ignored. And then what do they do? Seek out someone who has the knowledge and will help them?''

"Someone like you?"

The sadness in her voice pierced him to the core. "The woman who taught me warned that I would find the knowledge a hard burden. She was right."

"What are you going to do?" he asked.

"I don't know. Right now she is too afraid to consider any alternative and I cannot really ask her to spend a great deal of time doing that. Time is of the essence in such matters. 'Twere done, must be done quickly.''

"But the child—''

"I know," she broke in. "Sweet Lord, I know. All life is precious, the babe's *and* Sarah's. She is so very afraid. If only it had been the sailor on your ship and not Mayano. If she could marry, build a new life, believe in a future, it would be different.''

"This is Owenoke's grandchild," Garrick pointed out quietly. "He may well want to rear it himself, or at least share in the rearing. Sarah should not forget that.''

"I don't think she's considered it," Amelia acknowledged. "She knows Mayano was at odds with his father. Perhaps she just presumes Owenoke would not help her.''

"She may well be wrong. At the very least, she should find out.''

"I could talk with her about it," Amelia ventured. Garrick was right. Perhaps this child might even be the means of bringing the Pequot and the settlers closer together. God truly did move in mysterious ways, ways not always understood by man.

"There is something else," she said softly as they stood together. Briefly, she told him what Sarah had revealed about Holling. "I should have believed you," she concluded. "He does seem intent on sowing trouble here.''

Garrick nodded grimly. "Leave him to me," he said with such deadly chill in his voice that for a moment, Amelia did not dare even to look at him. She shivered inwardly, almost pitying Holling, as she would have if he hadn't been so set on wreaking havoc on Belle Haven. For that, he deserved no mercy.

But Sarah Fletcher did, and somehow, in some form, it had to be found. Owenoke might hold the answer, but first she would have to talk with Sarah.

And for that she would have to find her. But she could not. Although she searched everywhere she could think of, there was no trace of the girl.

By nightfall, it was clear that she was gone.

"Gather your courage, my friends," the Reverend Holling said. "For we must speak of painful things. A flower of our community, a young woman in the first fresh blush of life, has vanished. We are left with no sign from her, no hint of where she may have gone. She has disappeared as though she no longer existed."

In the clearing before the meetinghouse, Sarah's parents stood close together, sobbing softly. The others were all clustered around them. Only Garrick stood off to one side, watching the proceedings with eyes that revealed nothing of his thoughts.

Holling was on borrowed time. The furor over Sarah's vanishing had bought him a stay but that would not last. He would have to answer to Garrick soon enough.

But first he would have his say.

"God is warning us," Holling intoned. "He has sent an unmistakable message of His displeasure and how has He done it? By taking from us one who was too pure and innocent to be left dwelling among us."

Sarah's mother sobbed even more heavily. She clung to her husband as her anguish became unbearable. Amelia stepped closer to her, putting a hand on her shoulder. This was too much. People needed to grieve, but to have it suggested that they had lost their daughter through some sin of their own, that was not to be borne.

Yet the young pastor was fiery in his oratory. He held his audience in the palm of his hand and he did not intend to let it go.

"Think," he exhorted. "Seek deeply into your souls. Pray God to reveal to you what can be done to earn His forgiveness. Reflect on the sin of pride and the rejection of authority. Consider how easily we step onto Satan's path when we seek only the fulfillment of our own desires."

He raised his arms, black against the sky, and lifted his head to heaven's glare. "Sarah, sweet child, is gone. But we remain. Lest more evil befall us, we must cleanse our path and repent our sins to Almighty God. Heed me, my brethren! Do not turn away from what may be the last chance for your salvation. Let us all return to our dwelling places and pray sincerely, for holy guidance that we may know what must be done."

Slowly, the assembled group did as he bid. Everyone was far too shaken and saddened to do anything else. Bette wept softly, as did Lissy and many of the other women. The men looked grim. Several paused to say a few quiet words to the Fletchers, but they were beyond consolation. For them there was only the deep anguish of unbearable loss.

Late in the moonless night, the reverend went to answer a call of nature. Returning, he was deep in pleasant contemplation of the great success that was about to fall into his hands.

He would bring Belle Haven back into the fold. For that, he would achieve great honor in this world and the next. He would be among the elect, chosen to rule over lesser men and receive the reward due them when, in the fullness of time, they passed beyond this world.

All this he would do and more. Once the elders knew what he had achieved, he would tell them of his fears about Amelia. He would stress that she was fundamentally a good woman, only a misguided one. He would urge them to let him prove through her that Satan truly could be defeated. She would have to be turned over to him, of course. He would require a free hand in everything he did. And in time, she would be saved. He was sure of it.

It did not occur to him that Peter Harkness had thought along similar lines—and that he had been mad. He thought only of the great pleasure such a notion gave him and trembled at how much greater it would be once she was actually his.

Indeed, he was smiling when he happened to look up and see the dark man standing just a little beyond the trees.

Garrick saw the smile, and smiled in return. But his was merciless. It held a world of meaning, all unpleasant for the Reverend Holling.

"Good morrow, pastor," Garrick said politely. He was always courteous, but never more so than when he was contemplating mayhem.

"Good night, you mean," Holling said nervously.

"Dawn comes," Garrick said. "It will grow light in an hour. And with the light a new day."

"Oh, well, then," the pastor said with a weak laugh, "good morrow to you."

"Indeed," Garrick said and thought of Amelia, of her sweet, proud strength and of what it provoked in twisted men, "a very good morrow." And he walked toward the smaller man.

Chapter Twenty-Nine

Sam Whitler's barn floor was turned to gold. A fine dust rose over the rough wooden planks and danced on the air. It drifted upward to the long, slender shafts of sunlight that shone through the unshuttered windows near the roof, and vanished out the double doors through which people came and went. It clung to their hair and their garments, to their faces and their smiles. Children chased after the floating tufts of grain while their parents watched indulgently.

In the long, slanting light of afternoon, it settled on leaves from which the green of summer was swiftly fading.

Reaping time, gathering time, threshing time, all passing now in quick succession. Some mornings when Amelia and Garrick woke wrapped in their blankets, there was even a nip in the air.

The week before, they had slept indoors, inside Amelia's house, for the first time. Slept there and made love there, sweetly and lingeringly, not with their accustomed fierce passion but with slow gentleness, as though each knew that what time remained needed to be drawn out.

Threshing time, somber with the memory of lost Sarah fresh among them, but pleasant still with the ancient songs to lighten their work, and with the joy of labor well done, rewards well deserved.

And now, beyond Sam Whitler's barn, the first graying autumn storm was blowing at them off the water, driving them inside, away from the dripping day.

Garrick got the fire going. He was satisfied that the chimney drew well, but since it was the first one he had ever built, he tended to worry over it a little. Amelia thought that endearing. She stretched out on the floor, lying on blankets, and she thought of what the room would be like someday when she had furniture.

A table first, hewn of pine, and several chairs to go with it. A bench near the fireplace for which she would make a softly padded cover if she ever had the time. A wrought-iron rack with hooks to hold her pots and, someday, a cupboard to hold dishes. It would be a cheerful place, filled with good smells and happy laughter.

Or it would be empty.

She could see it either way. The dual, conflicting vision ate away at her, making her feel hollow inside.

She turned from it and deliberately stared into the fire, blanking the vision out.

"I still don't understand about Holling," she said. "He left so suddenly."

What she really wanted to ask was what Garrick had done to him. She had seen the reverend before he departed and there hadn't been a mark on him. But he had been in a desperate daring hurry to leave, so much so that he had accepted Passicham's offer of an escort up the coast to the next settlement.

"He decided this wasn't the place for him," Garrick said lazily. He lay back and smiled at her.

"What did you do to him?"

His eyes widened in pretended amazement. "Me? What makes you think I did anything to him?"

"You said you would."

"I did?"

"Well, then, you thought it."

"And how would you know what I thought, Melly girl?"

"I'm not sure," she said slowly. "It comes to me from time to time."

His smile deepened, becoming so intimate that her breath caught in her throat. He knew her so well, this strong and tender man who held her with such possessiveness and raised her to such aching joy.

"Then what am I thinking now?" he asked.

She blushed, which earned a laugh from him and the proof, if she needed any, that her guess had been right.

Much later, in the night, she woke by the embers of the fire and found him watching her. His smile was gone, his eyes deep set.

"The harvest is done," he said softly.

She bit her lip and slowly nodded. All day it had been coming, and for days before. In their lovemaking, she had felt it. In the breath of the dying summer's wind. In the rustle of the leaves turning gold. In the flight of geese across the moonlit sky, fleeing, fleeing toward another land.

"I know," she whispered, and feared she would cry.

He touched her cheek, stared at his fingers and slowly touched his lips to the tears he found there.

"Come with me," he said. "There's a whole world out there, Melly. Let's share it."

Emotion welled in her. There they were, the words she had never even dared to hope she would hear. So simple, so direct, so infinitely tempting. Go, leave Belle Haven, journey with him out into the greater world.

"You can swim now," he said softly. "Truth is, you can do all sorts of things. I never thought to ask a woman to share my life, but I'm asking you. I don't want to leave you."

"I don't want to leave you, either," she whispered.

"Then don't. Belle Haven's on its way. You did what you set out to do. There's no need to stay any longer."

She drew back slightly and pulled the blanket closer around her. Despite the fire, it was suddenly so cold.

"Nothing's that simple," she said. "We've done well, it's true, but there's still much uncertainty. Sarah's gone, and the pain of that weighs heavily. Holling's sudden departure upset everyone—even those who were glad to see him go. Winter lies ahead. What if some of these people become ill? They are counting on me to be here. And what of Lissy and Bette's babies? They believe I'll be there to help them when their time comes."

"There are others who can help," he insisted. "You've given them their beginnings. They've no right to expect anything more."

She stared at him for a long time before she rose and went to stand near the window. Still holding the blanket around her, she pushed the shutters open with one hand and looked out.

The night was crystal clear. Moonlight poured over the clearing around the house to the trees and the river beyond. In the distance, she could hear the crash of the waves against the shore.

All around her, the peace and beauty of Daniels Neck wrapped itself around her like the blanket her fingers clutched. This was her place, the home she had always sought, the land she had struggled to make her own.

Yet she could give it all up, walk away and be one with this man she loved.

If only she could forget the duty she had to others and to the faith—in God and in freedom—that had brought her so far.

"I cannot," she said and let the pain take her, knowing it would never end.

Lady Star sailed on the tide. The settlers lined up along the shore to see her off. The boat hauled anchor with a smaller crew than the one she'd carried when she arrived—ten of the sailors had chosen to stay and make their home in Belle Haven. They would be replaced in Nieuw Amsterdam whither *Lady Star* was bound to take on cargo and provisions.

Garrick stood on the wheel deck with Jacob beside him. The first mate had been the last to board. He'd stood on the beach, holding Amelia's hands in his, and bid her a gentle farewell.

She could not speak and he did not expect her to. "Love is a harsh master," he said. "Love of God, of principle, of home. But truly it is all we have in the end."

She nodded and did not try to hide the tears she had kept so valiantly from Garrick. Jacob understood. He kissed her gently on the cheek before stepping into the longboat.

The wind increased. As the villagers watched, the proud ship swung around to catch it. The anchor was up, the mainsail out. Quickly, tide and wind seized the vessel.

Amelia could watch no longer. The others would remain on the beach until *Lady Star* was out of sight, but she had seen enough. Quickly, she turned, lifting her skirts, toward the trail to Daniels Neck.

She did not see the man whose eyes strained after her until she was no more than a small, dark speck vanishing along the haze of land.

For a week, Amelia did not leave her house except to venture outside for water and her other needs. She stayed away from the clearing and the meetinghouse. Company and conversation were more than she could bear. She needed to be alone with her grief.

And with something more.

Her time of flowing had not come. When she woke in the morning on her pallet of blankets, her head swam. Her breasts were tender, and it was all she could do to swallow a few sips of water with dried bread.

Life stirred within her. As it had in the fair land she planted her feet on, and as it did in Bette, Lissy and the vanished Sarah.

The knowledge thrilled her. This was what she had wanted almost as much as she had wanted the man himself. This she loved, as she had loved him, yet differently, with a maternal protectiveness that sprang fully from the first tentative knowledge that the child existed within her.

Marvelous, she thought, like the sudden unfolding of a flower. No hesitation, no waiting, no need to accustom herself to the idea. There it was like a strong flowing current within her—to protect, cherish, love.

So simple, so eternal. So miraculous.

So alone.

But not for long. While the knowledge was still achingly fresh, the world intruded. With a vengeance.

"Holling is back," Sam Whitler said. He stood at her door, early on the third day of her discovery, his cheeks red and his chest rising and falling with the speed of his coming. "He looks like a scared rabbit, or at least he did until he learned that the captain is gone. He says he has news.''

''What news?'' Amelia asked. She had a blanket around her, for she was not yet dressed, nor had she broken her fast or put a comb to her hair. The night had been long and she had slept deeply despite all that was in her mind. The demands of the child on her body would not be ignored. They held sway over all else.

''The settlement to the east of us,'' Sam went on, while she struggled to listen. ''Danford they're calling it. The elders up in Boston and the Massachusetts Bay Colony have expanded the settlement's borders. They include us now, and they've sent Holling to announce it.'' His mouth thinned in derision. ''According to them, Belle Haven no longer exists.''

''Indeed?'' Amelia demanded. The self-protective fog that had wrapped itself around her was lifting. Her shoulders stiffened. ''I cannot imagine how anyone would think that. We have a clearly written deed from the Pequot.''

''Tell it to Holling,'' Sam advised. ''I've already tried.''

''It does not matter,'' the pastor interrupted. He stood tall and austere in his black garb and refused to look directly at her. As Sam had said, there was still an air of fear clinging to him. But it was overridden by burgeoning confidence. He was feeling surer of himself by the moment.

''A deed from the Indians means nothing. All this land is claimed for the Massachusetts Bay Colony. It is entirely at the discretion of its leaders that allotments are made.''

''Maybe so,'' Amelia said, ''but we are here and we are not going to leave. What do the leaders say to that?''

Holling hesitated. This had, in fact, been a prime subject for discussion in Danford. But then anything to do with Belle Haven absorbed the good people of that settlement most intensely.

Belle Haven had a better landing than they did. More land was cleared and it was more fertile. They even went so far to say that though they were only a few miles separate, it rained better in Belle Haven, more gently and more often at night, instead of during the day.

They even believed it.

It was envy, of course, this the reverend knew, his old, well-known friend. That, and the fear of having something so different near to them. Belle Haven was prospering, they heard, while for them everything seemed a struggle. If they could expand, take it over, make it their own, they would feel their righteous obedience to the elders of Boston was vindicated.

"They say," Holling intoned, "that there is depravity here. It must be rooted out. Joining with Danford is the best way to assure it." He looked around at the newly gathered crowd, raising his voice so they would all be sure to hear.

"You have already lost an innocent young woman. How many more will have to vanish before you realize that Satan is abroad among you?"

Despite herself, Amelia shivered. Sarah, too, had been unwed and pregnant. While she refused to believe that anything supernatural had happened to her, she still felt a cold finger of dread down her back.

Nonetheless, she would not let Holling see that he affected her in any way. Stalwartly, she faced him.

"What depravity?" she demanded. "We are all good, industrious people. Our success to this date shows it."

The people around her murmured their agreement. They were caught within their own minds, not sure that Holling was completely wrong but unwilling to be slurred by him either.

Instinctively, they looked to Amelia to help them.

"There is no depravity," she said firmly, "and no evil. This land will not be taken from us."

Holling hesitated. She stirred him as she always had, but he dared not think of that. It was imperative that he keep his composure and do exactly as he had been told to do.

"Perhaps you are right," he said. "No one wants to judge you without evidence. All due procedure must be followed. Danford is applying to the Royal Commission for a town charter. Belle Haven can do the same."

He paused and looked directly at Amelia. For a moment, she had the horrible sense that he was trying to gaze into her soul. "If no irregularities are found, it is possible that Belle Haven could be chartered on its own. Were that to happen, you would be left undisturbed. However, if it is found that all is not as it should be, you will be incorporated into Danford."

"So what if we are?" Sam Whitler demanded. "It doesn't have to mean anything to us. We don't have to accept it."

"You don't?" Holling asked. "Let me assure you, such defiance would carry a high price. It has been decided to base a garrison in the Connecticut Valley to protect the rights assigned by the Crown. You could find yourself barricaded, unable to trade, perhaps compelled to billet royal troops. I assure you, this will happen. England is reaching out, taking what is hers alone. You sought protection from the Dutch, but soon they will have all they can do to protect themselves. For you, the only hope lies in surrender."

There was a quick intake of breath around the circle as people bent their heads together, murmuring over what they had heard. Faces were angry and defiant, but also deeply concerned.

What Holling had described was believable to them all. It was how the lords in London reasoned things out. When they thought further, they realized how lucky they had been to get as far as they had without running into trouble.

"But wait," Benjamin Fletcher said. His voice sounded rusty, for since his daughter's disappearance, he had spoken little. "You said they can only take us over if they prove irregularities. What if they can't?"

Holling hesitated. There had been much talk of this. He had assured the men in Boston that sin abounded, but he was counting on being able to point to Amelia in order to prove it.

Only Captain Marlowe was gone, and she was standing there before him looking the very vision of purity and strength.

He needed proof. Without it, he could not take Belle Haven from her.

He knew that full well and there, in that moment, standing in the circle in the full glare of the sun, Amelia knew it too.

Chapter Thirty

"I don't understand," Lissy said. "Why do you want to leave us?"

"I don't," Amelia murmured. She had her head bent over her bundles and did not look up. If she did, Lissy would see her crying and be all the more disturbed.

"I just think it is for the best, that's all. We've made a good start here. You will do well on your own. There is a doctor over in Danford who is well spoken of. He has already agreed to tend everyone here if they have need."

"I don't want any doctor," Lissy said stubbornly. "When my time comes, I want you."

Amelia looked up then, despite herself. She gazed into the kind, worried eyes staring at her and choked back a sob.

"I want to be with you, too," she said. "But it cannot be. I must leave now. Please, just accept that."

"It's because of what that fool Holling said, isn't it?" Lissy demanded.

"Fool? He's far from that. He's a wily and dangerous man. We must defeat him."

"Then stay and help us do it."

Sadly, Amelia shook her head. "I cannot. If I stay, I will be giving him exactly what he wants."

For a long moment, Lissy looked at her until, at last, understanding dawned. Her face filled with sympathy as she reached out to Amelia.

"Sweet child, I should have known. You loved the captain and he loved you. It was clear to all who saw you."

"Not clear enough to me," Amelia said shakily. "He asked me to go with him. I said no, my place was here. But now it seems that it is not. I must go anyway."

"Then seek him. It is said he is in Nieuw Amsterdam."

"Only for a day or two. He will be gone by now. No, the best thing for me is to return to England. I have family there who will help me." She touched a hand to her belly lightly. "I do not want my child to be alone."

"He would not be, here."

"In what will be part of Danford?" Amelia asked. She shook her head again. "No, Lissy, there is no choice. Belle Haven must survive, else all we've done means nothing."

She blinked back tears and squeezed the other woman's hand. "I'll be all right, really I will. I have much to be glad of, not the least that Garrick and I made this babe together for me to cherish always. I will keep him safe, especially from the Hollings of the world."

"I am so sorry," Lissy said. "Of all of us, this is your place more than any."

"I will find another," she said, but the words were empty and she knew in her heart they could never be true.

Still, she had to try.

Lifting her head, she picked up the bundle and stepped outside the small house she had so briefly occupied. Surely, it would not stand empty long. Someone else would come to plant the flowers she had not the time to do, to fill it with children, to make it the place she had seen in her dream.

Someone else, not her.

"I must go," she repeated to herself as much to Lissy, and started down the path.

Passicham was waiting at the water's edge. He had come the day before, staying in the background, listening to what Holling had to say. When the pastor was done and all dispersed, he had sought out Amelia.

Few words were said between them, but he would take her southward to Nieuw Amsterdam. *Lady Star* was gone from there, having sailed several days before. But there were other ships on which Amelia could buy her passage.

But now, as she joined him on the beach where one of the large seagoing canoes was pulled up, he seemed to hesitate. He fiddled with this and that, checking and rechecking what she could not tell, and several times he glanced out over the water.

"We must go," she reminded him, for each passing moment hurt her more.

"Tide coming in," he replied.

"But surely we can paddle against it."

He shrugged. "We can."

"Then why," she asked, bewildered, "do we wait?"

He smiled at her gently. "Are you in such a hurry to go?"

"No," she admitted, her throat tight. "I don't ever want to leave."

"Yet you do." He shook his head. "Strange ways your people have. Much confusion where there should be none."

"Is it easier for you then?" she asked.

He sighed. "No, but I would like to think it is for someone."

Despite herself, she laughed. He had succeeded, for just an instant, in penetrating the shroud of sorrow hanging round her.

And in that moment, sunlight glinting on the water, seabirds soaring, and all around her the promise of Belle Haven shining under the blue helmet of the sky, something moved far out on the water.

Something large and white, coming fast, cleaving the sea in its path, throwing foam to heaven.

"Run aground, he keep going like that," Passicham muttered and shook his head again at the vagaries of men and women.

"He," Amelia breathed, sweet word on her lips, promise in her breath, hope suddenly surging in her heart.

"He," she said again and began to run down the beach, for out there on the water *Lady Star* was slowing and the longboat was being launched. But the man on the deck would not wait for it.

He stood for a moment silhouetted against the sea and sky, joined by the proud ship to both. Then he dived, strongly and cleanly, and swam with powerful strokes toward her.

She came into the water to meet him, wading hip deep so that her clothes were quickly sodden and clung to her. He took her in his arms, not particularly gently, but with the fierce strength of all his love.

"Damn you, woman," Garrick said, his voice roughened by the fatigue of the anguished days alone without her, "you've made a landsman of me."

Passicham threw back his head and laughed, but the pair in the water did not hear him. Far above, the seabirds whirled, timeless, enduring, over the land that was Belle Haven, now and forever.

* * * * *

Author's Note

I hope you've enjoyed this first book about Belle Haven and that you'll return with me in THE SEDUCTION OF DEANNA, Book Two of the Belle Haven Saga.

More than a century later, flowers bloom around Amelia's house and children fill its rooms with laughter. But the Revolutionary War threatens this serenity and divides the families of Belle Haven. Garrick and Amelia's great-granddaughter, Deanna Marlowe, is torn between the man she always expected to marry and a dangerous rebel who threatens everything she holds dear.

I look forward to my visits there and I hope you will too.

Maura Seger
Stamford, CT

ROMANCE IS A YEARLONG EVENT!

Celebrate the most romantic day of the year with MY VALENTINE! (February)

CRYSTAL CREEK
When you come for a visit Texas-style, you won't want to leave! (March)

Celebrate the joy, excitement and adjustment that comes with being JUST MARRIED! (April)

Go back in time and discover the West as it was meant to be... UNTAMED—Maverick Hearts! (July)

LINGERING SHADOWS
New York Times bestselling author Penny Jordan brings you her latest blockbuster. Don't miss it! (August)

BACK BY POPULAR DEMAND!!!
Calloway Corners, involving stories of four sisters coping with family, business and romance! (September)

FRIENDS, FAMILIES, LOVERS
Join us for these heartwarming love stories that evoke memories of family and friends. (October)

Capture the magic and romance of Christmas past with HARLEQUIN HISTORICAL CHRISTMAS STORIES! (November)

WATCH FOR FURTHER DETAILS IN ALL HARLEQUIN BOOKS!

Harlequin Historical

THREE
UNFORGETTABLE
KNIGHTS

First there was Ruarke, born leader and renowned warrior, who faced an altogether different field of battle when he took a willful wife in *Knight Dreams* (Harlequin Historicals #141, a September 1992 release). Now, brooding widower and heir Gareth must choose between family duty and the only true love he's ever known in *Knight's Lady* (Harlequin Historicals #162, a February 1993 release). And coming later in 1993, Alexander, bold adventurer and breaker of many a maiden's heart, meets the one woman he can't lay claim to in *Knight's Honor,* the dramatic conclusion of Suzanne Barclay's Sommerville Brothers trilogy.

If you're in need of a champion, let Harlequin Historicals take you back to the days when a knight in shining armor wasn't just a fantasy. Sir Ruarke, Sir Gareth and Sir Alex won't disappoint you!

IN FEBRUARY LOOK
FOR *KNIGHT'S LADY*
AVAILABLE WHEREVER
HARLEQUIN BOOKS ARE SOLD

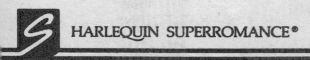

HARLEQUIN SUPERROMANCE®

HARLEQUIN SUPERROMANCE NOVELS WANTS TO INTRODUCE YOU TO A DARING NEW CONCEPT IN ROMANCE...

WOMEN WHO DARE!
Bright, bold, beautiful...
Brave and caring, strong and passionate...
They're unique women who know their
own minds and will dare anything...
for love!

One title per month in 1993, written by popular Superromance authors, will highlight our special heroines as they face unusual, challenging and sometimes dangerous situations.

Dare to dream next month with:
#541 CRADLE OF DREAMS by Janice Kaiser
Available in March wherever Harlequin Superromance novels are sold.

HARLEQUIN®

my Valentine

1993

The most romantic day of the year is here! Escape into the exquisite world of love with MY VALENTINE 1993. What better way to celebrate Valentine's Day than with this very romantic, sensuous collection of four original short stories, written by some of Harlequin's most popular authors.

ANNE STUART
JUDITH ARNOLD
ANNE McALLISTER
LINDA RANDALL WISDOM

THIS VALENTINE'S DAY, DISCOVER ROMANCE WITH MY VALENTINE 1993

Available in February wherever Harlequin Books are sold.   VAL93